# Alice

## MARSH SAGA SERIES BOOK 4

## AnneMarie Brear

AnneMarie Brear

# Chapter One

London, October 1929

Lady Alice Mayton-Walsh tapped her pencil on the polished desk. Rain dripped against her office window on the south bank of the Thames, and she sighed. The gloomy weather matched her mood perfectly, which annoyed her. She wasn't one for gloom, for despondency, hated it in fact. Yet, here she was, unable to concentrate, to work as she should on her brilliant fashion magazine, *Sheer*.

Her head pounded slightly from a headache behind her eyes. She'd drunk too much last night at a jazz bar in Soho. Her feet ached from dancing until dawn. It was becoming more difficult to be out all night and then turn up at the office for a day's work.

She swung around on her brown leather chair and looked out over the murky river, which today resembled dirty bath water. Too many times this week she'd wasted time looking out of the window.

She watched the boats plying the river, the people walking past on the street below and the non-stop flow of motor cars, trucks and buses, the odd horse and cart, and a few men on bicycles. Everyone seemed to be in a hurry. They had somewhere to go or someone to meet.

Standing, she stepped closer to the window and craned her neck to peer along the city scape, its skyline dominated by the cranes along the docks in the east and church spires in the west. If she opened the window, she'd hear a boom of noise, honking motor cars, boats' horns and the sounds of construction in this great bustling city.

Progress was happening all around her. She'd always loved the edgy vibe of London. She'd been a part of it for the last six years since she became a magazine owner and editor. Launched on a bright sunny day in May in nineteen twenty-three, Alice had plunged her time, energy and money into its publication and now, six years later, the magazine had become a complete success, surprising everyone but herself. She knew that her magazine would be popular with the young women of the upper classes, those who had money and time on their hands went shopping. *Sheer-*, like *Vogue* became the fashion bible for women needing to out-style the next woman at the races, garden parties, tennis clubs and so on.

*Sheer's* readers were her people, women like her. Privileged. A class where they spent their days not only shopping but making calls, as their mothers and grandmothers did in a time-honoured tradition which only paused during the Great War. After the war young women wanted to be free and freedom meant many things. Dress styles changed as well as attitudes. Lifestyles became faster, more daring. Young women didn't want to stay home all day with their mothers. No, they wanted to learn how to drive, dance to jazz, cut their hair short, raise eyebrows with what they wore. They drank and smoked and loved in a way they'd never done before the war.

*Sheer* captured the fashion of all that. Day wear, evening wear, sportswear, party wear and all the accessories that went with it were spread over the pages of the magazine, drawn by Alice's excellent artists from the clothes designers' own etchings.

It wasn't all her doing, of course, she had a wonderful team: her brother Brandon, sister-in-law, Prue, and family friend, Vince Barton, plus all the other staff working in the offices. She knew them all, from the editorial team to Gloria, the tea lady, to Sam, the building's maintenance man. The last six years had been the best of her life, she knew it for a fact.

The excitement of realising a dream, of working as the head of a talented crew all pulling together for the same cause – to make the best women's fashion magazine Britain, indeed, Europe had ever seen. *Sheer* rivalled the celebrated *Vogue*. It was coveted by women of the upper classes, their own fashion bible to study and to learn from, or to simply just browse through on a lazy afternoon while sipping tea.

Everything had gone to plan from the outset. She'd bought a rundown building south of the Thames and had it gutted and remodelled into office spaces, a canteen, and meeting rooms. They even had a mini catwalk and shooting studios for the models to parade the latest designer wear. She had plunged all her money, and some of others, into the magazine in the biggest gamble of her life.

Brandon had guided her on the financial issues of starting a business, while Prue had a good eye for detail and exciting ideas to push the magazine further, to make it modern and unique. While dearest Vince had bought shares in the company and was the marketing manager. He had the natural ability to promote *Sheer* so that it was talked about in all the right circles and all the best parties. Between him and herself they had everyone talking about *Sheer*. They were a success. A hit. The readership grew each month, demanding more copies to be printed. It was all Alice had wanted to achieve, all she had hoped would happen.

So why was she having these increasing days of misery? Had it all come too easily? The success of *Sheer* meant the long hard days of getting the first editions into shops and sent to people's homes were long gone. Now there was a high demand for it. Fashion designers came to her to be featured. Advertisers came to her to pay for page space. Gone were the long and exhausting days of her knocking on industry doors asking for meetings and selling the value of being featured in *Sheer* to companies. Was that the problem? Was there nothing left to fight for, no hunt, no chase to keep her mind sharp?

Did she need another challenge perhaps?

She thrived on defying the odds, of being unconventional, of causing a stir. Family and friends knew her for her outspoken opinions, her impulsive decisions, her fast life. She'd toured the world, stayed in so many capital cities that she was on first name basis with a good many doormen at all the expensive hotels.

However, lately, the idea of travelling to another country, of spend countless hours in meetings with difficult fashion designers, attending business dinners with boring businessmen and sometimes even fending off her fair share of those men who saw her as easy prey for the night was becoming tiresome.

Being a single wealthy woman, a widow, gave her independence, but also made her a target for men who felt she needed a husband, or a lover. During the war, she had married her dashing husband, Sir Thomas Mayton-Walsh, after an engagement of only weeks and had only known him for six months in total. They had shocked everyone, but the war changed how people thought and behaved. Everyone lived for each day, not thinking of the future, especially not soldiers who might not see another dawn. Getting married seemed the right thing to do. In the end, it turned out that they spent only three short days together as a married couple before he went back to France and was killed soon after. She didn't regret it. She never regretted anything. Life was too short for regrets.

A ship's horn blew outside the window, dragging her back to the present and her current state of mind, which was becoming a concern. After six years of being at the helm of *Sheer*, she was finding the excitement was missing. Something was definitely *missing* from her life, but she didn't know what it was.

Some changes were occurring that might be the reason for her mood. Prue had just found out she was pregnant again and naturally she'd have to stop her activities with the magazine. Brandon insisted on it as Prue had sadly suffered several miscarriages after the birth of their son Henry four years ago. Brandon blamed the punishing work load that Prue put on herself and he refused to discuss the prospect of her continuing work this time.

Alice was over the moon to become an aunt again. She knew Prue would still secretly come into the offices at least once a week to discuss ideas and projects for *Sheer*. Prue was as stubborn as herself when wanting her own way and she enjoyed working for the magazine. Therefore, the change wasn't too damaging in the structure of the magazine and Prue's talented assistant, Maisy would take over Prue's role. So, Alice couldn't understand this feeling of being unsettled, of discontent. She wished she could put her finger on the reason.

A knock on her office door broke into her brooding. She glanced at the ornate clock on the wall. Twelve-thirty. Too early for any of her appointments. She sat back in her chair. 'Enter.'

Vince popped his head around and gave her a cheeky grin. 'Good afternoon, my lady.'

She smiled at him, feeling immediately better at his appearance. He always had that effect on her. His happy demeanour brightened every room he entered. Since her marriage and gaining her title, he had always called her, *my lady*, not in deference to her status but as a joke that the girl, whose pigtails he used to pull, was now a titled lady. That was Vince. He smiled the whole time and took nothing seriously. He was the only person she knew who could lighten the atmosphere at a funeral, who got the mourners laughing at antics of the deceased instead of crying for their loss. He excelled at finding the best in every situation and she and the magazine would be lost without his enthusiasm and drive. 'Vince, darling. I wasn't expecting you today. Is something the matter?'

'Not at all. Do I need a reason to come and see you?'

'Gosh, absolutely not.'

He sauntered in, his manner relaxed and carefree as it always was. Nothing bothered Vince. Well, nothing she knew about. She'd known him since childhood, he was her brother's best friend, and he was known for his happy-go-lucky attitude to life.

She lifted her cheek for him to kiss. 'Have you come to take me out for an expensive luncheon? I simply must escape this office.'

'You escape the office? You're usually chained to this desk.'

She glanced at his suit, the same charcoal grey one he'd been constantly wearing recently. 'Yes, I know, but the latest edition has gone to the presses and I'm in need of a break before the editorial staff meeting this afternoon. So how about it? High tea at the Savoy?'

'Ah... not today unfortunately, sorry.'

'Tomorrow then? Shall we take a drive into the country? Or we could head for the coast, Brighton perhaps, and stay in some hotel and get roaring drunk on brandy cocktails until the sun comes up? Oh, let's do that, Vince! We've not done anything thrilling for simply ages. Do say yes.' She was suddenly eager to be away from London and her responsibilities.

'Sounds like the grandest of ideas, dearest, but alas, I am unable to at this time.'

She frowned at the pensive expression he wore and looked at the gold-embossed envelope in his hand. 'Is that for me?'

'It is.' He handed it to her and then sat on the corner of her large walnut desk and fiddled with the square crystal vase that held her pencils.

She pulled out the invitation and read it with surprise. 'We are invited to the *Corden-Greens'* annual winter ball next month? I honestly don't believe it.'

'We are,' he boasted, his brown eyes smiling at her. 'Are you impressed?'

'Suitably. How did you jolly well manage it?' She stared at him. 'An invite to the Corden-Greens' annual ball is almost impossible to acquire. It's a closed shop. The same people go every year, it's *select*. They have, in the past, turned away royalty, and even *me*!' She laughed at her own joke.

'I know. But as luck would have it, we are on the list. You and me.' He tilted his head, eyebrows raised. 'Care to go and slum it at the country's most exclusive ball of the year?'

Her thoughts scattered. It was a coup. The one occasion she'd always wanted to attend and never thought she would was now within her grasp. Her late husband's family were Knights of the Realm and even they had not made the list. She tapped the invitation. 'Seriously, how did you get the invite? Who did you sleep with?'

'No one.' Vince strode to the window and watched the rain, shoulders slumped.

'I don't believe you. Was it Janice Plumpton? She's had her eye on you for years, or has your latest mistress revealed she is a member of the art world, you know how the Corden-Greens love to advocate the arts.'

'I don't have a mistress at the moment, can't afford the expense, and I wouldn't sleep with Janice even when drunk. It was simply contacts, my lady.

You know how it works. A word in the right ear, being in the right place at the right time, all very boring.'

'Stop playing me about, Vince, I know how it usually works, but not for the Corden-Greens,' she scoffed, eager to know how he had done what many couldn't achieve. And why was he swiftly down in the mouth? She relied on him to make her laugh. But he was different today. Actually, now she thought about it, he'd been a little edgy since June when his father died, and it wasn't just grief.

A shiver trickled down her back. Something was wrong. Alice frowned, her fingers tight on the invitation. 'You seem awfully depressed, darling. Have you been out all night and not gone home to bed?'

'I wish.'

She glanced down at the invitation with its gold-embossed writing on white card, wondering how she could get him out of this mood. 'Is everything all right?'

'You will laugh when you hear,' he said mockingly, continuing to stare out of the window.

She waited, watching him closely, the stillness of him. There definitely was something strange in his manner, the stiffness of his shoulders. A flash of guilt squeezed her chest. She'd been so wrapped up in her own unexplained misery that she'd missed the signs in Vince. What a pair they were. 'Vince?'

He turned and stared at her, his expression sombre. 'I'm to marry Miss Diana Corden-Green.'

Alice felt her mouth drop open in shock and her stomach twist. 'What? What are you talking about?' She didn't believe him. 'You are to *marry* Diana Corden-Green?'

'So, it seems.' He shrugged as though they were talking about nothing more important than the weather.

'*So, it seems?*' Was she hearing this correctly? He was jesting, surely? Always one for a joke he was. 'Vince!' She forced a laugh, alarmed at her own reaction. 'Really, you are a buffoon. You had me there for a moment. What a joke! Shall I ring for coffee?'

'It is true.'

Suddenly, she felt cold, despite the expensive blue wool suit she wore. 'I don't believe you,' she whispered.

He held up his hands in surrender, the look on his face was closed, distant. 'Don't, Alice. Don't question me.'

'Don't question you?' she repeated, annoyed, no, furious with him. 'You spring this astonishing news on me, and I'm not allowed to question you about it?'

'It's none of your business,' he murmured, staring at his fingernails.

'You are my friend, of course it is my business when you make such an outlandish statement!'

'I have to go.' He pushed his hand through his silver-flecked dark hair, which had a tendency to curl when not cut short and stepped to the door. 'I'll see you on Monday for the marketing meeting.'

'Don't you dare leave!' She pushed up from her leather chair. 'How did this happen? I didn't even know you two were properly acquainted, never mind courting. I can't believe this. How have you kept this a secret? And why her, for God's sake? I don't understand. It's so sudden. *Why her?*' Her voice rose and she quickly took a deep breath to calm down.

'I've known the family vaguely through my mother's sister's husband. It's all very complicated.' He shrugged again. 'By chance I bumped into Diana and her mother some time ago at the Ritz, and since then we've exchanged the odd letter, met for walks in Hyde Park, that sort of thing.'

'And, *that sort of thing* has led to you both falling in love and you asking her to marry you without any of us, *your friends*, knowing a thing about it?' She couldn't hide the suspicion in her voice. Vince talked in the tone of someone discussing a business deal, not the love of his life. Was it possible that was what he had done, a business deal? Diana wasn't a beauty. In fact, she wouldn't draw any man's attention with her plain mousy looks, but gossips had it that she was sweet enough, just a little uptight and quiet. Someone totally opposite to whom Vince would be engaged to.

She glared at him as the silence stretched between them. None of this made sense. She couldn't consider it to be true. A hard rock of emotion lodged in her chest at the very thought of Vince being married. 'Well? Have you no more to say?'

'It is to be done. That is all you need to know.' His lips quirked into a semblance of a smile. 'Imagine how good this will be for *Sheer*. It'll open so many new doors for us.'

'Sod the magazine!' Alice stormed around the desk and poked him in the chest. 'Tell me this is what you want because I positively don't believe for a minute that it *is*.'

'Alice...'

'I want the truth.'

A flash of something crossed his face but he masked it quickly before she could identify the emotion. He bowed formally. 'I do not have to answer to you, my lady. What I do privately is my business. Good day.' He left the office before she could utter a reply.

She stared at the closed door for several moments, resisting the urge to chase after him, but it would never do to behave in such a way in front of the office staff.

Instead, she lit a cigarette held in a long ebony holder and walked to the window to gaze out at the grey sky, the grey Thames and the grey buildings on the other side of the bank. Vince couldn't marry. He was her escort to all the parties and dinners, the theatre shows and garden picnics. *He was hers...*

Alice drew in deeply on the cigarette, the smoke curling about her head. She felt every one of her thirty-three years.

How dare he leave her alone.

She stubbed out the cigarette and reached for her fox fur coat. Damn him. She didn't need Vince Barton. There were plenty of men wanting to be her companion.

God, she needed a drink!

'Winifred.' Alice left the office and stopped by her receptionist's desk. 'Cancel all my appointments for this afternoon.'

'Certainly, madam.' Winifred, a woman in her early sixties with neatly curled grey hair and usually dressed in sensible skirts of varying shades of brown, pulled out a thick ledger. She was used to Alice's whims and impulsive changes.

'Thank you. Have a good weekend.'

'And you, madam.'

Alice hesitated at the door leading from her office into the central office area where her five staff sat at their own desks, busy creating the next edition of the magazine. She gazed around the productive room filled with potted palms, previous magazine covers in frames hanging on the walls and, as always, the amiable hub of noise as her staff went about their work. Only, right now, Alice didn't feel the normal excitement of being in the room. She felt... nothing.

What was happening to her? This magazine had been her sole focus for the last six years. Where had her drive gone? And what's more, how could she get it back?

Annoyed at herself for feeling so low when she had absolutely no reason to be, she left the room, determined to drink and party the whole weekend and forget this wretched misery.

# Chapter Two

Vince nodded to Mrs Cunningham, the housekeeper, as he stepped into the hall of Barton Court, the family's townhouse in North London. The housekeeper took his hat and coat and disappeared with them. Once an elderly butler had done the job, but he'd never been replaced after he died because the men returning from the war no longer wanted to be subservient and earn pittance wages as domestic servants, and he couldn't blame them.

Having survived the war himself, he understood the need to not return to the old way of life. He and Brandon had resigned from the army and then spent the next few years travelling around Europe climbing mountains to challenge themselves and to forget the horrors of war. It was in Italy where Brandon met Prue, who was holidaying there with her grandmama, and it was there when Brandon fell injuring himself badly. That had stopped their escapes on mountains. The time had come for them to return to England and find some way to start again.

Brandon had married Prue, but Vince had struggled to settle. Alice, inviting him to be a part of *Sheer* saved his sanity as his father suffered several strokes over several years, until he died recently during the summer. The responsibility of helping his mother through such a terrible time became Vince's heavy burden, as did managing the Bartons' dwindling finances.

His gaze flashed to the right to the pale square on the wallpaper where, until last week, a Joshua Reynolds painting had hung. It was now waiting sale in the auction house along with many other works of art and valuable furniture unearthed in the attics and unused rooms.

He strolled through the drawing room, noticing keenly the missing valuable figurines, the Chinese vases and Japanese cabinetry. Such possessions he never cared for or even realised were there until they were gone.

Other changes caught his attention. No longer did flowers decorate every room. His mother always enjoyed flowers filling each of the rooms and hall tables, but flowers in winter were an expense long considered extravagant.

Advice from the family's solicitor had them contemplating every aspect of their lives. What money could be saved by making alterations to the way the house was managed, their entertainment, indeed every detail of how they lived was now under scrutiny. And all because of the death duties they had to pay from his father's death, the high taxes and the rapid decline of the family's wealth since before the war.

'Is that you, Vince?' his mother's serene voice called to him from the conservatory.

He joined her, standing by the white wrought iron table where she sat sipping tea from a plain green china tea service, the expensive pink and gold-edged set had sold at the last auction, along with numerous other sets that had been in the family for centuries.

He kissed her cheek. 'Good afternoon, Mama. What are you doing sitting in here? The drawing room is far warmer.'

'I needed a change. I seem to spend all my days in that drawing room. The conservatory is cold, yes, however, I have my wrap and it does benefit me to fiddle with my old plants. They and I have been through a lot together.'

'If that makes you happy.' Though the drop in temperature made him shiver inside his suit. He wished he still wore his coat.

'You have been into town?' Sylvia Barton's grey eyes were shadowed, her manner listless.

'Yes.'

'And?'

'It is sorted. Diana has agreed to marry me.'

She sucked in a breath. 'And the money?'

'Her father is discussing it with his solicitors. They will draw the papers up and I'll meet with him again in a couple of weeks.' He let out a long deep sigh, disgusted with himself for selling out to the Corden-Greens. They wanted their only daughter married to someone with an excellent pedigree. He needed the money she would bring to keep his family's estate, Barton Downs, in Sussex from going bankrupt. It was a good deal. Except he didn't love her, or she him.

Diana wanted to be married and have children and the sooner the better. At twenty-eight, she was tired of people whispering that she'd be single for life. She had told him all that this morning. They both agreed that this marriage, although unconventional, did suit them both and each would get from it what they wanted. Happily, they did like each other and got on well enough to be friends, and they both hoped that from there, friendship would develop into something more, something that would last. But Diana had shocked him by saying that if he decided he needed the odd affair, done discreetly, of course, that would be acceptable.

The marriage was business. A contract for survival, for them both.

'A couple of weeks? Let us hope we can endure until then.' Sylvia crumbled a small lemon tart on her plate, then pushed it away.

'The wedding isn't to be for six months or more, Mama. The date hasn't been set yet, but likely to be June. We have to survive until then at least.'

'Can we?'

'Yes. The auction will help.'

'Ah, the auction. Our disgrace goes public again. I will never recover from the shame. Some friends have stopped calling, you know. It is to be expected I suppose. We can no longer offer the hospitality we used to or are known for.' She rose carefully from her chair like an old woman, which until his father's death, Vince had never believed her to be. Her once blonde hair was completely grey now and she had lost the will to hide it with dyes. Gone was her spritely walk, her ready smile, her engaging wit. All replaced with an old woman he hardly recognised.

'All will be well. I promise. I will do my very best to reclaim the life you are used to, Mama.'

She paused next to him and cupped his face with her hand. 'Your father and his father are to blame for not safeguarding you and your heirs from this catastrophe. You have suffered enough with all that happened in the war and now you must suffer again by marrying a woman you barely know and do not care for, all because of the money she brings with her. It is wrong. Oh, I know it has often been done in the past, but the world is different now, changing, or has changed from what it was when I was a girl. I do not like this situation at all. I do not like you giving up your freedom for a contract.'

'Diana and I will rub along well enough,' he said with more confidence than he felt. 'Please don't worry. She is a good person.'

'Yes, I know she is, but is it enough? How do you know from the little time you have spent with her that you can get along sufficiently?'

'I have to trust my instincts.'

'It is for life, Vince!' She gripped his shoulder. 'Do you not see? Life. You shall always be tied to her. This is not like buying a horse or a house. You cannot walk away from her or sell her on. You cannot divorce her, that will be written into the solicitor's contract, mark my words. Her family will not ever want a hint of scandal attached to their name. Can you do this momentous thing, my son?'

'Do I have any choice?' He looked at her in despair. 'What is the alternative? I have to take care of you and the estate.'

'No!' She backed away, a horrified look on her face. 'I will not have you sacrifice your life, your happiness for me! I thought you were going through with it for your own reasons, not for me.'

He pulled out a chair and sat down heavily. 'It's not just you, but the Sussex estate, the family name, our history and reputation, and for myself, too, I suppose. My pride.' He paused. 'Though, to be honest, I wouldn't mind if it all went.' He waved his arms to encompass the whole room. 'It's like a noose around my neck. If I could just have enough to live peacefully in a townhouse somewhere, with perhaps... the odd holiday in a villa somewhere warm, then I'd be happy.'

Mama folded her hands together. 'Would you? Honestly?'

He thought for a long moment, finally accepting the truth of it. He wasn't cut out to play the lord of the manor. True he'd been educated and brought up to be so, but it wasn't in him. It wasn't who he was. The estate of Barton Downs was enormous and cost a fortune each year in its upkeep. He didn't see the need of it, and he felt guilty for feeling that way. As the eldest, and only son, he should be doing everything he could to keep all the family properties intact. Yet, the truth was, he preferred the city to the country and Barton Downs needed more money than he could make with the few investments he'd inherited.

'Vince? Talk to me.'

He sighed deeply. 'Yes, Mama. I truly do think I could be happy without the estate.'

'Then do it. Instruct the solicitors to sell. We'll get rid of the lot. If you do not want the estate, I shan't beg you to change your mind.'

'You won't?' He was surprised and couldn't hide it.

'That estate was never a home to me. Your father's mother ruled the place even after we married. She never wanted to give up being the mistress of it. I was happy to let her stay in control and so I made this house my home. Selling the estate and all the problems that go with it will be the best solution.'

Vince stared up at her. 'You know it's not as easy as that. No one is buying large country houses anymore, unless they are American. Barton Downs will take a long time to sell, and the expense of its upkeep will continue on, forever increasing as the house gets older. No one wants that. I doubt we'd get good price on this house never mind a sprawling country pile in the green fields of rural Sussex.'

He glanced around the conservatory, blind to the leafy green plants collected from exotic parts of the world, but instead seeing the structure properly for the first time, the peeling paint, the warped wood. 'We need new glass in here.'

'Yes, it's the least of our problems though.'

'True. I've been sent quotes for repairs at Barton Downs. The price for replacing the roof on the east wing is enormous. Then there is damp in the attics and some of the bedrooms, the cellar floods, the stables are in ruin, the gardens are overgrown, and then there are the debts from the death duties we have to pay as well as the income tax invoices. Need I go on?'

She shakily took the chair opposite him and shook her head. 'No. Do not say anymore. But think of this. Will Diana's father want to pour his money into Barton Downs when he knows of the extent of the debts, the upkeep? What does he get from buying all this for his daughter?'

'He gets her married into an old noble family. The Corden-Greens have enormous wealth and are powerful, but they have no pedigree that really matters. It's a known joke that they are only one generation from trade. The Corden-Greens want grandchildren. Diana's father told me so himself. He wants his lineage to continue. And let's face it, Diana's brother doesn't look in any hurry to marry and produce an heir.'

'That is probably because he prefers his male friends...'

'Mama!' Although shocked that his mother knew about such things, he grinned.

'I have lived a life, you know, my dear, and I do have my sources.'

'So, it's down to Diana to fulfil her father's wish for grandchildren. Only, no man from a decent family has shown any interest and she's not getting any younger. Apparently, there hasn't been any attention at all and she's getting desperate.'

'That is because she has the features of a field mouse and the character of one!' His mother huffed. 'No one is eager enough to take her for whoever does has to take on the father as well and he is a man used to getting what he wants. Diana's husband will become her father's puppet.'

'And yet I must do it.' He groaned inwardly. Mr Corden-Green was a difficult man to like, arrogant and selfish, vastly wealthy and full of self-importance. The old man had already told Vince that he had found him a position in one of his businesses, a sort of marketing figurehead. He'd not even consulted with him about it. Vince hated the thought of working for his father-in-law as though he was some young pup straight out of school.

His mother reached for his hand and held it tightly. 'No, my darling son. I will not let you do it.' She too now gazed about the room. 'This is a house. Nothing more. I will not allow you to give up your life for houses or even the family's reputation. Your happiness is more important to me than bricks and mortar.'

'Mama...'

'No, Vince. It has been plaguing me since you mentioned your plan a few weeks ago. I have had many sleepless nights with my mind in turmoil about what all this entails. I do not like it. None of it. I will not allow you to go through with it. I am adamant in this.' She stood and straightened her shoulders, the old spark returning. 'Call it all off. Now. Go to Diana, tell her everything—'

'It's not possible!' He jerked to his feet. 'Contracts are getting drawn up as we speak.'

'Of course, it is possible to finish it! Diana is an intelligent girl, she will understand.' She headed for the door. 'I shall speak to Dunsten and Hickory. Those solicitors have charged this family enough over the years now they can earn it by helping us out of this mess once and for all.'

'But, Mama—'

She turned at the doorway. 'No, Vince, I will not stand by and let this happen. It was weak of me to allow it to continue for as long as it has.' She took a deep breath. 'A small house is all we need. We can manage to afford that, I am sure. All this,' she said, sweeping her hands wide, 'means nothing anymore now your father is gone. Unless, of course, you want to try and keep it for your children, *yours and Diana's children*?'

He shuddered at the thought of lying in the same bed as Diana, for whom he felt no attraction whatsoever. Liking her wasn't enough. He could not imagine performing the act of love with her at all. In fact, he knew he couldn't. He was famous for chasing and bedding pretty women but in the last year he'd felt himself change. He wanted something permanent, something real and important like Brandon had with Prue. Someone to come home to, and not just his mother, but a woman who wanted to share his life. He wanted Alice. He had done for years. Yet, he knew she could never be his. Alice didn't feel the same. No one measured up to her fallen hero husband. Alice was a free spirit, his friend, and could be nothing more.

Diana was a nice woman, but it also meant he'd not have the passion, the deep love he knew he wanted and was capable of achieving with someone else.

Alice, the woman he had loved since he was a youth, but who had never seen him as anything other than a brother, would never consider him. If Alice had given the slightest hint that she was attracted to him, he'd have declared his feelings for her, but she focused only on *Sheer*. He had lovers, and so did she and yes, he escorted her to all the parties around London, they were known for being friends as well as business partners. He had stakes in *Sheer* and was the senior marketing manager for the magazine. They were part of the wild set of London and not once had she asked for anything more intimate.

So, he thought to marry Diana. Diana and her money would save the family's reputation and save his mother from living out her years in poverty.

For the last few weeks all he considered was the money, the debts being paid, no more embarrassing auctions, the family's honour being restored and keeping his mother safe to live out the rest of her life securely in this house as she deserved and was her right.

To have all that meant marrying Diana, giving her children.

Sweat broke out on his forehead despite the coldness of the conservatory. A life with Diana, as kind as she was, would suffocate him, he knew it would. He would become a man he didn't like. A man who didn't want to return home to a wife he didn't love.

He groaned in anguish. God, he was but a stupid fool! How had he got himself into such a mess?

'Drive over there now, Vince, please.' His mother broke into his reverie. 'Explain it all to her. I am certain Diana does not want to be married to a man who does not love or desire her.'

'She says she doesn't mind. She understands and accepts it.' They'd had the brutal conversation last week. Even then they had been dishonest to themselves and to each other.

'Then she is lying to herself. It is not fair to either of you. Someone else will marry her, I am sure of it. But she is not for you. Money will not buy the happiness you need to live the rest of your days, and they could be a great many indeed. I will not let you do it. Marriage is hard enough when you do love the other person, but without it, you are doomed. Is that what you survived the war for, what you fought for? Is that the freedom your fellow soldiers paid with their lives for?'

Vince nodded. She was right. Mama's words struck a chord deep in his chest. He owed it to his fallen men to live the best life he could.

'Darling?' his mama prompted.

'I don't think I've ever gone back on my word in my life, Mama.' He sighed deeply, feeling wretched.

'This is too serious to simply brush aside and ignore, my son.' Her eyes softened. 'No one knows about the marriage deal outside of a few people. It has not been announced in the newspapers. If you are going to end the agreement between the pair of you, and I hope you do, then I suggest you get on with it.'

'Diana will hate me.'

'Better that she hates you now and not in the years to come when there is more at stake.'

'I'll telephone her now and ask to meet with her on Monday at the Savoy.'

She kissed his cheek. 'We will survive all this. Trust me.'

Vince remained silent as she left the conservatory. Poor Diana. Her hopes had been raised and he was going to dash them. The moment he voiced the wedding out loud this morning to Alice the reality hit him, that and the shock on her face. He didn't want any of it. Diana meant nothing to him and never would.

He drummed his fingers on the table just as the rain started to beat on the glass roof above him. The rain clouds had drifted north from the city, and he thought of Alice once more. When she asked him this morning about marrying Diana, he felt ashamed, ashamed and humiliated that his affairs had come to this. The stunned look on her face haunted him. He couldn't admit to her that he felt like he was drowning, that his life meant nothing to him. How could he tell her of his unhappiness? What right did he have to speak of it to someone who has always known him to be the light of every party? Only now, his light was diminished, he no longer wanted to smile and make people laugh. He'd had enough. More than enough.

With each dreaded step, he walked to the hall and picked up the telephone handset. Less than a minute later he heard Diana's soft voice on the other end.

'Diana, it's me, Vince.'

'Vince? How lovely.' He could hear the smile in her tone and his gut clenched.

'Could we meet at the Savoy for lunch on Monday?'

'Monday, no, sorry. I am hosting a morning tea here at the house for the Chelsea Women's Art Society.' She sounded apologetic.

'Tuesday then? It's important we speak.'

There was a pause before she answered. 'Important?'

'Yes, terribly.'

'I see.' Another long pause stretched. 'Are you having second thoughts?' she whispered.

He closed his eyes and swore under his breath. 'Diana...'

'Tuesday at eleven o'clock is fine.'

The line went dead in his ear.

# Chapter Three

Alice swallowed the last of her red wine and glared at her brother, Brandon, who sat across the dining table in her townhouse in Notting Hill. 'Well? We've finished the first course and discussed the family and trivial things as etiquette requires.'

'But now you want to dispense with niceties and verbally attack me over something of which I have no control?' Brandon shook his head as he topped up her wine glass and his own. 'What exactly do you want me to do?'

'Something, anything, I don't know, but we can't let Vince waste his life married to someone he doesn't love!' Agitated, she moved the crystal salt and pepper shakers an inch or two in the centre of the table.

'Why do you care, Alice?' Brandon reclined back in his chair while Esme, the maid, cleared their soup bowls. 'Vince is a grown man who can do as he pleases. He always has done.'

'Do you think what he is doing is the right thing?'

'He's getting married, Alice, not murdering children in their sleep. Why are you so against this? Who he marries won't affect what he does for *Sheer*. He'll be even better at promoting the magazine once he starts to move within the circles of the Corden-Greens, they know everyone, including a good many rich families in America. I heard it mentioned only the other day in the club that Diana's old man has invested in some scheme in India, at least I think it is India, anyway, apparently, it's made him even more wealthier than any man has the right to be. So, you see, Vince will be within a powerful family, and he can push *Sheer* in directions we can only dream about. You mustn't be worried he'll forget us.'

She spluttered. 'You think this is about the magazine? I don't care about his role with *Sheer*. It's far more important than that. This is our friend, Brandon. Vince has been your best friend since you were children. How can you calmly sit there and allow him to make this mistake?'

'Who says it is a mistake? You?' He grinned.

'Can it be anything else? He hardly knows the girl!' She took a moment to calm down. She didn't want a screaming match with Brandon because she rarely won. She became too emotional while he remained calm and rational.

All weekend she had thought about Vince's announcement. It filled her head, pushing out all attempts to have a splendid time at a friend's house party near Oxford. None of the drinking, dancing and party games had pushed her concerns away. She'd barely slept and come home early on Sunday with a roaring headache and in a bad mood.

Inviting Brandon to dinner on Monday, while Prue was away in France visiting her sister Millie, to talk about Vince seemed the right thing to do, but he was being a typical man this evening and stubbornly refused to be of any use in the matter.

'Believe me, Alice, if I thought Vince was doing something ridiculous, I would talk to him, but I fail to see why this is such an issue. The man wants to marry, he's thirty-six, it's about time.'

'But why her? He's never been one to look for a suitable wife before.' She waited until the maid, Esme placed their second course of lamb and vegetables in front them and left the room before continuing on a softer, earnest tone. 'I just feel something isn't quite right about this. What do you know? He must talk to you about it.'

There was a long pause before Brandon spoke. 'Money.'

'Money?'

'He's inherited debts, death duties.' Brandon poured gravy onto his meat from the gravy boat and then offered to do the same for Alice.

She nodded her thanks. 'Yes, he mentioned the death duties to me months ago.'

'Well, to put it simply there is no money left to keep the London house and Barton Downs estate going beyond another year. He's selling everything he can.'

Letting this information sink in, Alice played with the slices of lamb on her plate, her mind working. 'I see.'

'Do you?' Brandon raised one dark eyebrow at her. 'Bankruptcy looms. He's scared, not for himself, but for his mother. He doesn't want to disappoint her. They thought they had time to deal with the financial problems, to claw back some money through investments. I was trying to help them. There just wasn't time in the end.'

'So, marrying Diana gains him access to the Corden-Greens' millions?'

'Well, yes, as vulgar as that is.' Brandon cut into his potato and forked some into his mouth.

'A business deal in effect.'

'It's not unheard of. It still happens.'

'I'm surprised he's not found an American heiress.'

'He doesn't need to. Diana is an English heiress of sorts. He brother will inherit most of the wealth, but Diana won't be without.'

Alice nibbled on a small piece of sliced lamb. 'And the brother won't be giving his parents an heir, not with his... tendencies being inclined towards his male friends.'

'True. It's London's worst kept secret.' Brandon chewed thoughtfully. 'I feel sorry for the fellow. He can only ever be happy in secret. On the outside he must pretend to be a different person.'

'And Diana's father wants grandsons,' Alice added.

'Grandchildren that Vince can provide.'

They ate in silence for a while, but Alice's thoughts whirled around in her head, and she barely tasted anything on her plate. She looked up as she realised Brandon had stopped eating. 'What is it? The food?'

Shaking his head, he laid down his knife and fork. 'The food is fine, not that you've enjoyed it. Alice, Vince is our dearest friend, but I am amazed at your response to his news.'

'Why amazed? As you say he is our friend. I want him to be happy.'

'So do I, but you don't see me reacting as strongly as you are.'

'I... I... you see, I... well...' She faltered to a stop, not sure of what to say. Why was she feeling so strongly about this? She didn't know. All she knew was that since Vince sprung the news on Friday morning she had felt out of sorts.

'Do you have feelings for him?'

She sipped her wine thoughtfully. Good God. Did she? How could she? Vince was... just Vince! Someone she'd known for as long as she could remember. He was like a brother...

'Alice?' Brandon studied her. 'Am I right?'

'I... I don't think so. He's important to me, certainly...' She cared for him, of course she did, but love him? It seemed too *sensible*, too *real*.

'Then you need to think about it and find out your true feelings. Though to be brutally honest with you, I don't think it will make any difference to Vince because you don't have the money he needs.'

'So, he'll sacrifice himself for a house,' she muttered, irritated and confused.

'Vince will do what he has to.' Brandon reached over and took her hand. 'I wish with all my heart that he wasn't in this situation and that you and he could, well, be together. I want you to be happy, and him, too.'

'I am happy.'

'Are you?' He scowled at her and sat back in his chair. 'No, you are not. You cannot lie to me, dearest sister. I know you too well. I've noticed this last year how you seem to be pretending to be happy.'

'I love my life,' she defended hotly.

'Really?' he scoffed. 'I don't believe you and I don't think you believe yourself.'

'You know nothing.'

'Trust me, I know more than you are aware. For instance, I can see you are losing interest in *Sheer*.'

'That's not true!' She glared at him.

'Don't lie to me.' He held up a hand as she went to protest. 'And I'm not judging you, just stating the facts. You've lost your drive for the magazine. When you first started it, you worked twenty hours a day, barely sleeping or eating, to make it a success. Your passion and focus was exemplary. Everyone admired you and were thrilled to be a part of the journey.'

'But?' she prompted, miffed at him for bringing it up.

'But now, you have slackened the reins. Others do the majority of the work.'

'Because that's what I pay them to do. I cannot do it all by myself.'

'No, but you used to watch over them like a hawk seizing its prey.'

'My staff are well trained now, they don't need me to be hovering over their every move.'

Brandon nodded. 'Very true.'

She glared at him knowing there was more to come. 'And?'

'Nothing.' He sipped his wine.

'I will admit that the magazine has become so well run and my team are so competent that I don't need to think about *Sheer* during every waking hour, not how I did when it first started. I've worked hard and long hours to make it successful.'

'No one is denying that.'

'You seem to be,' she remarked, annoyed.

'I am proud of you, as you well know, but I feel that now the pressure is off, you're missing something in your life. Alice, you spend your life partying.'

'What's wrong with that?' she snapped.

Unfazed at her brutish tone, Brandon sipped more of his wine. 'Prue and I just want you to be happy.'

'Just because I'm not married to the love of my life like you are, doesn't mean I'm not happy, too.' She refilled her glass and gulped the wine.

'Tell me then, why haven't you had a serious relationship with any man since Tom died over ten years ago.'

Her heart sank. She glanced at the framed photo on the mantelpiece of Tom in uniform. 'I've not met anyone who can replace him.'

'You haven't even tried.' Brandon finished eating his dinner.

'We aren't all destined to be like you and Prue.' She smiled sadly.

He squeezed her hand. 'Yes, but I want that for you. I want you to experience a love like we do. There is nothing better than being loved by someone you love.'

'It's easier said than done.' Alice doubted she'd ever find love again, and definitely not the kind of adoring love Brandon and Prue shared.

'Perhaps. Which, coming back to the original discussion, is why Vince needs to walk his own path, and if that is with Diana, so be it. I will not interfere, and nor will you.' He raised his eyebrows at her in warning.

She smarted at his high-handed tone. 'I'm allowed an opinion, Brandon.'

He laughed. 'No one is ever in doubt of that, dearest.'

\*\*\*

Vince left the Savoy and walked blindly along the street, not caring in which direction he was going, or that a strong cold wind carrying spots of rain buffeted him. He'd never felt so low in his life, not even in the trenches, because then he'd been surrounded by fellow men suffering the same as him and there was a perverse comfort in that. However, at this moment, he'd never felt more alone in his life.

Back in the Savoy, no doubt Diana and her mother still sat at the dining table. Her mother had been speechless with fury at him. Diana had been quiet, resigned. No tears, no tantrums. Just downcast eyes and slumped shoulders.

Vince had explained himself as clearly as possible, apologising profusely, wishing he didn't have to hurt Diana. In the end, he'd left quickly, not wanting to prolong the awkwardness, to suffer the strained silence from Diana or the muttered angry words cast by her mother.

He continued walking, the rain lashing down now, dripping off his hat. Umbrellas opened all around him, but he'd forgotten his. His best coat would be ruined.

Eventually, the cold made him stop his depressing stroll and he stood on the corner of a street. A motorcar took the corner and splashed water onto his leather shoes. Swearing softly, he squinted up at the sign on the side of a building to get his bearings. Fortuitously, he was only around the corner from the family's solicitors' office.

It took only a moment to make a choice. If today was going to be the day of life decisions, then he might as well do it all now. All these indecisions were making him ill. He'd lost weight and felt lethargic most of the time. The stress was giving him grey hair and he was tired of feeling so low. It wasn't his nature. Changes had to be made, drastic changes, not the small adjustments they were doing, selling the odd painting and furniture at auctions. No, the time had come to strike out and remove the noose from around his neck.

Within five minutes he was seated in front of the desk of Mr Arthur Dunsten, a greying older gentleman of an undefined age, but who Vince had known all his life.

It didn't take Vince long to inform him of the day's events, and when he'd finished, Mr Dunsten leaned forward in his chair, placed his elbows on his desk and rested his chin on his folded hands.

'Well, Mr Barton, I am sad to hear this news. Sad indeed. Your father, God rest his soul, has left you in such a desperate position that, well, Miss Corden-Green's marriage settlement is urgently needed, very much so.'

'I am aware of that, Mr Dunsten. I wouldn't have gone into such an agreement otherwise, but my conscience, and my mother, will not allow me to go through with it. It wasn't fair to Diana or myself.' He ignored the whispered voice in his head that Diana's father would want his guts for garters!

'Then we are back to square one, sir. And if I can be so bold to say, your predicament is still rather severe and with no solution at present to fix it.'

'Actually, Mr Dunsten, there is.'

'Oh?'

Vince took a deep breath. 'I wish you to sell.'

'Sell what exactly? Another auction?'

'Everything. The entire estate of Barton Downs and anything else in the Barton portfolio, except one house for us to live in.'

Dunsten reared back. 'The entire portfolio? Oh sir, let's not be hasty. Perhaps we can—'

'No, Mr Dunsten. It is decided. My mother and I are in total agreement in this. We sell everything and, hopefully, it is enough to make us debt free.'

'But the whole lot? That is a monumental decision.'

'And one that has taken a lot of thought, believe me. However, it is the only way forward as I see it. It is the only way we can be rid of the debts, you know that.'

Dunsten nodded sagely. 'Indeed, it is, and I'm sorry that it has come to this, deeply sorry.' He wrote some notes in a ledger. 'Do you have in mind which property you wish to keep to live in?'

'I believe my father has a cottage in Yorkshire with some acreage attached, but for my mother's sake I would like to keep the London townhouse if that is at all possible?'

'Hmm...' Dunsten stood and stepped to a large floor-to-ceiling cupboard and opened the doors of it to reveal sets of drawers. He riffled through two drawers before finding the folder containing the Barton assets. 'This is everything that your father and grandfather bought over the years.'

Once seated again, Dunsten flipped through the folder of numerous papers, reading aloud as he went. 'Your father inherited from your grandfather the Barton Downs estate, the London townhouse, the five warehouses in Cubitt Town, London, the cottage and ten acres in Fulford, near York, and the four terrace houses in Limehouse, London.' The solicitor looked over his glasses at Vince. 'Barton Downs is the property that draws down most of your finances. I would advise selling it as soon as possible.'

'Yes, I agree.' Vince nodded unhappily. The estate had been in the family for generations, and he was the one to sell it. Not something to be proud of but he could see no way of keeping the estate viable.

'The warehouses are an income, one sorely needed. I would not be inclined to sell them.' The older man tapped the papers. 'The townhouse really should go, and the cottage in Yorkshire. The townhouse sale would clear many debts as would the cottage and land. It would give you a clear path ahead, Mr Barton. If you and your mother could live simply...'

'We are agreed to that, Mr Dunsten.' Vince nodded. He rubbed a hand over his face. 'But where to live? I'm loathed to rent a house at the rates being charged in the centre of London.'

'No, that is not a wise decision.' Mr Dunsten glanced at his papers. 'You could move into the terraces in Limehouse? It's not ideal to be certain, but it is still close to London and no rent.'

'Limehouse?' Vince recalled going to the dock area only a couple of times with his father. It was a dirty, rough place, full of dockers and pubs and narrow grimy streets filled with raggedly dressed children. 'I could not allow my mother to live there, Mr Dunsten.'

The old man shrugged. 'Needs must, Mr Barton. It may not have to be for a long period of time, but it could get you out of your present bind. No rent to pay.'

'I will think about it.' Vince fidgeted in the leather chair, his mind whirling with the prospect of a dismal future with reduced finances.

'Shall I ring for some coffee and let us get down to details?' Mr Dunsten asked, pity in his eyes.

Over an hour later, Vince left the office feeling lighter of heart than he had for many months. Although the outcome of selling most of their property portfolio wasn't something he could be happy about, at least he'd be debt free, and that gave him hope. He strode in the darkening afternoon, heading for his club and a stiff drink.

'Vince!'

Above the noise of traffic and pedestrians, he heard his name called and turning, he smiled as a sleek white Rolls Royce pulled to a stop next to him.

Alice. She was the only person of their society he knew that drove her own car. That was the type of woman she was. Independent. Stubborn. Adventurous.

He opened the door and climbed in. She looked stylish wearing a pinstripe navy skirt suit and a small navy hat sporting a large red bow. 'Good afternoon, my lady, going my way?'

'Which way would that be then?' She smiled back, her green eyes full of caring.

'Anywhere I can have a drink.'

'That kind of day?' She pulled swiftly out into the middle of the road causing the other vehicles to toot their horns at her in frustration as they braked.

'Yes, that kind of day, that kind of week, that kind of month and year.'

She glanced at him, the laughter gone. 'Talk to me, Vince.'

'What is there to say?' He looked out at the passing people. 'The marriage is off, you'll be frightfully pleased to know.'

Her grip slipped on the steering wheel. 'It is? Why?'

'I couldn't do it to Diana, or myself. It must have been the shortest engagement in the history of society.'

'Well, bravo! I am pleased, I won't deny it.' She drove faster, dodging around other cars, wagons, electric trams and horse-drawn carts. 'It would have been a positively terrible mistake.'

'Yes.' He held on as she took a corner too fast, making a man hurry across the road.

'Though it means we won't be going to their coveted ball.' Alice sighed and gave him a wink.

'I won't be going but you have the invitation, take someone else.'

'No, they gave the invitation to you.' She shrugged. 'I don't mind, really. I like being one of the few who haven't been invited. Shall we make a club for all members who haven't been to that ball?' She laughed.

'Sounds exclusive, yes, let's do it.' He grinned. She always lifted his mood.

'So, what now?'

'The entire estate is to be sold, the townhouse and the Yorkshire cottage. We'll try to keep the warehouses and the terraces in Limehouse.'

'Oh, gosh. I am sorry to hear it, old bean.'

'Mine and my mother's life as we know it will never be the same.' How would they recover from it all? He had no idea.

'You were in an impossible situation. You've done the best you could.'

'Have I? I hope so. Or have I not fought enough to keep it all? Did I not try hard enough? I just don't know anymore.'

'Stop it, Vince,' she snapped at him, nearly hitting a man on a bicycle. 'If the decisions you've made today are the right ones, and they must be or you wouldn't have made them, then get on with it. The future is out there for you now. Yes, it's not how you wanted or expected it to be, but it is there.'

'Can you slow down? You're going to jolly well kill us both!'

'Oh, absolutely. Sorry.'

The car instantly slowed and as they left the centre of London, he realised she was driving him to her home in Notting Hill. He raised his eyebrow at her. 'Did I say I wanted to go to your home?'

'Oh, do be quiet. You wanted a drink and I have a very smashing supply of all sorts of alcohol, as you jolly well know.' Her jaw clenched. 'But you also need a decent meal down you. You're nothing but skin and bone. In fact, you look appalling. Just like you looked when you and Brandon returned from France. And I'll not stand for it.'

He remained silent as she parked the car in front of her white townhouse with its black iron railings. Inside, the maid, Esme, took his hat and coat and Alice told her to inform Mrs Jones, the cook, that she had a guest tonight for dinner.

Following Alice upstairs to the warm reception room, which was littered with collectibles from all her travels around the world, Vince had to smile as she went straight to the small bar area at the back of the room and poured out two large whiskeys on ice.

Alice handed him one glass and raised hers. 'Here's to a brand-new life that is exciting and full of happiness. Cheers!'

He laughed. 'You're such an optimist, Alice.'

'You used to be too! Now just say cheers, for heaven's sake!'

'Cheers!'

She waved him to the big red sofa that held plump cushions you could sink into, and over the years he had done that often at her famous parties when they'd drunk so much they could no longer stand.

Alice sat at one end and he on the other. She gave him a long look. 'I know this is going to be a terribly awful time for you, but I'm here. I insist you lean on me. I want to help, and if I had the Corden-Greens' millions I would offer myself in marriage to you and save you from all this ghastly business!' Her laugh was strained. 'But failing that, I do have some money, as you know. Most of it is invested in *Sheer*, and I bought a lot of American stocks, especially with Tom's money. However, I can sell some stocks.'

'Alice...'

'No, listen to me.' She straightened her shoulders and lifted her chin. 'I want to help you, and money is what you need. I'd enjoy giving some to you, or loan it to you if that's what you'd prefer. It might not be enough to keep the estate—'

'Stop it, Alice.' He jerked to his feet, humiliated by the fact that she wanted to bail him out, and her pity.

Her green eyes narrowed, and he saw the exasperation on her face, for it was the same expression he'd seen for years when she didn't get her way. 'Don't be stubborn, Vince, please.'

'I'm not. I'm being dashedly practical. I have to do this on my own.' He threw back the drink, embracing the burn down his throat.

'But you don't have to do it on your own!'

'Yes, I do. You don't understand.' He ran one hand over his hair, suddenly tired. 'I will sort it all out. I will take care of mother and with what is left... I'll manage my own affairs.'

'You aren't alone in this, Vince, I promise you that,' she said softly.

'Thank you.' He stared down at her, his chest felt tight. He had the insane urge to gather her into his arms and hold her close, to smell the freshness of her hair, to bury his face in her neck and never come up for air. He was going mad. How could he have these thoughts about Alice? He *must* treat her like a sister, one of his best friends. His fantasies had no place in his life.

'Well, this positively won't do at all. I think that for this evening we are not going to talk of anything serious.' She suddenly stood up. 'I'm going to go change and then we are going to eat and drink and laugh all night. We'll go to a splendid jazz club and dance until dawn. All talk is to be of a silly nature. We shall gossip and make jolly fun of other people we don't like. We shall reminisce about the old days and make exhilarating plans of what we're going to do next summer. Agreed?'

'I have no money, Alice, so all summer plans will consist of me packing up the houses.'

'Uh uh!' She waved her finger at him. 'No talk of anything serious tonight, Vince. You've just broken the rule.'

'All I'm saying is—'

'No, no! Absolutely no serious talk. I forbid it. Now agree to the rule, if you don't mind.'

Relaxing, Vince nodded and gave her a smile that was genuine for the first time in a long time. 'All right. I completely agree.'

# Chapter Four

A week later, laughing and slightly drunk, Alice gripped Simon Delamont's hand as he twirled her around the dancefloor. Her emerald-green silk and chiffon dress twirled around her legs and the long pearl necklace she wore swung from side to side. The jazz band played on the stage behind them and surrounding the dancefloor were white-clothed tables seating the honoured class of London's elite. Gilded light shades cast the large ornate ballroom in a myriad of gold. Men in black dinner suits and women wearing silk and taffeta smothered in jewels danced, ate and drank.

Every night, if someone wished it, there was a place to go in London to enjoy themselves. Theatres, restaurants, jazz clubs, cocktail bars and private homes were the haunts of the privileged. Alice loved the freedom of mixing with a select social group of friends who all had a fast lifestyle. She counted on them to keep her entertained as she entertained them. Aside from Vince, her closest friends were Sally Stuart, Gordy Elliot, Helen Blake and Ronnie Holden. With them she could be wild and expressive all she liked. They were as carefree as she was, always up for a laugh and an adventure. The six of them shared homes and secrets and a day didn't go by without one of them seeing the other in some way or talking to them on the telephone.

Right now, they were all dancing, having drunk too much and eaten too little. Swaying dramatically, Gordy had lost his partner but didn't care and danced alone. Helen laughed at some foolish thing Ronnie said to her, while Sally only had eyes for the man who held her rather too close than was acceptable, not that anyone cared.

'Want a drink?' Simon asked in his educated American accent.

She nodded as the band finished one song and went straight into another. She led the way back to their table, smiling and nodding to those people she knew. She blew a kiss to an older man she once had dinner with last year before deciding to end it before anything even begun.

At the table she waited for Simon to refill her champagne glass from the bottle in the ice bucket.

Watching him, she felt a flare of desire. His blond dashing good looks and handsome smile never grew old. Simon was the son of a rich man and had been introduced to her at a party on his first visit to London two years ago. They'd clicked immediately. Seeing in each other an undeniable attraction.

Simon was in London for the whole month of October, and they were picking up where they'd left off when she was last in New York during the summer. Simon had begged her to stay in his Fifth

Avenue apartment and take their friendship to the next level of intimacy. She'd agreed and for a few weeks she'd toyed with the idea of becoming dreadfully serious about him. But in the end, she missed London and her family and friends and knew America would never be her home.

Not one to be downhearted for long, Simon remained upbeat, in his typical American fashion, about her decision and declared they would always be friends. Which was why they were together tonight. Simon had returned to London for business and immediately telephoned her to meet him.

London social gossip had them as lovers, but there wasn't any proof and Alice preferred it that way. Simon never stayed overnight at her home in Notting Hill. Not that it stopped the gossip and rumours. As part of the London 'wild crowd' meant her activities were always up for discussion, though her title and position of being Lady Mayton-Walsh saved her from outright backlash. Tom's family had been admired and respected and she tried not to bring their name into disrepute. Alice had made sure she kept as discreet as possible with any man she took home over the years.

'Where is your friend Vince?' Simon asked. 'He's usually stuck to your side whenever I'm in London. I've been here for a week and not seen him once. I'm not complaining. I enjoy having you to myself, well, most of the time.' He grinned and inclined his head to her four friends on the dance floor.

Alice stared at the bubbles in her wide champagne glass. 'Vince is currently in Sussex.'

'I for one hope he stays there.' Simon sipped his champagne, his eyes watching her over the rim of his glass. 'What shall we do tomorrow? Take in a show?'

She nodded. 'Sounds smashing.'

'I'll get tickets in the morning. Anything in particular?'

'We could go to the new Dominion Theatre that's recently opened?' She'd read about the opening in the newspaper. 'They are showing a musical comedy called, *Follow Through.*'

'Excellent. Shall we have dinner before or after the show?'

'Definitely after, but we can have drinks first. I know a lovely little bar in Oxford Street.' She looked up as the others came back to the table. 'Simon and I are going to the Dominion tomorrow night, do you fancy it?'

'Oh, I say that's a jolly good idea.' Gordy filled his glass, emptying the bottle.

'Love to,' Helen said, crashing into a chair with a laugh. 'Hey, order another bottle, Gordy. Heavens, you're meant to pour for the ladies first.'

Simon frowned at Alice. 'I thought it would be just you and I, babe?' His unhappy expression made Alice feel guilty.

'Sorry. I wasn't thinking.' In truth she didn't want to spend an evening alone with Simon.

Sally, all curly blonde hair, and dainty hands, sat next to Simon. 'We do rather hamper your time with Alice, don't we? Awfully sorry, dear chap.' She hiccupped and slumped against his shoulder. 'I need another drink.'

Simon sat her upright. 'I don't think you do, actually.'

Ronnie, a terribly tall man who stooped because he was conscious of his height pulled Sally over to him. 'Shall I take you home, sweet pea?'

A rumbling of fraught conversations rippled around the room. Suddenly, gentlemen's heads were close together in whispered conversations. Looks of anxiety were exchanged by their wives as they were spoken to in harried undertones.

'What's going on?' Alice asked, sitting straighter, glancing at the men's pale faces.

Simon stopped a waiter and asked.

'News has come through from America, sir. Something to do with a stock market crash, whatever that means.'

'Again?' Alice worried. Throughout the month of October, the American stock market had wobbled and crashed numerous times. The London stock market had fallen at the end of September causing concern amongst some of her friends, and especially Brandon. He'd urged Alice to sell her shares and stock in the American markets, but she'd not managed to get around to doing it. Although she wasn't an expert at share buying and selling and left it all up to her stockbroker, she knew the market fluctuated at times and didn't feel the need to bother her broker.

Simon rose and went to a nearby table and spoke to an older man with a large stomach, who was running his hands through his well-oiled grey hair. Simon was gone so long that Sally fell asleep, and Alice no longer felt like partying. People were leaving, the happy atmosphere seemed rather glum now.

She stood and said goodnight to her friends, giving them a kiss on each cheek, before going to where Simon stood talking.

'So sorry,' Simon apologised to her, his face full of worry.

The older man stood and nodded to Alice, shook Simon's hand and then helped his much younger wife up from her chair. 'It is time we went home,' he mumbled. Alice noticed she was pregnant.

'What's happening?' Alice asked as she and Simon walked to the foyer to collect their coats.

'Telegrams are being sent from home...' Simon passed the tickets to reclaim their coats to the girl behind the counter. 'The news isn't good. I need to speak to my father.'

'Should we be worried here in London? Usually, the markets right themselves in a day or so.'

'I think the entire world should be worried if what is happening in New York is true.'

Out on the street, Simon signalled for a black taxi.

'I have shares in a few American markets. I invested heavily a few years ago, as did Brandon. He's been telling me in the last couple of weeks to sell them.' She yawned and huddled into her long fox fur coat. The chill of the night air bit at her cheeks.

'Did you sell?' Simon opened the car door.

'No. I never got around to it,' she replied, slipping into the back seat.

'Let us hope you don't live to regret that decision.' He gave her a small smile to help ease the worry. 'It'll be fine. America is incredibly strong. Nothing can bring us down.'

*** 

A shaft of blinding sunlight forced Alice to close her eyes again as she raised her head up from the pillow. Esme was in the process of opening the tall drapes that covered the long narrow sash windows in the bedroom.

'Esme!' Alice flopped back onto the pillows, wishing she could throw one at her maid.

'I'm sorry, my lady but you did ask to be woken by nine, and it's ten past now. Also, there's a telegram for you.'

Alice groaned and held out her hand. 'Give it to me.'

'I've put it beside your plate at the table. Your eggs are boiled, and I'll make some fresh toast.' Esme swept up the expensive gold silk dress Alice had worn to dinner last night.

As Esme left the bedroom, Alice wrapped her satin dressing gown around her naked body and climbed from the bed. She went to the cheval mirror and peered at her face. Traces of makeup still lingered. She needed a bath.

Staring at her reflection, she scrutinised her face. Simon had kissed her passionately when they reached her home but hadn't suggested coming into the house. He wanted to telephone his father in America. She'd been pleased he didn't pressure her into sleeping with him. She wasn't sure if she'd been able to say no. But it felt such an age since she last was held and loved. Though it had only been months since she was in his bed in New York.

She studied her face and neck for signs of aging. She was thirty-three. Should she settle down, perhaps? Did she even want children? Usually, her answer was no. Yet, that answer was becoming more difficult to say. Was it time to get married?

Perhaps marry Simon? He was immensely wealthy, and fun to be with but was he a man she could spend the rest of her life with? She wasn't too sure about that. Simon was an oil baron's son, who'd never been to the Midwest where his father earned all the family fortune. No, Simon lived in Manhattan and London and Paris and wherever his urges took him. He survived by his family's wealth and spent each day in pursuits of his own pleasure.

Was Simon the man she wanted to marry?

The answer of no came much quicker.

Simon was a lady's man and Alice knew she wasn't his only lover. There were rumours of him having a son with some Parisian social butterfly. That sounded messy and complicated to Alice. Although she did like him a lot, and she believed he felt the same about her, *liking* wasn't enough to be united in marriage. She couldn't be a hypocrite and do what she'd warned Vince not to do.

Strolling into the dining room, Alice sat at the end of the polished oak table and smiled as Esme brought in the coffee pot and a silver stand of fresh toast. 'Thank you.'

Left alone, Alice opened the telegram and read it as she poured a cup of coffee and added milk.

Frowning, she read the telegram again from Mr Henderson her New York broker. She couldn't quite take it in.

PRICES PLUMMET STOP

SOLD TOO LATE STOP

SHARES WORTHLESS STOP

LETTER TO FOLLOW STOP

Alice heard voices downstairs in the hallway.

Brandon entered, having given Esme his hat and coat. 'Pour me a cup, will you?'

'Pour it yourself while I go and get dressed.' She quickly ran into her bedroom and pulled on her underwear, a satin slip and topped it with a woollen rust-coloured skirt and a cream silk bouse. Her mind was stuck on the telegram and what it meant for her future.

When she re-entered the dining room, Brandon was munching on buttered toast, his expression drawn as he read the newspaper which blasted the spectacular headlines of the American stock market crashing.

She poured the coffee with a hand that shook slightly. 'I've received a telegram from Mr Henderson in New York.'

'That's why I've come over. He sent one to me, too. I managed to contact him last night by telephone.' He stared at her in such a way Alice wanted to cry and she never cried.

She gave him the telegram to read. 'It's all gone, isn't it?' She bit her lip, trying to accept the news.

Brandon rubbed his forehead. 'Don't panic. It looks bad but we might be able to salvage something.'

'And what about you and Father?'

'The family's fortune has halved overnight.' He looked haggard. 'I left it too late to sell my shares and stocks. My gut was telling me to sell but Father said to wait it out and that nothing would happen. I shouldn't have listened to him.'

'Is Father terribly upset?'

'Yes. He's lost more money than I have, and I've lost enough.' Sighing, Brandon pushed away the plate of toast. 'I've been up all night trying to contact our other brokers in New York. It's crazy over there at the moment. I'm leaving for New York tomorrow. I'll sail from Southampton.'

She nodded. Possibly tens of thousands of dollars had simply vanished from her portfolio. Tom's money. She'd invested the money that came to her on Tom's death. Money she always felt a fraud for having since they'd only been married such a short time, but with his parents dead and him an only child, the money was hers alone.

On Brandon's advice she'd invested it years ago in American companies that were profiting better than the regular British companies her family invested in. America soared after the Great War whereas England floundered. British coal prices had fallen when Germany was allowed back into the market. British exports had suffered from union strikes and the pound sinking. America seemed the golden goose. She had willingly placed her money in the broker's hands and reaped the dividends for years.

Brandon walked to the window to look out on the street below. 'I don't know how long I'll be gone. So, Prue is staying in France with Henry for longer. She'll go between her mother in Paris and Millie's chateau.'

'What about Prue's grandmama? I thought Adeline was rather frail now and Prue wanted to be in London to be near her?'

'Cece is coming down from Scotland to stay with Adeline for a month, after that, we'll work something else out. Adeline has a new nurse who is apparently much better than the previous one, so Prue feels reassured. While I'm gone, I'll have the house packed up.'

'Packed up?' Alice frowned.

'As it stands now, with the losses from America, I need to sell our townhouse. Prue and I will move back to Yorkshire with Mother and Father.'

'It has come to that?' She was astonished. Never would she have thought Brandon would move home to Hazel Grove the sprawling estate on the outskirts of Whitby.

'I'm afraid so. It'll take me some years to rebuild my portfolio again. To save on costs, if I sell our townhouse then I can use that money to reinvest.'

'And Father?'

'He's being stubborn as always. He refuses to believe it is as bad as it's being reported. He's putting on a brave face in front of Mother, but from what I know, from what he and I have spoken about and discussed in the last few years, then I think Father will have to curtail their lifestyle substantially. We may have to sell some land.'

'It's as bad as that?'

Brandon nodded.

Alice played with her teaspoon. 'I've not been home for so long. Whitby seems so far away.'

'Mother says it was last Christmas since the whole family has been together.'

'Has it truly been ten months?' Guilt filled her. She should travel home to Yorkshire more often to visit her parents. Telephone calls weren't enough.

'Could you run *Sheer* from Yorkshire?'

'Lord, no! I need to be in London.'

'I simply thought you could rent this house out and come with us. It'll be a saving for you in the present situation.'

'I'll not be returning to Yorkshire to live. London is my home.' She sipped her coffee thoughtfully. 'I will get by.'

'Alice, you're my sister. We need to stick together when things are tough. I feel there *will* be tough times ahead for us all.'

'I'll be fine. My focus is getting the magazine through any upheavals.'

'The profits from the magazine won't keep you in the lifestyle you're used to. You need to talk to Father and I about your financial situation.'

'No. I am perfectly fine. You both have enough to deal with. Besides, I've been self-sufficient since I was eighteen and I married Tom. You should know by now that I'm not the type to go running back to Father when times get tough. I didn't ask for Father's help to build *Sheer*, and I'll not worry him now. Besides, I can ride this out, I'm certain. *Sheer* will continue to sell and be profitable. If it means that for a little while I must stop buying diamonds and furs, then I'm sure I'll cope.' She shrugged with a forced smile.

'This isn't to be taken lightly.'

Alice hated seeing the worry crease his forehead. 'I know and understand that.'

'Do you? Really? If the markets don't rally, we could be in for some hardship. This has affected thousands of people on both sides of the Atlantic.'

'Yes, I heard talk at a party the other night that the British markets are in a terrible state, too.' She was worried for *Sheer*. The advertising they offered to companies kept *Sheer* going. Without it, she'd have to scale back on content and expenditure. The magazine might be her only income now.

Brandon thrust his hands in his trouser pockets. 'It's not looking good. The US stocks have rallied slightly, but none of the reports I'm reading regarding the US are reassuring.'

'What can we do?'

'Hold our nerve in the British shares we have. We have to hope this country doesn't plummet as the US has done.'

'A man at the party told me that whatever happens in America has a knock-on effect here. Is that true?'

'Yes, in differing degrees.'

'But America will rally, won't it? Simon says it will.'

'The coming months will soon let us know.'

'What do we do until then?'

'Go about our lives as normally as possible, but perhaps for the first time in this family's history we might have to watch what we spend.' Brandon returned to the table and took a sip of coffee. 'Can you continue to live as you do without the money coming in from America?'

'I'll have to cut back somewhat. Now I'll have no dividends from America, I'll be relying on the profits of *Sheer* and my other small investments.'

Brandon rubbed his hand through his black hair, the same shade as her own. 'Will it be enough? *Sheer*'s profits have been steady, but they aren't growing, which is a worry.'

'I'll make it so.'

'I can help you. I'll know more once I'm in New York and all the reports come through. I need to visit the bank. If the London trade exchange takes a hit, then we need to be ready.' He kissed her cheek. 'Talk to me if you need to, about anything. Promise?'

'I promise.' She walked with him to the door. 'Any news on Vince?'

'He's still in Sussex but I think he's coming back to London next week.'

As Brandon left, Simon came up the staircase carrying a bunch of red roses. He, too, looked anxious.

'I wasn't expecting you,' she said, receiving his kiss and the flowers.

'I must return home. Father insists. I leave tonight. I've managed to get a cabin on a ship leaving from Southampton. My train departs in an hour.'

'So soon?' She led him into the sitting room and placed the flowers on the low walnut table near the sofa.

'Will you come with me, Alice?' His earnest smile gladdened her heart.

'On such short notice?' She shook her head. 'It's not possible.'

'Then settle your affairs here and join me. You can run the magazine from New York or start an American version. Just think of that!' His enthusiastic manner touched something in her, an answering call to begin again, to accept the challenge. But the feeling died as quickly as it sparked. She didn't want to start another magazine in New York.

'Please, Alice. We'd have a wonderful life together.' He took her hands and kissed her gently. 'We're good together, sweetheart.'

A small part of her urged her to say yes, to take the leap and move to another country. However, a larger part of her was already distancing herself from him. She knew he wouldn't stay loyal to her. In time he'd have liaisons and she'd be hurt. Though the main reason she wasn't saying yes was because she didn't love him. Simon wasn't enough for her to leave everyone and everything behind.

She stepped back. 'I'm sorry, Simon. It's not what I want.'

'What *do* you want then?' he asked with a cheeky smile, as though he believed only *he* could give her what she needed.

'I don't know. I feel myself changing and I don't know why or what to do about it.'

'So, come and make that change with me in New York.'

'Thank you, but no.' She squeezed his hands and kissed his lips. 'Have a safe journey home.'

When he'd gone, Alice glanced at the red roses and wondered if they'd be the last roses she'd have for a while.

# Chapter Five

Entering the *Sheer* offices, Alice smiled and nodded to her editorial team, before entering her own office. 'Good morning, Winifred.'

'Good morning, madam.'

'It's nasty out there.' Alice spoke of the heavy rain falling and the gale force wind blowing down the Thames as she collapsed her umbrella and took off her black sable hat and long black coat. She wasn't keen on autumn weather and darkening days. She much preferred the warmth of summer.

'I was drenched just walking from the train station to here.' Winifred handed her a pile of letters. 'You've an appointment at ten o'clock with Mr Isaacs.'

'Thank you.' Alice headed to her office door.

'Coffee or tea, madam?' Winifred asked, rising from her chair.

'Tea, please.'

'Late night?'

'Terribly.' Alice, ignoring her slight headache from attending a wild party with Sally, Helen and Gordy, walked behind her desk and leafed through the mail and selected an envelope at random. Opening it, she quickly scanned the contents and gasped. The rent on the *Sheer* offices were being raised by over a quarter. She had ten days' notice. The cheek of the man, who only two weeks ago promised he'd not change the rent amount.

As Winifred carried in a tea tray, Alice slammed the mail on the desk. 'Mr Carter is raising the rent on the building. This is all I need on top of everything else.'

Winifred's eyebrows rose to nearly her grey hairline. 'But why has he done that?'

Alice waved the letter in the air. 'Current property climate and all that nonsense!'

'What will you do?'

'I'll not be paying it. I'll look for new premises.'

'Shall I start searching straight away?'

'Yes, make it your priority, please.'

When the door closed behind Winifred, Alice strode to the large window and stared out. She didn't need this. Although the magazine's sales were still good, prices were rising for the magazine's content, especially the printing costs.

Her meeting with Mr Isaacs this morning was to discuss the increase in printing costs and if he didn't reconsider, then she'd have to up the price of the magazine and she was loathed to do that. But it wasn't just Mr Isaacs, the venues where they shot the models wearing the latest fashions were asking for more money, as were the models themselves and the artists and writers who worked on the magazine. She had combated that in the last issue by increasing the advertising space and charging more for it, but such a move had lost her clients and she knew this month her advertisers had dropped by a tenth.

If she hadn't lost money on the American market, she could have ridden out the new expenditures and worked hard to create more sales with clever marketing. Only, she now had to be careful of every penny spent and what's more, she didn't have any enthusiasm to drive a big marketing push.

Despite the consistent sales, she had no choice but to cut costs more and that meant letting go of some of the staff. She hated the thought of it, especially with Christmas creeping up on them, but it had to be done. Thankfully, Prue had resigned from her role within *Sheer*, but she was only one person, one wage gone. Others had to go, and Alice needed to make that dreadful decision today. Talking it over with Sally, Helen and Gordy last night, she had decided to reduce *Sheer* to a bimonthly magazine. The change would affect her entire staff and the business.

A knock on the door heralded Vince. He came in giving her a small smile. 'Are you busy?'

'I should be but can't make a start. I wasn't expecting you until later in the week.'

'I couldn't wait until later.' He kissed her cheek.

She slid into her chair and faced him. She'd barely seen him in the last month. He'd lost more weight. 'You didn't come to the McDonalds' party last night. We had a marvellous time. Johnny Fletcher taught us a new dance, lots of close embraces.' She smiled. 'You'd have enjoyed it.'

'I've sold my car and I didn't fancy catching the train.'

She blinked at the frank admission. 'I would have come and collected you. You should have telephoned me.'

'Maybe next time.'

Alice gazed at him, seeing the tiredness in his eyes. 'What's this visit about? Not that you need a reason to call in, obviously.'

Vince sat in the visitor's chair instead of perching on the corner of her desk as he usually did. 'I'll come straight to the point. I need to sell my shares in *Sheer*.'

'What do you mean? Sell your shares? Why would you do that?'

'I need the money. The estate sale has fallen through.'

'Oh, Vince. I'm sorry to hear that.'

'It came at a dashedly bad time.' He shrugged. 'The mortgage is due. I must sell the estate and make some money and not let the bank just jolly well take it.'

'Your ten percent in *Sheer* won't make you rich.'

'It'll be enough to cover the next mortgage payment.'

'Then what?'

'Then hopefully I'll have another buyer.' He ran a hand over his face. 'Mama's not well. She caught a bad cold in Sussex, and it's developed into a terrible cough.' His gaze bored into hers. 'Can I sell my shares to you?'

'What do you want for them?'

He told her a large sum that made her frown. 'What have you based that price on?'

'The last quarterly profit margin.'

'This quarter will be drastically different. Much lower than any of us expect.'

He shrugged. 'Those figures are what my solicitor has told me to ask for.'

She did calculations in her head of what money she had left in her bank. 'I don't think I can buy them. The stock crash has changed everything. I have to curb my spending.'

'Sell your car then. A Rolls Royce like yours will fetch a decent price.'

She bristled. 'I'll not sell my car.'

Vince tapped his leg. 'I've spoken to Brandon, and he can't buy them either. It leaves me no choice but to go outside our circle, Alice.'

That he called her Alice and not my lady told her what mental state he was in. 'I'd rather not have a stranger invest. Leave it with me. I'll ask some of my friends first.'

He nodded and rose to his feet. 'Let me know as soon as you can, by Friday preferably.'

'Friday? Are you mad?' A flame of anger ignited in her chest at his demands. 'Vince, the magazine has to be downgraded somewhat. I'm making it bimonthly. The profits are dwindling, and content prices are rising. I must find new office premises as Mr Carter has put the rent up. I don't think it'll be an easy pitch to sell shares to people, but I'll do what I can.'

'Don't take this personally, Alice.'

'How else can I take it?' She fumed. 'You're my friend, yet you're acting like a stranger.'

'I'm acting like a man drowning in debts!'

'How is that my fault?'

He paused by the doorway. 'It's not. I'm just trying to do whatever I can to survive. That means I must sell everything I own. My shares in *Sheer* will go. I should have sold them months ago, but I didn't out of respect for you.'

'But now you don't care?' She felt wounded.

'Don't twist my words. You know the situation I'm in.'

'Then perhaps you should stop your membership at your club, too, and all the other nonessential things you do,' she snapped.

Sadness etched his face. 'I already have. So, don't tell me how to run my life, please. The world is shifting, Alice. You need to come out of your ivory tower and realise that.'

'How dare you speak so rudely to me.'

'I dare because you need to wake up. People are out of work, businesses are closing all around us and you skip about publishing a fashion magazine for the women of this city who don't even understand that soup kitchens are operating just streets away from their front doors.'

'Do not lecture me, Vince.'

'Someone has to. Do you see what is out there, Alice? Do you see the strikes and the poverty? I do. I see it. I've had to as I'm about to live it. I've spent the morning visiting flats for Mama and I to live in and they are dire, believe me. Visit the East End of London and see for yourself.'

'Why are you speaking to me like this? I barely see you and when I do you behave like a cad. Losing your friends won't help you, Vince. You need us.'

'Do I? Do you think my friends will still entertain me when I live in a poky little place with bare cupboards? When I can't go on shooting weekends or summer house parties. When I can no longer meet them at the club or have long boozy afternoons? How many friends will I have then, Alice?' Pain was in his brown eyes.

As much as she wanted to refute his statement, she couldn't. They both knew that once the money goes, so too the 'so-called' friends. Unless you can return their hospitality and join in with all the parties, excursions, holidays and entertainment you were soon shown a cold shoulder. She'd seen it happen many times before. She'd even been guilty of behaving that way herself. Many a time she'd lost touch with someone simply because they could no longer afford to live as lavishly as she did. It wasn't meanly meant, just how life progressed.

'I'm sorry,' Vince murmured on a long sigh.

'Me, too.' Her heart broke at the sadness on his face.

'I don't want to fight with you. You mean too much to me.'

She nodded, her throat full.

'Let me know about the shares. But perhaps it's time you got out while the magazine is still making a profit.'

'Sell *Sheer*? I couldn't possibly.' The thought horrified her. It was all she had.

'Maybe its wiser to do it now than before it folds completely.'

'It'll not come to closure. We are still in profit.'

'But for how long?' He let out a deep breath. 'Sorry, dearest. I carry a fog about me that infects my every thought and I lay it on others. Of course, *Sheer* won't fold. Not with you at the helm.' With a wave, he was gone.

Alice leaned back in the chair. Was Vince right? Would *Sheer* fold? The world was rapidly changing. America reeled from the crashing stock market and Britain was floundering. Did women want to spend money on a fashion magazine anymore? She had hoped to make her magazine available to everyone, but she knew deep down only the wealthy bought *Sheer*. Female factory workers, nannies, servants and the like couldn't afford to waste precious wages on a magazine about clothes they could never afford.

When she started *Sheer*, her goal had been to make a magazine to enrich women's lives. Had she done that? Women of her class raved over *Sheer*, it had become their fashion bible and the success gave her great satisfaction. She'd entered a man's world of publication and joined their elite status. Yet now, when faced with the reality that one of her best friends couldn't afford to pay his mortgage, and many other friends had taken a hit with the stock market, she wondered if a fashion magazine really mattered.

Winifred knocked on the open door. 'Mr Isaacs, madam.'

Alice stood, alarmed that the last hour had flown by, and she'd not done any work. 'Mr Isaacs.' She walked around her desk and shook his hand. 'Would you like refreshments?'

'No, thank you. I'm afraid our business won't take very long,' he said in his slightly accented voice. As usual he wore all black.

Heart sinking, Alice resumed her seat and faced the older man across her desk. 'Please, let us talk frankly.'

Isaacs nodded, his long black beard touching his chest. 'I understand your surprise and reluctance to pay more for the printing of your magazine. Raising the printing prices wasn't a decision I took lightly. But all aspects of the printing process have risen in price. Paper, ink, machinery, transport, wages. If I do not pass these increases on, I will close. It is not personal, madam, I assure you. It is simply business.'

'Business. Yes.' She tapped her pencil on her notepad. 'Although you must consider the increase on your clients could potentially put them out of business.'

He frowned. 'Do your words reflect yourself?'

'There is a possibility, in time, yes, but I hope not.'

'I am sorry.'

'Me, too.'

He frowned and tapped his fingers together in thought. 'I will keep your prices the same until February. Yes?'

A few months. 'Thank you, Mr Isaacs.'

He stood and shook her hand. 'Forgive me for not being able to do more, madam.'

When he'd left, she heard Winifred talking on the telephone to one of their advertising clients. Alice could tell by the other woman's tone that she was trying to soothe ruffled feathers. No doubt that client had received the letter about the increased fees.

Walking out of her office, Alice crossed the reception to the small offices which were used by the editors, writers, designers and marketing team. Eight faces turned to her as she entered. These people were brilliant at their jobs. How was she to lay them off? They depended on her for wages to live. The weight of responsibility grew heavy on Alice. Two people would have to go this week. Which two? How would she decide?

Unable to make a decision, Alice smiled warmly at all of her team. 'How is the Christmas issue coming along? Deadlines are looming. Show me what you have.' She put on a false manner of everything being fine. Yet, later she'd have to call a meeting and announce the magazine would be going bimonthly after the Christmas issue and staff numbers were to be reduced.

As they guided her through the mock pages they'd created, pointing out the Christmas theme and asking her opinion on certain qualities of the layout, Alice couldn't help but realise that the buzz of excitement wasn't as high as it usually was. The layout didn't thrill her as it normally did. The fashion designs Maisie had seen on her last visit to Paris didn't excite her. But it wasn't the styles of silk evening gowns and fox stoles, or the cocktail dresses of satin and lace for they were beautiful, it was her. She stared at the designs of beaded bags and feather headdresses, the tasselled sashes and silk stockings and none of it brought out the passion she had always felt.

What was happening to her?

Why didn't the magazine give her joy anymore?

Why had she changed?

'Madam, Lottie is leaving early today, if that is permissible?' Maisie asked.

'Oh?' Alice looked to the young woman sitting at the far desk.

Maise's voice lowered. 'Her family has been put out of their flat. Lottie's dad lost his job, and her mother is caring for her sick mother and can't work. They've fallen behind in their rent and been evicted. They leave today.'

'Where will they go?'

'They'll move in with an aunt in Deptford who runs a pub. They'll be living in the attics.'

'Sounds dreadful.' Alice knew Deptford wasn't an affluent part of South London. It worried her that an employee of hers was going to be living in such reduced circumstances.

Maisie glanced at Lottie. 'She's a good worker, as you know, but she's from a poor family. She doesn't like people to know her situation. Working here at *Sheer* has given her a chance to better herself. Her family are so proud of her. She's the first of them to work in an office. They want her to spend her wages on nice clothes, so she fits in, but she feels guilty...'

Alice gazed around the walls filled with gold-framed cover editions of *Sheer*. In the corners of the office were samples of fur coats and silk gowns, shoes and hats for the artists to draw from for the magazine's artwork. Such expensive garments just hanging about when Lottie's family were unable to pay the rent...

Vince's words whispered in her ear again. *Visit the East End of London and see for yourself.*

Was she living in a bubble? Was there a world out there she totally ignored? Did she live her life blinkered and selfish?

She knew the answers to those questions and hated herself for not doing enough for others. Her mother did more charity work in their local village in one week than Alice had done in years. Her mother would be ashamed of her if she knew.

'Can we help Lottie's family?' Alice asked Maisie.

'They are too proud to take charity and Lottie would be horrified if she knew I'd spoken to you about it. She idolises you.'

Alice thought hard. 'Not every garment goes back to the designers, does it?'

'No. Some let us keep them as they don't want clothes that models have worn or that have been bandied about the office. We keep boxes of clothes in the storeroom downstairs.'

'Then the clothes that don't go back are ours to do with as we please.' Alice tapped her chin in thought then straightened and addressed the room. 'Just a moment of your time, please. It has come to my attention that in the storeroom are boxes of garments from the designer companies that they no longer want returned to them. The clothes are in good condition. It is a waste to see them not being put to good use. Therefore, under Maisie's guidance, I am giving you all the opportunity to go through the boxes and take home those items you will wear, at no cost, of course. Be fair and sensible. What does not get taken, we shall will sell and the profits divided by all the staff. Call it a Christmas bonus, if you will.'

A round of gasps and applause followed her statement.

She smiled and turned to Maisie. 'I am certain there are some everyday wear in those boxes?'

'Indeed, madam. A good deal of day wear and coats, that sort of thing.'

'Excellent. Can I leave it with you to sell the rest and share the money?'

'Absolutely. Thank you, madam,' Maisie said on behalf of them all.

Alice nodded and whispered, 'Make sure Lottie gets her fair share of clothes. Her wage can then help her family better than being spent on buying clothes.'

\*\*\*

'Motor car racing this Friday. Will you come?' Sally Stuart asked, sipping her cocktail in the stylish Palm Court in the Ritz, which was festooned with Christmas decorations of red and gold. 'We're all going. It'll be rather fun.'

'No, not this time.' Alice watched the room, waved to a couple of ladies she knew, but was mainly hoping Vince would show up as he sometimes did, but then she realised he'd no longer be able to afford to spend afternoons sipping champagne cocktails. Truth be known neither could she, but for a little while longer she was putting on a brave face. The figures for *Sheer*-'s November issue were way down on this time last year. Sales for the Christmas edition weren't officially reported but early numbers also showed a lower number. The stock market crash affect was lingering, scaring wealthy gentlemen who usually gave their wives and daughters an open cheque book for spending, into being more cautious.

'You are becoming a bore, Alice, truly you are,' Sally whined. 'I'll not forgive you for pulling out of our holiday next month. Who wants to spend January in London when we could be in the south of Italy at Gordy's delightful villa?'

'I'm sorry, but there's too much going on with the magazine,' she lied. She couldn't afford to spend weeks in Italy, which she knew from past experiences would cost a small fortune. She'd managed to get through November by reducing her personal expenditure, but Brandon's return from New York had worried her as he spoke of the unsettled markets there. He saw nothing during his stay to bolster his confidence in the markets there or in London. He forecasted a dismal future. Unemployment was rising, especially in the north of England as British exports were falling. He expected the new year of nineteen-thirty to be a turning point in the country's history, and not for the better.

Sally ran a finger around the rim of her glass. 'I do not believe you. *Sheer* has never stopped you going on holiday before.'

'I must find new office premises. A task that is proving rather difficult.' She inwardly groaned at the days she spent all through November searching and visiting office spaces that were over-priced, or too small or too large.

'Let Prue take over.'

'I've told you, Prue is pregnant and is in Yorkshire.'

'How inconvenient of her,' Sally joked. 'I thought she was in France.'

'She was, but Brandon is home from New York, and they've sold their townhouse and moved home to Yorkshire.'

'Sold their townhouse? Prue will hate that. She loves London.'

'I'm not so sure.' Alice took a sip of her drink. 'Prue looked tired. She's worried about Brandon and their finances after the crash. Also, her mother's husband, Jacques, suffered a heart attack while Prue was visiting. He survived, but it was a difficult and upsetting time for them all.'

Sally waved to the waiter for more cocktails. 'Darling, Prue. What a shame she is pregnant otherwise we could take her somewhere positively smashing for a weekend to forget all the unpleasantness that's happening. Prue loves a weekend party, doesn't she?'

'She does, but the *unpleasantness* as you call it, has far reaching effects. Many of our friends will be troubled by the consequences of what has happened on Wall Street. It is affecting London trading. Brandon said the London market hadn't fully recovered from the crash here in September and then the crash in the States in October was larger and more alarming.'

'Goodness, how utterly boring it all is.'

'Has the stock markets affected your family at all?'

'Us?' Sally blinked as though she'd never given the volatile markets any consideration. 'Lord, no. Papa is too sensible to invest in America. Our money is in India, the rubber plantations. Though India is a terrible hotbed with Gandhi and his followers causing mayhem. Papa is most put out by it all.' She flirted with the waiter as he brought the drinks over to their table.

'India might not be the sensible choice your father thinks it is?' Alice quipped. Sally's father was a stuffy elitist who she couldn't stand. He believed because he was a descendant of a distant line of the royal house of Stuart that he was above normal people. Thankfully, most of the time, Sally was nothing like him.

Alice looked up as new arrivals entered.

'Are you waiting for someone?' Sally joked. 'You're watching everyone who comes in.'

'I was hoping Vince might stop by. I need to speak to him.' She'd not seen him since their awkward conversation weeks ago when he asked her to buy his shares in the magazine.

'Poor Vince hardly shows his face anywhere anymore. He's become a complete drab.'

Alice clenched her teeth in annoyance. 'That's hardly fair, Sally. His family fortune has gone.'

'Well, that's simply bad management then, isn't it? That's what Papa say, anyway.' Sally shrugged unconcerned.

'Vince's father dying is hardly bad management,' she snapped.

'All families know there are death duties to pay for. Papa has made sure that when he dies my brother and I do not have the indignity of selling our pieces of art to pay those duties. Papa says careful financial structure is a way of life in our society. Vince's father was foolish indeed to not care for his family and now poor Vince is selling *everything*. His life is ruined.'

Alice was about to defend Vince when Sally's eyes widened.

'Oh, I say, isn't that your Simon who has just walked in?'

Alice swivelled on her chair and stared at her former lover. She didn't know he was back in London, but by the rapturous look on his face as he gazed lovingly down at the slender blonde woman on his arm, it seemed as though Alice had been replaced in his affections. It hurt for a moment and then she let it go. Simon hadn't written to her at all since leaving in October and now it was the middle of December. The affair had run its course. It'd been fun but meaningless and she'd known that at the end of summer when she left him in America, and again when he asked her to go home with him a few months ago.

'How despicable of him to be with another woman.' Sally tutted. 'Who is she? Do we know her?'

'I don't think so.'

'I've a good mind to go over there and jolly well slap him.'

'You'll do no such thing. Simon and I were never serious.'

'I thought he wanted to marry you?'

'He did, but I didn't. We had fun, but I couldn't see a life with him.' Alice stood and gathered her bag and gloves. 'Come along, we'll go shopping.'

'Splendid. I do need more stockings. Maybe a new hat for the motorcar racing. I thought to buy...'

Alice stopped hearing Sally as Vince entered the restaurant with an older man and a stylish woman.

As if feeling her eyes on him, Vince looked up and saw her. He smiled and after a quick word to the man, weaved his way between the tables to Alice.

'This is a stroke of luck.' He kissed her cheeks and then did the same with Sally. 'I was going to call into the office and see you.'

'Oh?' Alice smiled for he seemed a little happier, not so withdrawn and sombre. He still wore the same suit though and his hair seemed overlong.

Vince took her hand. 'I'd like you to meet a new acquaintance of mine. He and his wife are interested in *Sheer*. Come over and meet them.'

Sally pulled on her gloves. 'If you two are going to talk business, I'll leave you to it. Alice, I'll see you tomorrow night at Gordy's house for drinks before we go to the theatre.' She gave Alice a farewell peck on the cheek and one to Vince.

'Yes, see you then.' Alice focused on Vince. 'Why is this couple interested in *Sheer*?'

'Walt Branning and his wife Sara are buying my ten percent.'

'Vince!' she hissed, annoyed. 'You've not given me enough time to find someone we know.'

'It's been weeks and you haven't found anyone.'

'It was an impossible task to find a buyer with such short notice.'

'Well, I've done it now.' He gave her a wry lift of his eyebrows.

Alice bristled. 'Who are they?'

'Come over and meet them. They're lovely, truly.'

She gave him a furious look. 'I feel betrayed by this.'

'Trust me. They are good people. In fact, Mr Branning has a proposition for you. Come and listen to what he has to say.'

Reluctantly, Alice made her way over to the table. Mr Branning, a large man with a friendly smile, stood and shook her hand. His younger wife, Sara, was simply stunning. She wore a fitted white dress with a row of small black buttons going down the middle. At her throat a diamond choker twinkled in the restaurant's lights and her dark-red hair was curled and arranged beautifully under her angled black hat. As someone who'd always had an eye for fashion, Alice respectfully admired the outfit.

'It is a pleasure to meet you, Lady Mayton-Walsh.' Mr Branning took his seat as Vince held out a chair for Alice.

'Forgive me for being a little startled, Mr Branning. Vince has only just told me about the deal you've struck.' Alice tucked her beige skirt tidily beneath her legs to give her more time to compose herself. Her outfit was professional, since she'd been at the office for most of the morning, and she was glad she wore the beige skirt suit with the rust-coloured silk blouse. It gave her confidence when talking business to dress appropriately.

Sara Branning leaned forward. 'I hope the deal is to your liking? Purchasing Mr Barton's shares is simply thrilling for us, especially me.'

Alice looked at her, sensing a quiet strength about the woman if the intelligent gaze was anything to go by. 'That I cannot answer just yet, Mrs Branning. I do not know you and I guard my magazine like a mother with her child.'

'Mr Barton said exactly the same, and so you should. *Sheer* is utterly brilliant. I've bought every copy since you started.'

'My wife devours the magazine the minute it's delivered. There is no sense talking to her until she had read it from cover to cover.' Mr Branning laughed.

Alice relaxed slightly. 'I'm pleased you enjoy it.'

Vince ordered a bottle of white wine from a passing waiter. 'I met the Brannings at the weekend. They came to view my house.'

'I see.' Alice stared at Vince, realising that he was moving on and she no longer knew what was happening in his life. He'd shut her out, but not just her, Brandon also.

'We got talking and Mr Branning offered on the house.'

'Congratulations, to all of you.' Alice could sense the relief in Vince. He had sold the London house, but had he sold the estate, too? She wished he'd talk to her.

Mr Branning adjusted his cuffs. 'When my wife noticed a copy of *Sheer* on a table, she spoke to Mrs Barton about it.'

'Mama told her I had shares in *Sheer* and that we knew the owner personally,' Vince supplied, smiling at Alice.

'And I mentioned to Mr Barton how I'd dearly love to own such a magazine.' Sara's gaze bored into Alice. 'Fashion has been something of a passion of mine since I was a little girl. You, Lady Mayton-Walsh, created the dream I always wanted to. A magazine to rival *Vogue*.'

Mr Brannigan laughed. 'My darling Sara has you on a pedestal, my lady.'

'I'm honoured, but please call me Alice.' She blushed and felt a little uncomfortable. Sara reminded her of herself years ago when she first decided to create a magazine. Sara was brimming with enthusiasm and life and passion.

Mr Branning rested his elbows on the table, his gaze locked with Alice. 'Which is why she wants to buy your magazine, not just Mr Barton's shares. Will you consider it?'

Alice blinked rapidly in shock. 'Buy the magazine?'

'Do not consider answering us right now. Take some time to think it over. A month if you wish,' said Mr Branning.

'But not too long!' Sara Branning jested, her face aglow with excitement, but in her eyes was a burning need.

'Now, darling, do not pressure Lady Mayton-Walsh.' Mr Branning gave Alice his card. 'I'll leave some figures with Mr Barton, or your solicitor.' He glanced up at the waiter who arrived with their wine in a silver ice bucket. 'Ah, excellent.'

Vince took Alice's hand. 'There's no pressure. It's simply an offer for you to consider.'

Jerking her hand free, Alice stood. 'I... I have an appointment and must go. It's been... nice to meet you both.'

Sara stood as well. 'Lady Mayton-Walsh, please do not be offended by our eagerness and desire to buy your business. Perhaps we have been too impatient by not contacting you personally in an official manner, and that is my fault. I asked Mr Barton to introduce us when he saw you. He was going to take us to your office this afternoon until he saw you here and I begged him to bring you over to our table. I was very keen to meet you. Do forgive my rashness.'

Alice could tell she was sincere, but this woman wanted *Sheer* and Alice didn't know how to feel about that.

'Good day.' Alice left the table and made her way to the cloak room to retrieve her coat from the attendant.

'Alice.' Vince met her at the door.

She turned on him. 'I feel ambushed, Vince. How could you spring that upon me in such a way with no warning, no time for me to be prepared?'

'I'm sorry.'

'I'm not selling *Sheer*.'

'Then decline their offer, but at least see what Branning is willing to give you for it.'

'Why? *Sheer* is mine.'

He grasped her hands. 'I saw the figures yesterday that your solicitor sends out to shareholders. *Sheer*-'s numbers are down, Alice.'

'Hardly alarming enough for me to sell.'

'Have you found new office space yet, or a cheaper printer?'

'Not yet. However, there are a few possibilities I'm investigating.' Her cheeks felt hot.

'Do you want all the hassle of moving everything elsewhere? And what has been the reaction to the magazine going bimonthly in the new year?'

She felt under attack. 'What do you care anyway, you're selling and so *Sheer* is no longer your concern.'

'I still care about you, even if I'm no longer a shareholder of the business. You're still one of my best friends.'

'Really? I rarely see you anymore,' she scoffed. 'I have no idea what is happening in your life. I didn't know you were selling the house until it was mentioned just now.'

'Do you make the time to find out what is happening in my life?' he replied, an eyebrow raised in question.

'I've been busy!' She glared at him, temper rising.

'So, have I. Do you think any of this has been easy for me? Mama has been ill, and we are having to move out of our home.' He ran a hand through his hair.

'I'm sad to hear Sylvia has been unwell.' Alice instantly backed down seeing the anguish in his handsome face. 'It's good you have a buyer. That must relieve some of your financial stress?'

'Yes, it does. If only we could sell the estate as quickly, but I spoke with an agent today who has someone interested. I shan't get my hopes up just yet though.'

'Come over for dinner,' she suggested. 'Tonight.'

They moved aside to let some people pass.

Vince nodded to one of the men, obviously knowing him, then looked back at Alice. 'I'd love to, but I can't leave Mama. She's taking this very hard, though she won't show it to me, of course. However, I can tell how difficult this all is for her. Packing our belongings is a tremendous wrench for her.'

'Are you going to Barton Downs to live until it sells as well?'

He grunted. 'No.'

'Where are you going then?'

'Believe it or not, I'm going to check out one of the terraces we have managed to keep. We will move in there.'

'A terrace? Where?'

'Limehouse.'

Alice blinked in shock. 'The dock area in the East End?'

'Sounds ridiculous, doesn't it?' He gave a short chuckle.

'Surely it would make sense to go to the estate?'

'Mama won't hear of it. She says it'll break her to have to move there and leave again within months if it sells.'

'But Limehouse?' Alice couldn't believe it.

'Mama and I go to tomorrow to visit the terrace and see what state it's in now the tenants have left.'

'Let me come with you. I can be of some support to you both.'

He smiled that wry smile he had, and her heart kicked over in her chest. 'That would be wonderful, thank you.'

'I'll pick you both up at ten o'clock?' Her gaze lingered on him. She'd missed him so much.

Vince kissed her cheek, lingering a little longer than necessary. 'I've missed you.'

'I just thought the same.' She squeezed his hands. 'No matter what happens in our lives, we must stay close. Promise me.'

'I promise.'

# *Chapter Six*

Alice drove her car slowly along Commercial Road, glancing often at Mrs Barton and Vince. Mrs Barton looked pale, her wrinkles doubled since the last time Alice saw her, and she'd lost weight. But she was elegantly turned out in a pale lavender skirt and matching coat, her grey hair neatly styled and topped with a round grey hat. Keeping up appearances was vital.

The unfamiliar streets of the East End were narrow and filled with wagons and carts. Horse-drawn vehicles vied for space with lorries and bicycles. Above the rooftops, tall cranes loaded or unloaded cargo from the bowels of ships in the Regent's Canal Dock.

They drove beneath an iron railway bridge before Vince pointed to the street to their right.

'Island Row, Alice.'

'Lord, I don't think the Rolls will make it down there, it's awfully narrow.' Alice halted the motor car at the start of the lane.

'It'll be fine,' Vince urged. 'The terrace houses on the right are ours.'

Alice edged forward just into the lane and stopped the engine. Further down the row she saw the brick arches of the railway line which carried the trains high above the street as it curved across the skyline.

'Vince...' Mrs Barton swallowed, her chin quivered as she stared around at the neglected terrace houses on either side of them. The scene was dingy and dull and not a pretty thing in existence.

'We are only having a look, Mama.' Vince climbed out of the car and assisted his mother.

Alice stood beside her car, not totally sure she wanted to leave it. A man walked by, giving them a sideways glance, while a woman pushing a pram nearly scratched the paintwork as she wheeled the pram past.

'We own numbers one to four, Mama. Number one is empty, while the other three are occupied.' Vince produced a set of keys from his pocket and opened the front door of the first terrace.

They filed into the hallway, which was so tight they had to stand behind each other and not abreast. In front of them a steep staircase went up to the next floor. The smell of damp and staleness wafted over them.

'This is the parlour,' Vince announced, opening a door to a small square room. Its only window looked out onto the lane. Mould patterned the walls and ceiling. Plaster was crumbling in a corner of the far wall and the worn floorboards had numerous gaps.

'I'm told the fireplace works.' Vince bent to examine the black dusty fireplace.

Mrs Barton clasped her bag tightly in her hands and remained silent.

'Shall we look at the other rooms?' Alice suggested brightly. Though she thought Vince was mad to even consider living here.

They went down past the staircase to the back of the house which was simply a tiny kitchen with a small scullery that consisted of a few cupboards and a stone sink. Outside was the lavatory at the end of a small garden, though no garden existed, not even a blade of grass. Dirt and paving covered the area up to the rickety wooden fence.

'The Aga works, Mama.' Vince stared about the kitchen. He turned on a tap and running cold water streamed into the sink.

'Will we be able to afford a cook?' Mrs Barton asked shakily, eyeing the Aga with distaste.

'Yes, but not one that lives with us, same with the maid. They'll have to come each morning.'

Mrs Barton nodded but seemed far from relieved.

'And upstairs?' Alice headed for the staircase, wrapping her thick black coat about her for the house was as cold as an icebox.

'Two bedrooms. I'm told they are of good size and a small boxroom.' Vince opened the three doors in turn, revealing plain, cold rooms. The two square bedrooms held small black fireplaces, while the boxroom was no bigger than a large storage cupboard.

'And this is where you want us to live, my son?' Mrs Barton asked, walking to the window of the back bedroom which overlooked the empty garden below. Opposite was the unkempt and ugly gardens of the terrace houses on Mill Place.

Vince tapped a wall, its colour a grimy yellow from years of people smoking in the room. 'I know it's not ideal, but if you don't want to go to the estate until it's sold, then we might as well come here. Otherwise, we'll have to rent somewhere in London, which will drain our resources. We have little time to decide, Mama. All this place needs is a fresh coat of paint, new carpet, that sort of thing.'

A tear fell over Mrs Barton's lashes.

Alice's heart broke for her. To be driven so low as to live in a slum area after having such riches, would be a bitter pill to swallow. 'Perhaps, Mrs Barton, you would care to live with me while this house is made comfortable? I have two spare rooms.'

Hope flared in Mrs Barton's eyes and then died. 'I couldn't impose, my dear. I'm an old woman and you are young...'

'You wouldn't be imposing at all. I'm out all day at the office. You'd have the house to yourself.' Alice smiled. 'I would like you to come.'

Mrs Barton gazed at Vince, uncertainly in her eyes.

'I think it a sensible idea, Mama. If you are staying with Alice, I can make a start refurbishing here and not have to worry about you.' Vince glanced around. 'There's much to do. It will take weeks. Is that too long, Alice?'

'Definitely not. You can both stay for as long as you like.' It would give her such happiness to have Vince and his mother staying with her. Sometimes the house felt too silent when she was on her own and Esme and Mrs Jones had left for the day.

'Then I accept, Alice.' Mrs Barton nodded, her wan expression matching her tone. 'Thank you, my dear.'

Hoping to make Mrs Barton feel happier, Alice put on a bright voice. 'Shall we make notes as to what needs to be done?' She turned to Vince. 'Your mother might wish to choose colours?'

Taking the hint from her, Vince tilted his head in consideration. 'Excellent idea. Mama? What are your thoughts to the colours of the rooms? Paint or wallpaper? Panelling?'

Mrs Barton's slumped. 'I do not care, Vince. We shan't be entertaining here. This is simply going to be somewhere for me to spend my days until I die. I care little about how it looks. I shall return to the car.' She coughed as she left the room and went downstairs.

Dejected, Vince pushed his hands into his trouser pockets. 'Thank you for offering Mama a place to stay.'

'The offer extends to you, too.'

He gazed out of the window. 'I think I'll stay here.'

'Here?' Her voice rose in surprise.

'We can't afford to hire all the tradesmen this place needs until the estate is sold. I shall have to do some of it myself until then.'

'What do you know about house decoration or plumbing and all that nonsense?'

'Nothing at all. But I'll learn. I'll borrow books form the library.' He flashed a grin. 'Adapt or die, isn't that what they say?'

'Vince...'

'I'll be fine, Alice. It's time I grew up and took responsibility for my life. It can't be all parties and champagne, can it?'

'I think you've been responsible for many things since your father died.'

'And the journey continues. I must see that Mama is looked after. If I can make this house presentable, then the shock of moving here won't be so extreme.'

'Very well, I insist on helping you.'

'No, there's nothing you can do. Besides, I am grateful enough that you are having Mama stay with you.'

They walked downstairs and out to the lane where a thin woman came out from next door, pushing a large old pram. It was filled with suitcases and on top of these were placed two small filthy children.

'How do you do?' Vince doffed his hat to the woman.

'Can I help you?' She eyed him up and down and then Alice. Her clothes were drab and threadbare, her hair lank from being unwashed.

'I'm Mr Vince Barton, madam. Owner of this terrace.'

'Owner?' The woman's eyes widened. 'Mr Barton, sir, forgive me. I know I'm late with the rent but I'm movin' out, see.' She waved a hand to the pram, luggage and solemn children. 'I can't afford to stay, not now my Cyril has been sent down. I'm movin' to Poplar to me muvver's house. She's been given a new place as hers was demolished.'

'You're leaving?' Vince frowned.

'Aye, so the place is yours to rent again.' She gave him the keys and rent book. 'I must get on or I'll miss the tram.'

They moved aside so she could push the pram down the row and turn the corner from sight. Alice watched her go, seeing up close for the first time a working-class woman in dire straits. She couldn't help but compare herself to that young woman. How would she have dealt with a husband in prison, being behind on her rent, trying to find money to feed her children? She didn't know if she could be strong enough to survive it. How did these families do it year after year, generation after generation?

Vince stared at the open door.

'You'll rent it soon enough,' Alice said positively, but was that true? The whole neighbourhood was deep in poverty.

Vince stepped inside and she followed him. The rooms were identical to the one they'd just viewed, just on the opposite side. The same staleness and rising damp mirrored number one. Each room reeked of neglect and poverty.

Returning downstairs, Vince tapped the wall between the two houses. 'This could work.'

'What could work?'

'I can knock down the adjoining walls and create a larger house. Bigger rooms both downstairs and upstairs. A friend of mine did that with his townhouse in Mayfair. He bought the house next door and knocked down the walls between them. It doubled the size of the house.' Eagerness brightened his brown eyes.

'And not rent it?'

'No. Mama would be much more comfortable here if the rooms were larger and that would outweigh the small amount of income of someone renting it.'

Alice didn't believe that was the case at all. Mrs Barton didn't want to live in Limehouse, even in a palace, that was her concern. 'It'll mean more money to spend though, Vince.'

'I wouldn't think it much more. Once the estate is sold, we'll have money to do the renovations and to live on, albeit in a more meagre way than we are used to.' He ushered her out of the house and locked the door behind him.

'What was all that about, Vince?' his mother asked him as Alice started the engine.

'We'll live in both houses, Mama. I'll knock the walls through.'

'Oh.'

'I'll make it nice, I promise you.'

'I still do not understand why we cannot buy a cottage in the country somewhere, at least it will be pretty in the summer having fields around us instead of cranes and docks...'

'I've explained to you already about that. No one would buy the terraces at a price we'd need to move to a pleasant house in the country, and what would we do out in the country anyway with no friends or places to go? At least here you can still shop and see your friends.'

'You think I will allow visitors to come here?' she scoffed.

Vince sighed. 'This house is free, Mama. It's just sitting here empty. We can make it nice and still live a decent life, especially when the estate is sold, and I am no longer burdened with tax debts.'

'Very well, Vincent,' her reply was toneless, and she turned her head to stare out of the window and said no more.

Alice smiled softly at Vince, understanding the pressure he was under. All of it was terribly tiresome.

\*\*\*

Alice left the warehouse she'd just toured in Bermondsey. It had been raining earlier but now a weak sun poked between scudding grey clouds. Christmas was only days away.

'What did you think, Lady Mayton-Walsh?' Mr Loveday, the agent inquired, locking up the large door.

'Not what I was looking for, sadly.' She stared up at the side of the warehouse which denoted its former use as a timber storage facility. 'It's too open inside. I'd have to spend a great deal of money on the refurbishment of the interior. I'd need to fit it out with offices, meeting rooms and storage. The openness isn't suitable for what I need. Plus, I'd need to have more windows for more light.'

'I do have another property on Albion Street?'

'I'll leave it for today, Mr Loveday. Thank you for your time.' Disheartened, Alice walked back to her car. For the last two weeks she'd been inspecting potential properties every day and was tired of thinking about it. Early sales of the magazine had risen for the Christmas issue, which was pleasing, but she was finding it difficult to be motivated. Since the offer from the Brannings to buy *Sheer*, it had been all she'd thought about, that and Vince and his decision to live in Limehouse. Both were as shocking as each other and both kept her awake at night.

Back at the office, she sat behind her desk and read the letters Winifred had placed there. Several were letters from advertisers closing their accounts, which sent a shiver down her back. *Sheer* needed advertisers. Amongst the pile were a few invitations to balls and parties, and the rest were bills.

'I need your signature, madam, for the wages.' Winifred placed a ledger on the desk.

Alice ran a quick eye over the figures which were the same as last week and signed her name, knowing Winifred wouldn't have made a mistake with the wages. She trusted her completely.

'Thank you. I'll go to the bank shortly, unless you need me beforehand?' the older woman asked, taking the ledger back.

'No.' Alice looked behind her to Maisie, who came in carrying the mock-up of the next edition.

'Shall I come back?' Maisie asked, her curly black hair was kept under control by a wide red ribbon.

'I'm just leaving.' Winifred scuttled out of the office and to her own desk.

Alice took the mock-up and turned each page slowly, eyeing the design, the details and the colours of each page's layout. 'I positively don't like the brown scarf with the teal evening dress on page six. Ask Geoffrey to draw a white stole instead. Draped over her arms.'

Maise nodded and took notes.

'And page eight... Tennis? I rather thought we were pushing the tennis outfits to the April edition for spring?'

'We did discuss it at the last meeting, but you didn't come back to us with a definite answer, so we added it anyway.'

'I didn't?'

'No, madam.'

Alice rubbed her forehead in annoyance. How had she let that slip her mind? She turned another page. 'Where are the Fontaine shoes we are showcasing for Mr Fontaine?'

'The samples didn't arrive.'

Her head shot up. 'What do you mean? Didn't arrive? Has anyone contacted the Fontaine office to ask why? I told Mr Fontaine they would be in the February edition.' Alice stood and went to the door where Winifred was putting on her coat. 'I need Fontaine.'

'Certainly, madam.' Winifred went straight to her desk and picked up the phone to speak to the operator.

Alice waited by her desk for Winifred to put her through to the Fontaine office. Her black and brass telephone rang once, and she answered it. The operator put her through.

'Mr Fontaine's office,' a female voice spoke in Alice's ear.

'Lady Mayton-Walsh here, from *Sheer* magazine. I wish to speak to Mr Fontaine, please.'

'I'm sorry but he's not in his office today and won't be back until after the Christmas break, may I take a message?'

'Yes, have him contact me immediately. The shoe samples we were featuring in our next edition have not arrived as promised. We cannot put them in our magazine if we cannot see the samples to draw them!'

'I understand. I will have Mr Fontaine contact you as soon as he returns to the office.'

'No, before that!'

'But I'm not sure...'

'See that you do or otherwise Fontaine shoes will not be featured in *Sheer*'s next edition.' Alice put the receiver down and flipped through the mock-up once more. 'Why is there a ghastly blank space on the inside of the back cover?'

'We assumed you'd want advertising to go there as it always does.'

'All advertising has been secured for this edition. If there are spaces remaining, fill them up.'

'With what, madam?' Maisie looked clueless.

'Surely we have something? Isn't there enough of you out there to think of something suitable to include? It's what I pay you for.' Alice thrust the mock-up at Maisie. 'I am not happy with this at all. It's well below par.' Then she paused. 'Golf! That's it. Do a feature on the back page about women's golfing attire.'

Maisie tapped her pencil against her chin. 'We have some golf items in the storeroom from last summer.'

'Have Geoffrey change the colours in his drawing so it's different to the last time we showcased golf. Shorten the skirt, just under knee height instead of calf length and add... pantaloons.' Alice relied on her quick thinking. Over the years it never failed her.

Maisie stared at her. 'Shorten the shirt?'

'Indeed. *Sheer* is a leader in women's fashion, and if designers haven't created it yet, then we will!'

'How racy!' Maisie chuckled.

'Now, if I remember correctly, last time the golf outfit was in navy and red... This time tell Geoffrey I want light colours, pinks and sky blue. The jacket white striped. If women don't play golf, they can be inspired by the image to use as a walking outfit. Have the text denoting that.'

Once Maisie had left, Alice sat at the desk. Satisfied, she'd once again made a decision that would make fashion designers sit up and take note. Many times, in the past, she had put something in the magazine that she hadn't seen in the shops, a different style of evening dress, a coloured blouse not commonly seen, or outlandish accessories to put together an unusual look. Her readers would ask their dressmakers to create what they'd found and within months, the idea Alice originally had would be adapted and be on every mannequin in women's clothing shops.

Usually, such fast thinking gave her a buzz. But recently she felt less than enthusiastic. Solving problems at *Sheer* was becoming a chore not a pleasure.

*Was* it time to sell? If the process of running the magazine was becoming less enjoyable each day, then surely that was telling her it was time to make changes? The Brannings wanted it. Could she part with something that she had created, nurtured and devoted everything to? She didn't know. Besides, what would she do with herself if she did sell it? She was thirty-three years old. Her life stretched out before her. What would she do with her days? She had spent the last six years coming into the office, having something to focus on. Could she spend the rest of her days having long lunches, late nights and shopping afternoons? Her friends did it, especially the married ones, but she had an awful feeling she'd be bored within months.

However, she couldn't deny the money selling *Sheer* would bring would be beneficial after losing the dividends from her American investments. Was it possible to start again?

# Chapter Seven

By the glow of the streetlights, Alice walked into her townhouse while the taxi driver pulled her suitcase out of his vehicle and carried it up the steps to hand over to Esme.

'Welcome home, madam,' Esme said.

'Thank you. Did you have a nice Christmas?'

'I did, madam.' Esme shut the door. 'I even went and watched a show on New Year's Eve. Afterwards, me and my friends went for drinks. It was a splendid time. How was your holiday in Yorkshire?'

'Quiet but comforting.' Alice took off her hat, gloves and coat and handed them to Esme.

'Tea, madam?'

'Smashing.' She went upstairs and into the parlour and found Mrs Barton sitting by the fire, reading the newspaper. The older woman looked tired, gaunt. She'd lost even more weight. 'Good afternoon, Mrs Barton.'

'Oh, Alice. How lovely that you have returned.' Mrs Barton's smile was wide and welcoming in her pale face. 'Gracious, it has turned dark without me knowing. How are your family?'

Alice switched on two more lamps. 'All well. Henry is growing up so fast and Prue is doing brilliantly with the pregnancy, much to everyone's relief, especially Brandon. Mother and Father are the same as always and send their best wishes to you.' She drew the curtains, wondering why Esme hadn't done it.

'That is wonderful of them to remember me. Was Christmas pleasurable?'

'Yes. Henry was too excited. Having him about gave us such memories to cherish as we laughed at his funny little escapades and sayings. He's obsessed with ducks at the moment. Can you imagine such a thing?' Alice laughed, missing her nephew already. 'We had only the family around the table on Christmas, but we held a small party of close friends to ring in the New Year.'

'It is impossible to believe we are now in nineteen-thirty. Where do the years go?' Mrs Barton folded her newspaper.

'Where you able to enjoy Christmas?' Alice asked sitting down on the sofa. 'It must have been jolly difficult being away from your own home.'

'I confess the holiday season is no longer pleasant without my husband. Vince and I had a very quiet day. We went to church and then returned here for a meal just the two of us.'

'You both should have come with me to Yorkshire. Brandon and my parents were disappointed you didn't.'

'It is sweet of them to think of us. But we must learn to live this new life that has been thrust upon us.' Mrs Barton sighed unhappily. 'We are adjusting. That is to say, Vince is adjusting, I am simply living each moment as it comes.'

'It will become easier.'

'I hope so but I am not sure.' Mrs Barton took off her reading glasses and placed them on her lap. 'I used to be such a busy woman...'

'You still can be. You simply must continue visiting your friends and taking part in those activities that you enjoy.'

'But I feel such a fraud now, Alice. To accept invitations when I cannot host functions myself is demoralising.'

'I insist on you using this house as you would your own. Have friends here, host dinners and do everything you used to do.'

'Sadly, my dear, the cost of hosting is no longer something I can justify. Vince will not support such events.'

'I'm certain he would if he knew it made you happy. Where is Vince, anyway?'

Mrs Barton scowled. 'At the terrace! He spends all day every day there. I was fortunate to have him for Christmas Day, for he was gone again the next day and every day since.'

'Bless him. He must be working hard.' Alice glanced at the clock, but it was gone past five and too late to venture to the East End of London now. Darkness in winter was all consuming, especially as when she was coming home it looked like a fog was rolling in off the Thames.

Esme brought the tea in, and Mrs Barton poured for Alice. 'You seem rather tired, my dear.'

Alice nodded and thought she could say the same to her but refrained. 'I am. The train seemed to stop at every station from York to King's Cross.

I think a bath and bed with a supper tray might be in order tonight.'

'Indeed, it is a long journey for sure. Tomorrow, you will feel more refreshed.'

The door opened and Vince walked in and smiled in surprise on seeing Alice. 'I didn't realise you were coming home today?'

Her heart skipped a little at his untidy appearance. He looked dishevelled and ruggedly handsome. More and more she was wishing to be in his company, and she couldn't deny her attraction to him. She'd missed him while away in Yorkshire. She raised her cheek for him to kiss after he'd kissed his mother. 'Look at the state of you. Is that plaster in your hair?' She laughed.

'Oh, that is nothing, Alice,' Mrs Barton scoffed. 'Some days he is covered in paint, or some sort of mortar or brick dust and all manner of things.'

Vince grinned, staring down at himself. 'I do wear old clothes and then change back into my suit before I come back here, but even my suit is looking worse for wear lately.'

Mrs Barton rose and stepped to the door. 'I shall go and fetch you a teacup, dearest, and instruct Esme to run a bath for Alice. Perhaps you should indulge in one afterwards?'

'Yes, Mama.' He perched on the edge of a chair, aware he might leave dust marks on the fine gold fabric. 'How was Yorkshire and the family?'

'All very splendid. They asked after you though. Brandon wished you'd come with me.'

He peered down at his broken fingernails. 'I'll visit him in a few months.'

'How is it all coming along at the terrace?' Alice asked him, sensing the need to change the subject. Vince had stopped seeing their friends and attending functions for months now. Talking about any of that caused him to close up.

'Surprisingly well. Walls are down and new plaster is being put up. The building team I hired are very skilful and quick. I bumble along behind them like a fish out of water, but I am enjoying it immensely.' He grinned self-consciously.

'Enjoying it?' She stared in shock.

'I know, it is genuinely absurd that I, someone who has never picked up a hammer in their life, can now understand rudimentary building techniques. I know of load-bearing walls, lintels, joists, how to plane a door and hang one, would you believe!' He looked extremely pleased with himself. 'Every day I learn something new, and I'm finding it most interesting and never a bore, or a chore.'

'Gracious!' Alice grinned. 'You sound like a changed man.'

'I believe I am, actually.'

She studied him for a long moment and saw the healthy colour on his face, his eyes were once more alive. The shadows had gone from under his eyes and that haunted look he wore had disappeared. This project had given him something, something that brought a spark back into his life, a purpose. She was jealous. Despite all his problems, Vince was finding a reason to get out of bed each morning. Whereas she was finding it more difficult each day to head to the office. Spending Christmas with Brandon and her father had given her the opportunity to discuss with them the idea of selling *Sheer*. Both her father and brother had been surprised she'd consider it, after years of working long hours to make it a success.

'Have I shocked you?' Vince joked.

She shook her head, focusing on him again. 'No, not at all. I was merely thinking how much I envy you. You have a purpose. Once I was the same.'

He tilted his head at her. 'If you're unhappy, only you can change it.'

'Indeed, but how does one do that? *Sheer* was everything to me, my life. Without it, what have I got?'

'What do you want?'

She sucked in a deep breath. 'Golly, I have no idea. None at all. Anyway, am I allowed to visit this palace you are building?' she asked him, quickly changing the subject.

He smiled with warmth. 'Of course. In fact, there are things I wish to hear your opinion on.'

'Oh?'

'Yes, paint colours, and wallpaper, or furnishings.'

'Gosh. Surely your mother should choose those? It is going to be her house.'

'Mama isn't interested. I believe she wishes to stay here and never move to Limehouse.'

'Then why upset her, Vince? Both of you can stay here as long as you want. Why make her live in a place so unsuitable to her?'

'This is your home, Alice, not ours. We cannot stay much longer. We are an inconvenience. Now you have returned from Yorkshire, I'll stay at the terrace. I was only sleeping here while you were away to keep Mama company. I will get more done if I stay at the house.'

'I'd like you both to stay.' In all truth she enjoyed having them both with her. It was tiresome to always return home and have no one to spend an evening with, which is why she went out most nights.

'I cannot blame Mama for not wanting to move to that part of London, but the house will be comfortable enough and that's all she needs now our lives have been reduced in every way.'

'Who are you talking about?' Mrs Barton said, coming back into the room.

'You, Mama, and the house.'

Mrs Barton gave a strained smile. 'Do not worry about me, Vince. I have told you numerous times. I am content to live there. I am certain you have made the place habitable.'

'Vince needs your opinion on the paint colours, and wallpaper,' Alice told her. 'I'm interested to know what you are thinking of choosing.'

'I have not given any of it a thought.' Sylvia frowned with a dismissive shrug.

'Then perhaps we should go shopping tomorrow, just you and I and we can select some colours and furnishings together.'

'What about going into the office in the morning?'

Alice waved away her concerns. She wasn't in any hurry to go into the office and deal with potential problems. 'I'll go in the afternoon. A few hours more away from the office will be fine. You being happy is more important.'

Mrs Barton's smile was more convincing this time. 'I would like that, Alice. Thank you.'

Vince gave Alice a small wink in thanks, and she grinned.

As Esme brought in fresh tea, Alice excused herself to go and have a relaxing bath before supper.

***

Standing on a ladder, Vince squinted through the dust as he, and the other two builders he'd hired, pulled down the old plaster from the ceiling in the hallway. The adjoining wall between the two houses had been ripped down the day before, leaving a large mess of dust, rubble, exposed bricks and timber. A carpenter and his lad worked on the two staircases to join them as one, while in the kitchen a plumber was laying pipes for water to be attached to the new boiler.

The expense of hiring professionals lessened his bank balance but no matter how many books he borrowed from the library to learn about building, he knew he'd never be good enough, or know enough, to do the important work, such as installing the plumbing and carpentry, gas or electricity.

The noise and dust created by the renovation made Vince open the front door and all the windows, despite it being a cold blustery winter's day. He climbed down from the ladder and, grabbing a shovel, began scooping up the debris into buckets.

Out of the corner of his eye, he saw movement. He turned and was surprised when two young children came and sat on his doorstep. He'd seen them many times before playing out in the street. 'Can I help you?'

'We're just looking,' the girl with long black plaits replied calmly, as though this was some sort of entertainment. 'Timmy loves watching men work on the docks, but Mam said we're to stay close to the house today.'

'I see.' Vince took the little boy to be Timmy. 'And what's your name?'

'Libby Morris. I'm five and this is Timmy, he's two.'

'My name is Vince Barton. Nice to meet you.' He grinned.

'We live at the end of the street,' Libby supplied. 'Our dad died at sea.'

'Oh.' Shocked by the sudden statement, Vince took a moment to reply. 'That is sad indeed.'

'Dad only saw Timmy twice in his whole life.' Libby watched the other workmen with interest. 'Mam says this is your house and we're to stay out of your workmen's way.'

'It is my house, yes.' He scooped up another shovelful of debris. 'And why are you not heeding your mother's words?' he joked with her.

'We aren't in your way.' She pulled Timmy back a little to show him that she was not impeding on the movement of the workers where they stood in the doorway.

'A building site isn't a place for you or your brother to be playing.'

'We're not playing, just watching. We won't touch anything.'

'In a couple of months, the house will be finished. Maybe you can come and see it then?' he offered, carrying the bucket outside to tip into a cart before coming back inside.

'That'll be good.' She nodded wisely and then tilted her head sideways to study him. 'I've decided to like you.'

'Have you indeed?'

'Mam says you can't be a real gentleman as they don't work.'

He laughed. 'I am a gentleman, but also one that likes to get his hands dirty.'

She considered this. 'Then you can be my friend.'

He bowed. 'I am honoured, my lady.' Saying those words reminded him of Alice, for it was what he used to call her but for some reason he no longer did. Not since he became engaged to Diana. That's when the shift of friendship changed into an awkwardness he couldn't stand, and which was why he was working long hours to ready this house so he could move in here and not see Alice for weeks on end. He'd given up his partying ways, the social drinking, the events and dinners. Changing his lifestyle was due to financial necessity but also to distance himself from Alice, the one woman he wanted but could never have.

'Do you have any children?' Libby asked, watching a man walk past carrying a long pipe. She and Timmy shuffled out of the way for him to take it outside.

'No, I do not. Sorry to disappoint.'

Timmy sat on the floor. 'I'm hungry.'

Libby shrugged. 'There's nothing at home.'

Vince paused, seeing the unhappy little face. 'Why don't we go to the fish shop and get some fish and chips?'

Libby's eyes widened and her mouth became a perfect O. 'Fish and chips?'

'I get them for the men at midday. If you help me bring it all back, then I'll get you some as well.'

'Come on, Timmy. Mr Barton is buying us some food.' She grabbed her brother's little hand and hauled him up.

Vince called out to the men that he was getting food and, taking his coat off the hook on the wall, walked out with the children.

They walked along Commercial Road to the fish and chip shop on the corner, passing a Chinese shop. The old man who owned it, bowed to Vince as he walked past and said good day.

Some of the locals, Vince knew, didn't hold with 'foreigners' and never mixed with the Chinese community that had infiltrated the Limehouse area years ago. However, Vince got along with everyone and was fascinated by the few Chinese men he'd met and spoken with.

At the fish and chip shop they had to queue, and Timmy sat on the floor, growing tired. Vince picked him up, amazed at the lightness of him. 'You cannot sleep on the floor, little man.'

'He's always tired,' Libby supplied. 'Mam says it's because he doesn't eat enough.'

Vince studied the little scrap in his arms. The boy was very thin, covered in bruises on his matchstick legs and had shadows under his eyes. 'Some fish will fill that belly, won't it?' Vince tickled him.

Eventually they received their order and walked back to the house. The men stopped working and they all sat in the rubble of the kitchen and ate the many pieces of fish and the huge bundle of chips wrapped in newspaper. Vince had also bought boiled eggs for them and for Happy — the old carpenter whose real name was Terry — he'd bought a pot of jellied eels.

Vince watched Libby and Timmy eat as much as they could. They sat on the floor and ate a whole battered fish between them and handfuls of chips. They didn't talk or look around, just sat and ate as though to stop might mean the food would disappear.

Eventually, with the food eaten and the men returning to work, Libby smiled at Vince and Timmy yawned and said he needed to pee-pee.

Vince hoisted him over the building work and out to the yard where the old lavatory stood with its lopsided walls and leaky roof.

Back inside, Vince set to work again, shovelling the debris created by Happy and his apprentice. Timmy fell asleep despite the banging and hammering, and Vince placed his coat under the little boy's head as a cushion.

'Will your mother be worried about where you are?' Vince asked Libby.

Libby shrugged one shoulder. 'She's at work.'

'At work?' Vince paused. 'Who is meant to be looking after you then?'

'I look after Timmy.'

Vince hid his surprise. He'd thought the mother was simply at home washing or something and wanting the children out from under her feet. But to be at work and leave these two home alone? It seemed neglectful. Timmy was barely out of babyhood.

'Where does she work, your mother?' he asked, filling a bucket.

'At the pub.'

'Which pub?'

Libby frowned in thought. 'The first one on Cable Road. I sometimes take Timmy and we sit out on the front step when the weather's nice. Sometimes we get a glass of lemonade.'

'Well, you can stay here with me each time your mother is at work. I don't like to think of you both being alone.'

Libby grinned. 'We can come every day?'

'Every day.' He kept working only to stop a few minutes later. 'Why aren't you in school Libby?'

She was drawing stick figures in the dust on the floorboards. ''Cos I need to look after Timmy.'

'You should be in school.' She was a child herself caring for another child. It wasn't right.

She shrugged again, her answer to any question she wasn't sure about.

Vince took the full wheelbarrow outside and tipped it into a steel tub he'd hired for the building waste to go into. His thoughts remained on Libby and her young brother. Such small children to be left alone all day every day.

He understood the working class around here didn't have a lot of choice in the matter of how they survived and most times work was put before their children's welfare, but they were unseen children he didn't know. Closer to home was Libby and Timmy and he suddenly wanted the best for them. He felt guilty every time he looked into their gaunt faces, or noticed their lean bodies. He might have hit rock bottom in his own society, but even that was way above the standard of living for those two little people. He couldn't stop comparing them to Brandon and Prue's son, Henry, a well-fed boy surrounded by love and attention living in a lovely home with every comfort he could wish for. The difference between Henry and Libby and Timmy was enormous. It made Vince uneasy.

Despite the cold, Vince stood outside and really looked at the decrepit houses in the row. Behind each paint-peeling door was a family suffering hardship and poverty. He and his mother were coming to live amongst these people, yet he had no understanding of them, of their problems, their struggles. The Barton family fortune was gone, but

Vince still had enough money to live well, perhaps not in the sphere he once did, but he'd never go hungry, or without clothes and home comforts as his neighbours did. What right did he have to live amongst them and complain about anything? To them he was a rich man, despite everything he'd lost. Was it any wonder that not every person in the surrounding streets said hello to him? They were suspicious as to why a gentleman would choose to live here in the streets of Limehouse.

He needed to help them. Win them around. Show them that he could be trusted. How he could do that he didn't know.

*** 

Alice woke before Esme entered to open the curtains. She stretched in the semi darkness, listening to the rattle of the delivery carts on the street. The evening before had been pleasant as she, Vince and his mother played cards after supper. The evening had passed quickly in the enjoyment of chatting, drinking and eating and laughter. Alice had sent Esme home and they saw to themselves. Vince kept the fire blazing, while Alice found her way around the kitchen enough to make them ham and cheese sandwiches and hot chocolate, with a dash of rum. They decided to finally go to bed just after one o'clock, with Mrs Barton declaring she'd not been up so late for years but it had been a lovely night.

'Morning, madam.' Esme breezed into her room. 'It has snowed overnight. My feet are frozen from just walking from the tram stop to here.'

'Really? I wasn't expecting snow. I had enough of that in Yorkshire over Christmas. What a bother.'

Opening the curtains, Esme peered out. 'It's stopped now and it's not too thick on the ground but icy cold. Wrap up warm if you're heading out.'

'Mrs Barton and I are going shopping.' Alice climbed from the bed and wrapped her thick wool dressing gown over her silk nightgown. She visited the bathroom and returned to the bedroom to apply her make-up.

'Shopping again?' Esme smiled, making the bed.

'Yes, Mrs Barton found it difficult last week to make any decisions. But she's had a think about it now and has chosen the curtains for all the rooms in Mr Barton's house.'

'Lovely. It's good to see Mrs Barton taking an interest. Mr Barton is spending so much time in Limehouse, bless him.'

Alice applied a spritz of perfume to her neck and wrists. 'He has really developed a passion for the renovations.'

'He's so keen, he's already left for Limehouse this morning without any breakfast.'

'Gosh. He must have left frightfully early.' Alice frowned a little. She barely saw Vince. He spent all his time in Limehouse, and she'd spent the last two weeks catching up with everything at the office after the holidays. Last night had been the first time he'd stayed over since she returned from Yorkshire two weeks ago and she found herself watching him more than she should. At some point her love for him had turned from simple friendship to something more and she didn't know what to do about it, or even if she should do anything about it. It was all a terrible muddle in her mind.

To add to that, she had also finally decided to sell *Sheer*. Her decision to sell felt right. After another discussion with Brandon on the telephone yesterday and again with Vince last night, her decision had been made. She just needed to put everything in motion to actually do it.

'Have you been into Mrs Barton's room yet?' she asked Esme, selecting a forest green dress from her wardrobe.

'No, madam. I thought to wake you first. Mrs Barton moves slowly on a morning, I've found. She's happy to stay in bed a bit longer and have a cup of tea.'

'Maybe I should start doing that?' Alice slipped on fresh underwear, stockings and then donned the dress.

Esme's eyes widened as she tidied the pillows on the bed. 'But you're always up early and heading into the office during the week.'

'I may be changing my lifestyle, Esme,' Alice told her as she opened her jewellery case and took out gold and diamond earrings, a gold bangle and a multi-strand gold chain necklace.

'That sounds interesting, madam.'

'I'm selling *Sheer*, Esme.' She put on the jewellery. 'Things will be different around here soon.'

'Heavens, madam, such a decision!'

'Indeed, it is, but one I am happy about.' In truth she was happy. It was time to do something else with her life.

'If you're happy, madam, that's all that matters.'

Alice brushed her short straight dark hair. 'Mrs Barton and I spoke last night about getting an early start. So, we'll take breakfast together. I'm sure she'll be awake now.'

'Very good, madam. I shall go and see if Mrs Barton needs a hand to get dressed.'

Alice went into the dining room and sat in her normal place at the head of the table. The first post and a letter opener were placed on a small round silver tray next to her fork. Seeing an overseas stamp, Alice sighed. Taking the letter opener, she split the envelope with dread.

Her New York broker, Mr Henderson's letter was lengthy, detailed and utterly depressing. Alice had lost more money than she thought in the stock market crash. Her shares were worthless. This would change everything. Selling *Sheer* would give her money in the bank and the means to live well until she decided her future.

Sighing, Alice pushed away the invitations not concerned about reading them. After shopping with Sylvia, she'd need to speak with her solicitor and contact the Brannings. They could have first refusal of the magazine.

Suddenly, Esme ran into the room, her face pale. 'Madam, I can't wake Mrs Barton. Come quickly.'

A shiver of fear ran down Alice's back. She hurried out after Esme to the guest bedroom.

'I opened the curtains, and she usually stirs...' Esme clutched her hands together.

Alice approached the bed cautiously. Mrs Barton appeared to be sleeping. 'Perhaps, she's in a heavy sleep?' she whispered.

'She's a light sleeper. She's told me that plenty of times.' Esme stayed by the door.

Alice kept her gaze on Mrs Barton's face, willing her to open her eyes. 'Mrs Barton? Sylvia?'

There was no response, no movement.

Gently, Alice shook the older woman's shoulder. Stillness. Coldness. Swallowing back a small gasp, she watched the dear woman's chest to see if it moved. It didn't.

A tingle of fear and dread shivered down Alice's spine. She gently grasped Sylvia's cool hand and felt for a pulse on her wrist. She couldn't feel anything. Heart pumping wildly, she tried the pulse at Sylvia's neck and waited. Nothing. Was she doing it correctly? She tried her wrist once more. Again, nothing.

'Oh God, no...' Alice breathed.

'Shall I ring for the doctor, madam?' Esme murmured, clasping her hands to her mouth.

Alice closed her eyes in utter sadness. 'Yes, and send a taxi to go and collect Mr Barton from Limehouse. It's the first terrace on Island Row. Tell the driver.'

Left alone, Alice straightened the blankets and folded Mrs Barton's hands over her chest. Her skin had a grey-yellow tinge to it. Alice had seen few dead people, mainly her grandparents and a friend from school, years ago. But this seemed so different. Her grandparents had been old when they died, and her school friend had been ill for a long time. Yet, none of them lived with her as Sylvia did. Last night they had laughed and played cards, drank hot chocolate laced with rum. She was Vince's dear mama...

'Poor lovely lady, I'm so sorry,' she whispered. 'Vince is going to be heartbroken.'

Taking a steadying breath, Alice tried to think what to do. What would Vince need from her?

The gold jewellery she wore flashed in the weak sunlight. She was meant to be shopping with Sylvia this morning...

Quickly, she ran back to her bedroom and stripped off all the jewellery and the dress. From her wardrobe, she pulled out a long black woollen skirt, a black silk blouse and a black tailored jacket. She brushed her short straight hair again, using a diamond clasp to pin one side up. In jerky movements she donned black court shoes.

Standing straight, she checked herself in the mirror. Black. So much black. Tears started but she blinked them away. She had to be strong today for Vince. Thinking of him made her chin wobble. Darling Vince. He would need her strength.

She hurried back to the guest bedroom and paused in the doorway. Mrs Barton hadn't moved, of course she hadn't! Slowly, Alice stepped to the corner of the room and carried the chair from there to beside the bed and sat down.

Alice took Mrs Barton's hand in hers. 'I will miss you,' she spoke quietly. 'Vince will be terribly upset, you know. We had no warning. But for you, it is the best way to go, isn't it? No pain, no suffering. Just go to sleep and not wake up.'

A slight tap sounded on the open door. Mrs Jones, her cook, came in carrying a cup of tea. 'I thought you might like a tea, madam, while you wait.'

'Thank you, Mrs Jones.'

'I've tied a black ribbon on the doorknocker to make people aware there's been a death.'

Alice nodded.

Mrs Jones, who rarely ventured outside of the kitchen, placed the teacup and saucer on the bedside table and left.

Alice glanced out of the window, a light snow was falling, the kind that melted as soon as it hit the ground. 'You know I'll take care of him, don't you?' she murmured to Mrs Barton. 'He's my best friend. Well, he's more than that. I'd like him to be...' She paused, still not even certain she could utter the words. 'Would you approve of him and me, Sylvia? I know you think of me as a bit fast. My lifestyle is extravagant, crazy and a little wild at times, or it was. I feel the future is going to be somewhat different. I've grown tired of all the partying, the meaningless men who I flirt and kiss with.'

She stared down at their joined hands. 'I want something solid, Sylvia. Something strong, something honest and profound. I'd like that with Vince, but I don't know if his feelings run that deep for me. He sees me as his friend.'

A small brown bird came to sit on the windowsill. Alice watched it for a moment, the snowy wind battering its tiny feathers, then it was gone. For a long time, Alice gazed out of the window hoping the bird would come back but it didn't. She hoped it was somewhere safe and warm.

Her tea went cold as she waited for the doctor and Vince. The doctor arrived first. An elderly man she'd not seen before but knew his name from the brass plaque on the wall a few streets away. She was rarely ill and could count on one hand how many times she had seen the doctor and when she had it was the family doctor in Mayfair.

She left the room as he did his examination, needing the lavatory and when she returned to the room Vince was there. He looked shaken and white. The doctor spoke in low tones, and Alice went to stand next to Vince and took his hand. He clasped it tightly but didn't glance at her, just concentrated on the doctor's words of possible heart failure.

'Your mother visited me only last week,' the doctor said.

'Last week?' Vince queried. 'She wasn't ill last week.'

'She has been ill for some time. Pains in her chest, you see. She told me that when out on one of her walks she saw our office and called in to speak to me.'

'We have our own doctor,' Vince said, as though the doctor was making it all up.

The doctor pushed his glasses further up on his nose. 'Yes, indeed. However, your mother didn't want to visit him. I was closer she said. Her life had changed, and she must change with it, she told me. She wanted a doctor only a few streets away not on the other side of town.'

'So, you knew she was ill?'

'She did mention pains in her chest, and I told her I'd like to run some tests at the hospital, but she wouldn't hear of it.'

'Then you should have insisted upon it being done!' Vince snapped. 'It could have saved her.'

'No doctor can force their patient to have tests. We can only advise, give the facts and let the patient decide.' He closed his black bag. 'There will be a post-mortem.'

'No there won't!' Vince dropped Alice's hand and ran his fingers through his hair. 'My mother will not be put through that.'

'Mr Barton, you must understand—'

'I understand that my mother has died, sir. The cause is heart failure while she slept. I think you can agree to that?'

'A post-mortem will determine that.'

'No, you will write that down on her death certificate. It's the least you can do after allowing my mother to walk from your office without going for tests. Do *you* understand, sir?'

'It is highly irregular!'

'I don't give a tinker's toss for what's irregular,' Vince growled between clenched teeth.

Alice gripped his arm. She'd never seen him so angry. An angry Vince was something she'd never witnessed, and it upset her greatly. 'Darling, please. Calm down. Think of your mother.'

The doctor, who had kind eyes, took out the paperwork from his bag and began writing. 'I shall record your mother died of heart failure, Mr Barton. I am certain in my professional opinion that is what it was anyway.'

'Thank you.' Vince turned away from the bed and stepped to the window. 'I want to arrange to bury my mother, Doctor. Send your bill to this address,' he dismissed him.

'Very well.' The doctor grabbed his bag and after a small bow to Alice went out of the room.

Alice watched Vince, waiting for a sign from him on how to act.

He turned and gazed down at his mother. 'She was a good woman, Alice.'

'Absolutely. One of the best.'

'Some mothers can be so irritating, demanding their children's time, or absence... My mother loved me and only ever wanted the best for me. Being an only child can be suffocating for some, but never for me, not really. Oh, I know after the war all parents wanted their sons home, and Brandon and I quickly found that a chore and decided to roam Europe climbing mountains. Mother didn't like it, of course. Feared for me, as I'm sure your mother did for Brandon. But never once did she ask me to come home...'

'She was selfless,' Alice agreed.

'And I was going to make her live in Limehouse.'

'Vince...'

'Why didn't I simply rent somewhere in the countryside as she wanted? A cottage in a village where it is green and has flowers. Why didn't I do that?' He gave a mocking laugh. 'Because I thought I knew best.'

'She would have gone wherever you decided to go.' Alice could see the emotions flickering over his distraught face.

'Yes, she gave me her complete trust and I expected her to adapt to the poor area of London. I was being selfish. She wouldn't have been happy there. I knew that and yet I went ahead with my plans, expecting her to fall in with them. I as good as killed her.'

'Stop that talk at once! None of that is true. You were being prudent with your money. She believed in you.' She touched his arm. 'Come into the parlour for some tea.'

'No, I must visit undertakers. I'll use the same firm we hired for my father. They were excellent.' He ran a hand over his hair again, making it stick up. 'Then I'll go to our church where Father is buried and speak with the vicar to organise a date for the funeral. There is a plot already there next to my father for Mama.'

'Shall I come with you?'

'Thank you, but no. I wish to do this by myself. Besides, I'd rather not have Mama left alone, if you don't mind?'

'Of course not. I'll stay with her.'

'Thank you.' He walked past Alice, then paused and kissed her cheek. His hand cupped her other cheek. The tender gesture meant so much to Alice.

She stared into his eyes, hating to see his misery. 'I have done very little.'

His thumb gently stroked her skin. 'Not so. You've been my very best friend. I'm truly sorry Mama died here in your home. It is a memory you should never need to be burdened with.'

His touch made her shiver with suppressed desire. 'It's not a burden, Vince. A great sadness, yes, but never a burden. I liked your mother very much. She died in her sleep in a place she was comfortable. Shouldn't we all wish to go that way?'

'But now you must have undertakers in your home, a body removed...' A muscle ticked along his jaw, and he took a steadying breath.

'And we shall oversee it all together. Go and do what must be done. I shall be here waiting for your return.' She kissed his cheek.

When he had gone, Alice went to her own bedroom and sat on the bed. Her emotions were raw and mixed. Vince held her heart, but she couldn't tell him that, not now, not when he had to bury his mother and grieve for her.

Instead, she'd be his strength when he needed it and his friend.

# Chapter Eight

Vince placed his teacup and saucer on the empty tray as Esme was walking past. He'd had enough of tea, of polite talk, of hearing people's sympathies. Alice's parlour was filled with black-wearing friends and acquaintances. People, especially the women who had been his mother's friends for years, sat chatting politely about how wonderful his mother had been. Yet, they had barely spoken to her once his father died and the money troubles became apparent. Those women had slowly stopped sending his mother invitations to their gatherings, or to meet for lunches when they found out the Bartons' were selling the estate, their London house, furniture and paintings to pay their bills.

He didn't want to talk to those people now. Their false friendship churned his gut. He didn't want their sympathies, their forced sadness. The only people who mattered were Alice, Brandon and Prue. Even his distant cousins annoyed him.

Why were they here, the children of his parents' relatives, who he'd not seen for a very long time? It was all so pretentious.

'Vince, dearest.' Prue came up to him, her pregnancy clearly visible at seven months. She and Brandon had travelled from Yorkshire, leaving Henry with his grandparents and nanny. He was deeply touched that they came, despite the foul January weather which created havoc with transport. Snow had fallen heavily up north, but Brandon and Prue had made it through, travelling all night, not letting delayed trains stop them from being by his side.

He smiled at Prue, such a beautiful woman and a true friend. 'You must be exhausted?'

'No, I'm fine.' She waved away his concerns. 'I'm made of strong stuff. However, Brandon was thinking to take you out for dinner later, if you feel up to it? I shan't go. I'll stay here and have an early night. Alice will keep me company.'

'Are you sure? I don't mind staying in.'

'I'm certain you'd rather have several drinks in a club somewhere than sitting about with me and Alice talking fashion, or some such nonsense.' Her eyes dimmed. 'To be honest I think Brandon needs it more than you.'

'Oh?'

'He's been working so hard, trying to rebound from the stock market crash. He's taken the whole family finances on board to ease the worry from his father's shoulders. For months he's done nothing at all fun. He needs a night on the town, drinking, playing billiards or whatever it is you men do in your secret clubs.' She grinned.

'Then I'll make sure he has a night off from thinking about money.' He patted her hand where it rested on his arm. 'The only good thing about not having any money is that it's no longer a problem to try and keep things going.'

'Alice told me the estate sold.'

'Yes, just yesterday. I signed the papers with the solicitor. Perfect timing, really. It is to become an elite boys' school.' The thought made him happy. To know hundreds of young lads would be running through the hallways, filling the old rooms with laughter and traipsing over the grounds gave him a lot of satisfaction. He'd rather have that than the place being torn down, and the land sold to create a housing development.

'Then you are free of that liability now and can relax a little?'

'Yes, I can. In a few weeks all my debts will be paid. For the first time in a long time the name Barton isn't associated with owing vast amounts of money to the government.'

'And what will you do with your time now? Be a man of leisure. Travel? Will you take a villa in Italy and while away your days reading the classics?'

He chuckled at the thought. 'No. I am renovating the terraces at Limehouse.'

'Still? But I thought now your dear mother has gone you'd be doing something else?'

'I need somewhere to live, Prue.'

'Gosh, but surely there is somewhere more...'

'Nicer?' He snickered softly.

'Well, yes. Rent some rooms somewhere in town.'

'No. Renting is dead money. Why rent rooms in a hotel when I own a house?'

'True. But surely Limehouse isn't going to be your home long-term? Why don't you come back to Yorkshire with us? Perhaps you and Brandon can go into business together?'

'Doing what exactly? I left university and joined the army. After the war I lazed about climbing mountains in Europe. I am not equipped to do anything much at all.'

'You seem equipped to oversee the renovations of the terrace though. Alice says you're never away from the place.' She gave him a cheeky grin. 'You'd get work as a foreman on a building site.'

'Actually, it is something I've been thinking about.'

'No!' Prue's eyes widened in shock. 'You can't be a tradesman!'

'What's this?' Alice joined them and his heart thumped faster as she slid her arm through his. 'What are you two gossiping about?'

'Not gossip.' Prue raised her eyebrows. 'Vince is talking about becoming a foreman on a building site.'

Alice stared at him. 'Is that true?'

He gave a wry smile. 'Not quite. I'm thinking of buying old buildings, renovating them and then selling them on.'

'In Limehouse?'

'No. I've been talking to some of the builders I've hired, and they say the government are knocking down whole swathes of the poorer areas in the East End. So, my thoughts are to buy an older, less expensive house in a better part of the city, perhaps the northern part and renovate it and then sell it for a profit, or create flats and rent them out.'

'When did you decide to do this?' Alice asked, keen interest in her expression.

'It's been something I've thought about for the last few weeks. Renovation has become rather addictive to me. I am enjoying what I'm doing in Limehouse a great deal. Now the estate is sold, and my debts will be paid, the money left I need to invest wisely. Property is the only thing I have any knowledge of and even that is still a work in progress.'

'I think it a wonderful idea,' Prue declared. 'This project of buying and selling property is just what you need. Now, excuse me, please. I need to sit for a little while.' She left them and Vince looked at Alice, noticing her frown.

'What is it?'

'Nothing.'

'It's something. I can see it on your face.'

'Well, it's none of my business, of course...'

'That's never stopped you before.' He grinned.

'I'm just worried whether you can afford to invest in property?'

'I plan to start small, Alice,' he told her, a little annoyed that she should think him incapable of making a sensible decision. 'I have done the sums and if I buy a house that is relatively cheap but in a poor state, then I can fix it up and sell it on.'

'But you don't have much experience in the building industry. You're not working class.'

'No, and I don't pretend to know everything I need to, at least not yet. But I can learn. I can hire tradespeople and learn from them.'

'But will it give you the kind of lifestyle you are used to?'

He shrugged. 'My old lifestyle has gone, Alice. It went yesterday when the estate sold. The estate and Mama's death were my last links to my former life. It's time to start afresh.'

'But what does that mean? What about your friends?' She looked worried.

'My friends are those who accept me as I am now and what I will be in the future.' In truth, he'd not been missing his friends. Oh, he missed the laughter, the jokes, but not the constant partying, the never-ending socialising that drain one's brain and wallet. He was becoming too old to keep up with all the new trends and found he didn't want to anymore. It was time to let the young ones take up that particular mantle.

'But you simply cannot turn your back on... everything.'

'No, I won't be. However, I'll not be spending my days on long boozy lunches, or my nights at extravagant dinners and all night parties. I'll attend some, but not all.'

'From you, of all people, I would never expect to hear such an admission.' She looked close to tears.

'I cannot pretend to be a member of our society any more, not when I can no longer afford to keep up appearances.' He turned to a friend of his mother's who was leaving. Shaking the older woman's hand and thanking her, suddenly became a turning point for the afternoon and many people began to leave. He spent the next hour chatting to those who were leaving in a steady line to the door.

Finally, Esme closed the door on the final guest.

Vince joined Alice, Brandon and Prue in the parlour for a pre-dinner cocktail.

Brandon mixed the cocktails and handed them around. 'So, Vince. Alice and Prue tell me you are looking to buy an old house and renovate it.'

Vince raised an eyebrow at them both. 'News travels fast.' Vince took his drink and sat down on the sofa next to Prue. 'Buy and sell houses. Yes.'

'It's a wise move.'

'You agree?' Vince was surprised.

'I do. If you have any spare capital left after the estate sale, then property is the next boom, or so

I've read. London is expanding, the population rising. People need houses. Do you remember Fred Jones-Smith from university? I had a letter from him last week. He's developing parcels of land on the outskirts of London and making them housing estates.'

'Isn't his family in the government housing sector though?'

'Yes, his older brother, I believe. Anyway, despite his excellent connections, the plan is simple and profitable. Land and houses. It's a winning combination.'

Vince loosened his tie. 'I must start small, Brandon. I've only just escaped the debtor's noose.'

'True, but if you have a partner...' Brandon grinned. 'Things could be very different.'

'You?'

'Yes. There's money to be earned in this country. I like the idea of bricks and mortar rather than stocks and shares in another country that I can't control.'

The idea grew on him. Vince took a sip of the cocktail, which was strong and fruity. 'It's something to think about, for certain. Only, my capital is not as large as yours.'

'You could always have another partner,' Alice suddenly piped up in a serious tone.

Vince stared at her. 'Are you saying you want to go into business with me?'

'Why not? We've done it before. You invested in *Sheer*. Perhaps now it's my turn to invest in your project.'

He rubbed his forehead. Things were moving too fast. 'My plans were to buy one house at a time, not develop a whole new housing estate. I'm not ready.'

Brandon nodded. 'Understood.'

Vince let out a long breath. 'Give me a year or so, when I have another house renovation under my belt, then we'll talk about it some more.'

'Shall we go for dinner then and leave the ladies to gossip?' Brandon smiled with a wink to his wife.

Standing, Vince placed his empty glass on the table next to the sofa. 'You'll have to vouch for me as I'm no longer a member at the club.' He stepped to the door, realising that usually he'd have made a joke about that, or laughed. However, today he'd buried his dear mama and already he was missing her. He missed his father, too. In fact, he missed everything about his old life and, for a glimmer of a second, he wished he had it all back again.

Then common sense returned. He'd witnessed too much recently to hanker after a frivolous life that held no meaning. He only had to think of Libby and Timmy, two children without proper food, who roam the streets during the day because their mother had to work. No. He could no longer justify spending vast amounts of money on a loose and easy life. His conscience wouldn't allow it.

\*\*\*

Wearily, Alice entered the house, glad the day was over. Once again there had been nothing but problems at the office. The staff were unhappy that she was cutting back their hours, but she couldn't continue as she was doing paying such high wages. The magazine was haemorrhaging money just as *Vogue* did several years ago. Only, her problem was she didn't have the financial backing behind her to stem the flow as *Vogue* did.

This afternoon she had telephoned Mr Branning and asked him and his wife to come in and see her tomorrow if they could find the time. She planned to ask him to make her an offer for *Sheer*. She was dreading the meeting but also eager to have it over and done with. Would Mr Branning offer enough with the downturn of sales and the rising prices of creating the magazine?

'Welcome home, madam.' Esme came to take her hat and coat. 'The fire's lit in the parlour. Would you like some tea?'

'No, thank you. I've had tea all day. In an hour, I'm heading out for drinks with Miss Stuart and Mr Elliot and then we are attending the theatre afterwards. So, could you run me a bath and lay out my silver silk dress with the black fringe hem, please? Then you can go home.' Alice collected the mail from the side table by the door.

'Yes, madam.'

'Is Mr Barton at home by any chance?' Alice asked, grimacing at the bills she held.

Esme hung up Alice's coat in the cupboard. 'No, madam. He informed me this morning that he was moving back to Limehouse permanently. I helped him pack his suitcase. He's left a note for you on the mantelpiece.'

Stunned that Vince had left without saying goodbye, Alice stormed into the parlour and grabbed the folded note off the mantelpiece.

*Dearest Alice,*

*Thank you for everything. You have been the greatest of friends to me and my mother and no amount of thankyous are adequate to express my gratitude.*

*I am moving to Limehouse permanently. Thank you for allowing me to stay while I organised the funeral, but that is all done with now and I need to begin this new phrase of my life.*

*You have your house to yourself again. Enjoy the peace.*

*Forever yours,*

*Vince.*

She read the note three times before the words had sunk in enough for her to think clearly. Vince was gone. He didn't even have the decency to speak to her face to face!

'Esme!' Alice strode into the hallway.

'Yes, madam?' Esme came running from the bathroom.

'My plans have changed. I'm going out.' Alice snatched her coat from the hanger in the cupboard. 'Lock up when you leave.'

'Shall I stay and wait for you to return?'

Alice pulled on her coat and hat. 'No, no need. I don't know how long I'll be gone. Oh, can you telephone the operator and be put through to Sally Stuart's number and pass a message along that I shan't be joining her tonight? Tell her I'll call her tomorrow.'

'I'll do it now, madam.'

'Thank you. Good night.'

Alice drove through the dark streets faster than she should have. She paid no heed to the pedestrians that she made hurry across the road, or the tram drivers who shook angry fists at her as she cut in front of them. Every mile she drove from Notting Hill to Limehouse in the sleeting rain fuelled her anger. She hated driving at night and especially in the rain. Visibility was horrendous and a wispy fog was creeping in from the Thames.

Finally, she stopped the car at the end of Island Row and turned the engine off. Her shoulders were hunched tight with the stress of the drive. She climbed out of the car, remembering to grab her bag from the seat and ran over to number one and knocked loudly.

The rain pelted her, icy, freezing her cheeks and toes. She knocked again. Was he not home? Had she come all this way in the dark for him to be not even there? Where would he be for God's sake?

She turned and peered across Commercial Road, a main thoroughfare, and on the other side she spied a pub. Was Vince having a drink? No doubt a warm pub would be preferable to a damp and demolished house.

Taking advantage of a break in the traffic, she ran across the road and opened the narrow wooden door into the pub. A blast of hot stale air and the noise of a couple dozen men hit her. Smoke hung like a grubby cloud over the men's heads as they turned and stared at her.

The barman stopped pulling a pint of ale and gave her a nervous smile. 'You alright, luv? Is summick wrong, as women aren't allowed in 'ere.'

'I'm looking for my friend.' Alice stood inside the doorway and searched the room for Vince.

'Who might he be then?' the old man sitting beside the door asked.

'Vince Barton,' she replied.

'Ahh, the toff?' another man said, taking a pipe from his mouth. He stood up and cupped his hands to his mouth. 'Oi, Billy!' he yelled. 'Get Barton from the snug. He's having a pie.'

A younger man wearing a flat cap who must be Billy, left the bar and disappeared through the crush of workers and dockers holding pints of ale.

'Thank you.' Alice nodded to the man.

'No worries, lass.' He looked her up and down but not in a disrespectful way. 'You're another toff then?' His tone was friendly.

'It would seem so.' She smiled thinly, not knowing if that was a good or bad thing to own up to in this working-man's pub.

'We don't mind Barton. He's not a bad 'un for a toff. He's been giving work to a lot of locals, and he's always kind to the kiddies.'

'The kiddies?' Alice frowned, confused.

'Alice?' Vince weaved through the dockers towards her with surprise on his face. 'Has something happened?'

'Nothing terrible, no,' she answered, amazed to see him wearing old boots, dusty trousers and a woollen pullover, which was splattered with paint. His hair wasn't combed or oiled and curled at his collar. He looked younger, carefree and utterly attractive.

'Ladies aren't allowed in the bar,' the barman told them. 'Sorry. It's the rules.'

'Can she come with me to the snug?' Vince asked.

'Aye, I suppose, just this once, but she stays in there. I don't want any trouble.'

Vince gave a nod to the barman then grinned at Alice. 'Are you hungry?'

'Um...' She rarely thought of food. It was either there or it wasn't at the appropriate times.

'They do a cracking pie and mash here.'

'Pie and mash?' She had no idea what he was talking about.

'Come.' He pulled her by the hand behind him. 'We'll have another pie and mash, thanks Rick,' Vince said to the barman. 'And a sherry for the lady.'

In the wood-panelled snug, Alice sat on the bench seat and placed her bag down beside her. The dark wooden floor had traces of sawdust and a low light swung from a chain. She felt like she was in a ship's cabin.

'Why did you come?' Vince asked, tucking into his pie and mash, which, now Alice could smell it, suddenly made her feel hungry.

'To find you. You left me a note? How cowardly.' She frowned at him. 'I don't know if I can forgive you for that. Why did you not wait to speak to me in person?' she asked him, not able to keep the hurt from her voice.

'Because I didn't want you to try and persuade me to stay.'

'I'm at a loss as to why that is so bad.'

'For your reputation, yes, it is. Without Mama there, we'd be two single people of the opposite sex living together.'

'As if I care about that!' she scoffed.

'Well, I do. For you. Besides, this is my home now, Alice. I have to start again.'

'No one is stopping you, but I... I mean we, your friends, don't want you to cut us out of your life completely.'

'Our lives are completely different now.' He sat back with a sigh. 'It's not possible for me to have a foot in both camps. It's too confusing, too hard to maintain. You do understand that, don't you?'

'Not really. I fail to see why you can't still do all the things you used to do, even if you are living here. We have artist friends who live in the scary parts of Soho that doesn't mean we don't socialise with them.'

'This is a little different and you know it. They are still wealthy, they've just chosen to live away from home. I must make a living, Alice. That's not going to be easy. There is much to contend with. My income is diminished. I don't have the money to idle away my days.'

'So, you will become a builder?'

He laughed, a delightful sound she'd not heard him utter in such a long time. 'No, not a builder. A property developer, I hope.'

She tilted her head in thought. 'Will you allow Brandon and I to invest?'

'I thought you were struggling financially, too?'

'I won't be once I sell *Sheer*.'

'You have totally decided that selling *Sheer* is what you want to do?'

She took a deep breath. 'Yes. It's a sensible decision. The magazine no longer holds the same interest it used to. The excitement isn't there. I made it a success and proved it could be done.'

He reached for her hand, and she clasped his tightly, feeling emotional. 'I'm proud of you. You've made a brave decision,' he said.

'Or a stupid one?' She was a little afraid to let *Sheer* go. It was her creation, after all. But the cord had to be cut.

'No. A magazine such as *Sheer* needs drive and spirit and constant coddling. You've given all that and more for six years without let up. I think you're burnt out from it.'

She nodded. She was tired. The late-night editor meetings, the deadlines, the constant deals with designers, printers, stockists, advertisers and so forth took the joy out of creating a stunning magazine. The long days, taking care of staff, the weeks of travelling to New York or Paris not for a holiday but to have meetings and delicate dinners with people trying to sell her their product, of always trying to be a step ahead of the competition, the full diary where every day and night was pre-booked had worn her out.

'You'll be all right, my lady,' Vince whispered gently.

She smiled at his nickname for her. 'I hope so.'

'You just need some time to adjust, to relax and make no decisions for a while.'

'Like you?'

'Yes, like me and I highly recommend it.' He smiled. 'I know this is a huge change for you but take it from one who has gone through the biggest upheaval one can imagine, there is light at the end of the tunnel. It might be a distant light, but it's there.'

'I'm frightened of the future.'

'That's a normal feeling when you are altering your life. I simply take each day as it comes. I've been doing that since the war when we had no choice but to take each minute and each hour as a blessing to still be alive. It's a habit I've not grown out of.'

Alice let out a deep breath. 'I'll be sad to see it go, but I have nothing left to give it.'

'Will you sell to the Brannings?'

'If their price is acceptable, yes.'

'They are good people.' Vince leaned back, breaking their contact. 'You're doing the right thing. Now, no more talk of business. Let us enjoy the evening. How did you find me, anyway?'

'I went to the house and then noticed this pub. I assumed you might be having a drink in here.'

'It's where I eat on an evening.'

'You can't have pie and mash every night.' She chuckled.

'It's not every night. Sometimes it's stew, or some dish from the Chinese stall. Sometimes I get fish and chips.' He shrugged as if it was no big deal and drank deeply from his pint of ale.

He paused as the door opened and a young lad brought in a tray holding the plate of pie and mash and a small glass of sherry.

'Thank you.' Vince gave him a coin as a tip.

The delicious smell made Alice's stomach rumble. She'd only had tea and biscuits all day.- The first mouthful of buttery mashed potato was heavenly.

'It's good, isn't it?' Vince laughed at her.

'I've never tasted anything like it,' she agreed.

'Not since we were kids.' He grinned. 'Eat up. You're all skin and bones.'

They ate in silence for a while until Vince finished and pushed his plate away. 'Meals like this might not get served in fine restaurants or at your mother's table, but it certainly fills you up, doesn't it?'

Alice wanted to wipe her mouth but no napkin had been provided and so she used a handkerchief from her bag. 'It was very tasty.'

'Did you want to see the changes to the two houses, or I should say to *the* house, as it's a larger one now.'

'I would, yes.' She sipped her sherry. 'But are you going to be comfortable there? Do you want to live around here?'

'I don't mind it at all. At first, I thought I'd hate it, but actually, now the house is taking shape and is half habitable, I'm finding that the area isn't too bad. It's poor and rough, but the people are kind, Alice.'

'But *they* aren't *your* people.'

'They seemed to have accepted me so far. They have so little, yet women have come and offered me cups of tea, or children will run and buy me some bread and cheese or whatever I ask them to buy for me.'

'I just want you to be happy.' What else could she say? He was living a life he never dreamed he would be and as his friend she wanted only the best for him.

'Shall we go, and I'll show you the house?'

She stood and gathered her things. Vince said goodnight to a few of the men at the bar and nodded acknowledgement to a great deal more. Outside it was raining and with their arms linked they ran across the deserted slippery road and into Island Row to Vince's front door.

Once inside, he flicked a switch to light the hallway, which, now the joining wall between the two properties had been knocked down, showed a much wider entrance hall and one main staircase going up to the next floor.

'Gosh! What a difference taking down a wall does.' Alice stared around, noticed the front room on the left was an open room, the wall having also been taken down, creating a large space and replacing the previous poky front room.

'This is the sitting room. The first room I had finished.'

'It's lovely and warm.' Alice remembered the ice coldness of how it was when she last visited. But now a fireplace with decorative tiles glowed beyond the fire screen, heating the room comfortably.

'I've had new radiators installed. The plumbing is what has taken the longest. The room opposite, the other front room will be the dining room,'

Vince explained, pointing to the closed door on the other side of the entrance. 'It's only a shell at the moment. It will be finished last. That room still needs work done. The adjoining wall to the next house is currently propped up until we can make it stable.' He opened the door to reveal a skeleton of a room, bare of plaster and showing exposed plumbing and electrical wires. Wooden posts were nailed to the wall and floor at an angle to strengthen the wall that joined with the neighbouring house.

Vince closed the door for the coldness seeping out made Alice shiver. 'Progress has been made in the kitchen. The original two kitchens are now one long room, giving much more space to have a decent preparation table and more storage.'

Following him down the hallway past the staircase, Alice stepped down into the kitchen and as he flicked more switches, it lit up to show this area was also a work in progress.

'I've turned one of the sculleries into a boot room and left the other scullery as a laundry-type room.' Vince showed her the unfinished parts of the kitchen.

'Will you hire a cook?'

'Yes, and a maid.' Vince added water to a kettle from a tap above a stone sink and then lit the green and cream enamelled gas stove. 'Shall we have some tea?'

'Show me upstairs first. Then you can dazzle me with your skills in the kitchen.'

He laughed and turned the gas off. 'Come this way, my lady.'

Emotional that Vince was once more sounding his happy self, Alice climbed the stairs. On the floor above, there were now four bedrooms. The two little box rooms, one from each house, and been joined into a bathroom. The bedrooms were not completed, fresh plaster was drying in three of them and the floorboards were bare. Only one bedroom held a bed and carpet, obviously where Vince slept.

'Gracious.' Alice stepped into the blue and white tiled bathroom. 'This looks wonderful, Vince.'

'Doesn't it? I assisted in the tiling, too. It's a skill I am striving to master.' He beamed, running his hand over the claw-footed bath. 'Look behind the door.'

Alice poked her head around the door and her eyes widened. 'You have an inside lavatory. How frightfully convenient and modern!'

'The first inside lav in all the streets around here. Everyone else must use the shared lavatories in the yards. The plumbing was a nightmare and has taken weeks to create, but all the hard work and money has been worth it. The children think it is magical and come in and flush it just for fun.'

'The children?'

'The local ones, from around here. They are always popping in and out.' He spoke as though it was a common thing for street children to wander in and out of a person's home. 'I have hot water too. There is a gas boiler in the kitchen and a water tank in the loft. All very modern.'

'And expensive. Why are you spending so much money on a place like this? It makes no sense. You're surrounded by slums and dockyards.'

'I am aware of that,' he said dismissively as he went downstairs.

In the front room, he took off his hat and coat and made them a glass of gin and tonic.

'I thought we were having a cup of tea?' She slipped off her coat and sat on the sofa, which she recognised from the Barton's townhouse. In fact, all of the furnishings in this room, the only room fully completed, came from the Barton's house.

'I'm not in the mood for tea,' Vince replied.

'Fine.' She gazed about the room, liking the cream wallpaper, the dark wood furniture. She noticed the framed portraits of Vince's parents. 'I'm pleased you brought things from your old home.'

'Yes, well, what was left. So much was sold at auction. I decided what was remaining of the old furniture could come with me.' He handed her the drink and sat at the other end of the sofa.

Silence stretched between them for several long moments.

Alice knew she had to speak to break the strained atmosphere. 'Forgive me for making you annoyed regarding my comments about living here.'

Vince sighed deeply. 'I understand that you find my decision strange. A year ago, I would have done too. However, I feel quite content here.' He sipped his drink and relaxed against the sofa. 'My old life was so frantic. I seemed to be rushing from one party to a dinner, to the theatre, to the races, to the club and back to another party.' He stared down at the glass he held. 'Don't get me wrong. I loved every minute of it. But sometimes, I felt it was no longer fun. Waking up hungover, sleeping in someone else's bed, or on someone's chaise, or even in my motor car was becoming more difficult to overcome.'

'I know what you mean. I used to be able to dance until dawn, have a bath and then socialise all day and only sleep for a few hours on an afternoon before doing it all again.' Alice grinned. 'Now, I prefer a good book and a hot chocolate in bed.'

'When did we become old?' Vince laughed, stretching his arm along the back of the sofa, His fingertips nearly touched her shoulder.

'I was thirty-three on my last birthday.' Alice frowned. 'In some ways I feel as though I'm missing out on something...'

'Like what?' he asked, his gaze intent.

She shrugged and then laughed self-consciously. 'I have no idea what and once I've sold *Sheer*, I'm even more worried I'll drift about aimlessly.'

'You won't. Something or someone will come along and sweep you off your feet and take you on another ride that you'll put all your passion and energy into.'

Their eyes met and held. Alice found breathing suddenly difficult. Her heart raced, desire flared in every part of her body. She turned her head to look at his hand lying by her shoulder. She leaned forward and turned his hand over to kiss his palm. It was impulsive and instinctive and felt completely natural to do.

His abrupt intake of breath made her glance at him. He hurriedly placed his glass on the floor, took hers from her hand and placed it next to his before pulling her into his arms.

The kiss was hot and hungry, aching in need and full of passion. Alice arched closer, needing to be nearer to him. His mouth tasted of gin and his hands toured her body in urgent caresses.

Sudden banging on the front door made Alice jump and she stared at Vince. 'What is that?'

# Chapter Nine

Vince ran a hand through his hair with a frown. The banging continued. With an apologetic look that also held a touch of frustration, he left her go and went to see who was making all the noise.

Alice heard frantic voices and Vince's calm tones. Curious, she went to join them to see what the fuss was about. 'Vince?' She stared at the two little children on the doorstep. The light from the hallway cast them into shadows but she could see the unkemptness of the little girl and little boy, who seemed no more than a baby.

'Alice, I must go with them. Their mother is ill.'

'I'm coming with you.' She grabbed her coat as Vince pulled on his and they hurried out the door and along the terraces to number four.

Opening the door, they paused to stare at an old Chinese man sat on the rickety staircase smoking a pipe. Alice balked at seeing him there and was confused to see several Chinese children up on the small landing above.

The little girl dragged Vince by the hand into a dimly lit front room where their mother lay on a bed, moaning.

Standing in the doorway, Alice held a hand to her nose for the smell was revolting. The room held a bed and a fireplace, which smoked badly, and the walls ran with damp. A small table had crates for stools and from the ceiling hung wet clothes no better than rags.

'Now, Mrs Morris, I'm here to help,' Vince crooned to the woman on the unmade bed.

Alice felt a small hand sneak into hers and stared down at the little boy, whose blue eyes were wide in his dirty face. He looked no more than two years old.

'Mr Barton...' The woman groaned, sweat causing her lank hair to cling to her forehead. 'The baby...'

Alice focused on the woman's stomach which was clearly rounded under the thin blanket, but she didn't seem very large, not that Alice was an expert on pregnant women. Her only experience had been watching Prue pregnant with Henry and the current baby.

'I'll fetch a doctor, Mrs Morris.' Vince patted her hand, but she held him tight when he went to leave.

'No money... for doctor.'

'I'll see to the bill, don't worry,' Vince reassured her. 'It's the least I can do for all the company your children have given me lately. Rest now.'

Troubled, Vince came to Alice. 'I'll go and fetch a doctor. I know there is one in Salmon Lane. Sit with her.'

'Me? Why would she want me? I'm a stranger.' Then, in a moment of horror, she wondered if Vince was the father and her knees wobbled. Why was he here attending to a pregnant woman? What did he have to do with her?

'And you're also an Englishwoman. Upstairs are Chinese, as nice as they are, they don't speak English well enough to help Mrs Morris, even if I could persuade one of the women to come and sit with her. Please, Alice.'

'Isn't there a midwife close by?'

'I've no idea. Can you just sit with her, please? She is a good woman and is in trouble. Can you turn your back on her?'

Alice gave herself a mental shake. Although this was by far the worst room she'd ever stepped foot in, this woman needed help. 'Of course, I'll sit with her.'

'I'll be as quick as I can.'

Alarmed at being left alone, Alice gave a grim smile to the little boy who still held her hand. 'Shall we sit with your mother?'

Alice stepped to the bed, giving a little squeal as a rat scurried out from under it. The girl ran after it with a pan but missed it as it bolted down a hole in the floor.

'They are always in here.' The girl put the pan on the table, looking fiercely at the hole.

Taking a steadying breath, Alice sat on the edge of the bed. 'Mrs Morris, Vince has gone for the doctor.'

The woman opened her blue eyes and Alice saw the pain reflected in them as she suddenly groaned and drew her knees up with a terrifying screech.

Alice jumped. 'What are you doing?'

'The baby is coming. It's too soon...' The woman panted, red-faced. 'I'm not far enough along.'

'Gracious me.' Alice didn't know what to do. She'd never witnessed a birth or even a woman in labour. She hadn't been in the same room as Prue when she gave birth to Henry. 'Hold on, the doctor will be here presently.'

'Where's Mrs Dawson?' the struggling woman asked her daughter.

'She's gone, Mam,' the girl answered. 'I went to her house, but she's gone. Moved to Mile End they told me. That's why I fetched Mr Barton.'

'Who is Mrs Dawson?' Alice asked.

'Midwife...' Mrs Morris, rested back on the lumpy mattress. The light went from her eyes as she closed them.

'Where's your father?' Alice asked the girl.

'Dead.'

Shocked by the matter-of-fact reply, Alice tried to think of something else. 'What's your name?'

'Libby, miss, and this is me brother, Timmy.'

'And how old are you?' Alice liked the little girl, who had a sweet face, despite the unbrushed hair and filthy clothes.

'I'm five.'

'Five? Only five?' Everything seemed to shock Alice. Libby spoke like an adult but was only five years old.

'Timmy is two. He'll be three on Easter Sunday, Mam says.'

Alice glanced at Mrs Morris, who lay with her eyes closed. She was a strange colour and her breathing shallow. 'Mrs Morris?' Alice shook her thin arm.

'Mam's been poorly.' Libby poured a cup of water from a chipped jug.

Taking the cup from Libby, Alice placed it to Mrs Morris's lips, but the water dribbled down her chin.

Suddenly, Mrs Morris moaned and squirmed on the bed. She drew her knees up and strained.

'I don't think you should do that, Mrs Morris. Can you not wait until the doctor arrives?' Alice panicked as the woman groaned and pushed.

Just as quickly, Mrs Morris slumped down again, her head rolled to one side.

Alice sensed something was very wrong. She glanced at the two children. 'Perhaps you should wait outside, Libby?'

'On the stairs with Mr Woo?'

'Yes.' She nodded taking that Mr Woo was the man sitting on the steps. 'Take Timmy so he isn't frightened by your mother's distress.'

Libby took Timmy's hand and led him out of the room, telling him that everything was all right.

'Mrs Morris.' Alice shook the woman's shoulder but received no response. 'Mrs Morris can you speak to me?'

The exhausted woman slowly opened her eyes, such beautiful blue eyes like her daughter's. 'Libby, Timmy... I don't want to leave them.'

'You won't. Indeed, you will stay strong for them, yes?' Alice offered her some water, but little went down her throat.

'My poor babies...'

'They will be fine.'

Suddenly Mrs Morris gripped Alice's hand. 'You must care for them, please! I beg you! See that they are cared for!'

'There is no need for such talk. You will come through this.'

'*Promise me!*' Her eyes held Alice's.

'I'll do my best for them. I promise.'

As if those words were a catalyst, Mrs Morris dropped back onto the mattress like a limp doll.

When the door opened and Vince came in followed by an older man carrying a black case, relief flooded Alice. 'Thank heavens you're back.'

'This is Doctor Hemming, Alice. Doctor Hemming, Lady Mayton-Walsh,' Vince made the introductions.

The doctor, tall and slim with a tired look about him, shook Alice's hand, surprise on his face at seeing a wealthy-dressed lady in such a decrepit room, but he made no comment and was quick to examine Mrs Morris. 'I need some more light in here and water, preferably hot.'

'I'll fetch a lamp and some water.' Vince stepped to the door.

'Towels if you can spare them.' The doctor glanced at Alice. 'Are you able to assist me, madam?'

'Assist you?'

'Is that distasteful to you?' he rebuked, glancing at her fine clothes, the pearls around her neck.

Not daring to let her emotions show, she lifted her chin in defiance. She hated any man who tried to put her down. 'I am happy to help in any way I can, Doctor.'

'Good. Stoke the fire up, burn whatever you can find to get some heat and light into this damn room.' He opened his case and took out a few instruments.

Alice set to raking the embers in the grate, coughing on the smoke that refused to go up the chimney.

'You're making it worse,' the doctor snapped.

'I'm doing the best I can!' She glared at him, but her words were drowned out as Mrs Morris screamed, arching her back and crying out in pain.

'There now, Mrs Morris. Calm down. Take some deep breaths. We'll have this baby out shortly.' Doctor Hemming worked quickly, wrapping an apron around his waist and rolling up his sleeves.

Finding bits of screwed up newspaper, Alice got the fire flaring briefly, but there was nothing to keep it going.

Vince entered with two towels and a jug of water and an oil lamp, which he lit with a match. Golden light lit the room, showing the decaying state of it more clearly. Mouldy wallpapered peeled off the walls, grime coated every surface.

'Thank you, Mr Barton. If you could bring me some more water, I'd be grateful.' The doctor washed his hands and settled himself at the end of the bed.

With Vince once more gone, Alice stepped beside the doctor, steeling herself at the sight of Mrs Morris's exposed lower half. Her legs were terribly thin, and her porcelain white thighs were splattered with blood. Alice saw the black wet hair on the crown of the baby's head. She stared in fascination.

'This baby is small, Mrs Morris. Push on the next contraction.'

Mrs Morris lay with her eyes closed, not listening. The doctor tapped her thigh. 'Mrs Morris! I need you to stay awake for me now. We must get this baby out.' He glanced up at Alice. 'Sit behind her. Lift her head and chest up. Talk to her, give encouragement.'

Doing as instructed, Alice knelt on the bed, ignoring the waft of foul smell that enveloped her as she moved the thin pillows and blankets. 'Come on, Mrs Morris. The head is nearly out. I saw it.'

Her energy waning, Mrs Morris strained, but she clearly wasn't mindful of the situation. Her head lolled on Alice's arm, her body went limp.

'Doctor?' Alice panicked.

'Mrs Morris!' the doctor barked. 'Stay with us now.' He used an instrument that resembled some kind of claw. 'Push, Mrs Morris!'

Alice shuddered as the doctor pulled the baby out on the next contraction. It lay still and lifeless on the mattress the same as its mother. Blood pumped from between Mrs Morris's legs onto the mattress in a red river.

'Mrs Morris!' The doctor slapped the woman's legs. 'Wake up now!'

Shocked by the treatment, Alice glared at him. 'What are you doing?'

'She's dying! We're going to lose them both!' Doctor Hemming ignored the baby and concentrated on its mother.

Alice scampered off the bed and stood watching in horrified fascination as he tried to revive her.

'No, no. No!' He lifted the woman's eyelids before checking her pulse. 'Damn it to Christ!' He thrust pillows under her buttocks, lifting her lower body up. 'Get me something to put under her, quickly!'

Alice jerked, not knowing what to give him. She grabbed a crate and Hemming snatched it from her and wedged it under the mattress, tipping the woman at an angle.

The baby, unattended, forgotten, rolled on the bed. Alice yelled and grabbed the baby, holding it close against her chest.

'Cut the cord!' The doctor snapped, working frantically to revive Mrs Morris.

Alice noticed the doctor had already tied the cord, but not cut it. She grabbed the scissors he left on the mattress and cut the thick cord, surprised by the rubbery feel of it. Freed from its mother, the baby mewled like a kitten.

She quickly wrapped a towel around it, amazed at the tininess of it. The baby girl hadn't cried properly, and she willed it to do so. 'Come on, little one.'

Instinct made her cradle the baby against her chest and rub its back, trying to instil some warmth into the fragile body. 'Come on, breathe now,' she whispered, rubbing harder.

'She's gone.' Doctor Hemming sighed and slowly straightened. His apron and hands were covered in blood.

'But the baby can still live.'

'I doubt it will.'

Alice glared at him and worked harder to make the baby cry properly. 'We must help this baby,' Alice snapped, rubbing harder, willing life into the limp delicate body. She kept blowing into the little face until finally, amazingly it gave a weak faint cry.

Alice sagged in such relief she stumbled. She rested against the wall, holding the baby tightly. 'That's it, little one,' she crooned, reassured at the pinkness colouring the tiny little face. 'Don't give up, sweet one.'

'Better the mother had lived instead as she had two other children to care for.' Hemming's matter-of-fact tone irritated Alice.

'What a thing to say.'

'Give it to me.' The doctor took the baby and unwrapped the towel to check her. 'She is very small. Unlikely to survive the night.' He was dismissive.

Alice gasped, staring at him. 'Then we must jolly well try and keep her alive!'

'With no mother?' He shook his head. 'She'll just be another child in an orphanage.' He wrapped the baby up and left her on the bed to wash his hands and write notes in his book. 'I'll contact the undertakers. There's an orphanage in Poplar. I can take all three children there in the morning.'

The baby cried lustily for the first time, surprising them both. Alice rushed and picked her up. She wouldn't let his harsh words become a reality. The sweet little thing was not an hour old and helpless. She couldn't wish for it to die as he did. She cradled the baby against her, gazing into her little face, shushing her until she stopped crying.

The doctor washed his instruments and packed them in his bag. 'Can you care for the children until morning? It's too late for me to waken the orphanage tonight.'

'I can,' she replied impulsively. 'Unless there are relatives who can take them in?'

'As far as I know, and I've called on Mrs Morris before, she has no relatives. Her husband died six months ago. He was an orphan himself, which is why he was a seaman. Ship masters usually take young boys straight from the orphanages to train them as seamen.'

'Gosh. And there is no one else?'

The doctor pulled on his coat. 'Not that I'm aware, but I'll ask around tomorrow.' He drew the blanket over Mrs Morris, covering her completely.

The act made Alice shiver. The woman had given birth and then died right before her eyes. She would never forget the sight for as long as she lived.

'Don't let the children come in.' Hemming opened the door and Vince got up from the step where he sat with Libby and Timmy. 'Mr Barton, may I have a word?'

Shutting the door on the children, the doctor told Vince what had happened. 'If you can care for the children until the morning, then I shall collect them and take them to the orphanage in Poplar. The undertakers will see to Mrs Morris tomorrow. A pauper's grave for her so it won't be a drawn-out process. I'll conduct the necessary interviews with the authorities and sign the forms.'

Vince looked as stricken as Alice felt. 'Poor, Mrs Morris. She was a kind woman,' he murmured. 'She often stopped for a chat when looking for Libby and Timmy. They came every day to sit on my doorstep and watch the builders work.'

The doctor grabbed his bag. 'I'll inform the children about their mother now.'

'No!' Alice put her hand out, which was shaking badly. 'We will tell them. They like and know Vince. It might be better coming from him.' She looked at Vince, willing him to side with her. The doctor's brusque tone wouldn't be kind to the children who'd lost everything. 'We'll take them back to your house for the night and tell them in the morning, yes?'

'Yes, of course.' Vince nodded instantly.

'The baby will need powdered milk and a bottle.' Doctor Hemming scratched his forehead. 'I have some in my office for cases such as these. If you'd like to come back with me, Mr Barton, I shall give you some to prepare a bottle for the baby.'

'Thank you, yes.'

'Well, shall we be on our way then? Good night, madam.' The doctor gave a nod to Alice.

'I'll be as quick as I can.' Vince touched her arm.

'I'll take the children to your house.' Alice followed them out, feeling guilty for leaving Mrs Morris alone. Someone should sit with her, surely? Alice feared the rats would nibble at her in the night and the thought made her shudder.

Libby and Timmy sat leaning against each other. Timmy was asleep.

'Vince, carry the poor darling to the house then go with the doctor.' Alice took Libby's hand and went out into the dark cold night, holding the baby close.

'Where are we going?' Libby mumbled sleepily.

'To Mr Barton's house. You're staying there for tonight, sweetie.'

Once inside Vince's front room, Alice laid the baby on the sofa before the fire and then helped Vince settle Libby and Timmy in his own bed. They were asleep instantly.

Vince stared down at them. 'Those poor little blighters. What a bleak future lies before them. Orphans at such a young age. And Libby is so smart...'

'I can't bear it, Vince, any of it.' Alice felt close to tears. The whole episode had been a ghastly nightmare. She could still smell the blood, see the dead woman.

He held her to him for a moment. 'I'll go get the powdered milk.' Vince reluctantly left the bedroom.

Downstairs, alone with the baby, Alice had a moment of panic as she started to whimper. Her experience with children was limited to the times she spent with Henry. Prue had engaged a nanny, so Alice had only seen newborn baby Henry when he was sleeping and had nothing to do with taking care of him. But as she scooped the baby up and nestled her against her chest, she felt an overwhelming rush of emotion for this tiny little scrap. Her small pink face calmed and when her starfish hand clenched over Alice's finger, Alice's heart somersaulted.

She had witnessed this baby come into the world, take her first breath. Nothing seemed the same now. It was as though a light had been shone into Alice's mind and heart, giving her a glimpse at something deeply profound. She had witnessed the miracle of birth, the highs of seeing a human come into the world, but also at the same time a life extinguished. This experience couldn't easily be forgotten. Something momentous had occurred right before her eyes and it was difficult to believe it had actually happened.

Gently, Alice unfolded the towel wrapped around the baby and studied the little body. The minute toenails, the thin legs and arms, tiny fingers. Her eyebrows were delicately arched, the sweet curves of her cheeks and the wisps of dark hair.

It pained Alice to think of this darling baby all alone in the world, no parent to love her, care for her. She had no name, no bright future. Alice wrapped her up tightly, holding her close, hoping the sweet soul would take some of her own strength and courage for whatever lay ahead.

Vince came in panting, raindrops glistening on his coat. 'I ran all the way back.' He put a large bag down by Alice's feet where she sat on the sofa. 'Hemming gave me a bottle, the powdered milk and some napkins and a smock dress of some sort. There is a note on how to prepare the milk.'

'We should get one made up. She must be hungry.' Alice followed him into the kitchen, holding the baby.

'She'll have to sleep on the sofa,' he said, lighting the gas stove to boil the water. 'And so will we.'

'I rather doubt we will get much sleep, anyway. What time is it?'

'It's gone one o'clock. I'll make us some tea.'

'She could do with a wash.' Alice could smell dried blood which had caked on the baby. The towel she was wrapped in was smeared with birth fluid. 'Do you have a basin we could wash her in?'

'There's bound to be something around.' Vince opened cupboards but they held tins of food and crockery. He went out to the scullery and found a tin bucket. 'There's only this or the bath upstairs.'

'The bath is too big. We have to be careful of her neck and head. I remember that from Henry.' Alice eyed the bucket doubtfully.

'Yes, I remember holding Henry so gently when he was first born. Now I tussle him on the ground.' Vince smiled.

'Perhaps we could wash her in the sink upstairs?'

'Yes. Splendid idea. The boiler is on as I was to have a bath after going to the pub. Then you arrived...'

Alice blushed, thinking of their kiss and heated embrace. They needed to speak of it, but now wasn't the time. 'I'll take her up and you make the bottle.'

'I'll come up and help you as soon as I'm done.'

One handed, Alice filled the sink in the bathroom, thanking the fates and whoever it was that invented piping warm water. Carefully, she held the baby in both hands and gently eased her into the tepid water, hoping it wasn't too warm or too cold. She'd never bathed a baby before and quickly realised she needed one hand to do the actual washing. Stuck, she stood there, her hands under the little body.

Her back was aching by the time Vince came up. 'You'll have to sponge her, Vince. I can't move my hands. I'm afraid I'll drop her.'

Grinning, Vince took the sponge. 'You didn't think this through, did you?'

'No. I'm a complete novice at this.'

'You and me both.'

Five minutes later, the water becoming too cold, Vince wrapped a clean towel around the baby and held her against his chest. 'I don't remember Henry being this small.'

'He wasn't. He was a good size when born, but this little one is very tiny.'

'Hemming said she might not make it.' Vince's gaze softened.

Alice flinched as she dried the baby's petite limbs. 'What a beastly thing for him to say. We cannot think like that.' She was determined to keep this baby alive.

Back in the front room, Alice sat before the fire with the baby and tried to get her to suck the rubber teat on the bottle.

'Is it working?'

'She doesn't seem interested,' Alice agonised. 'Come on, little one. You must have your milk.'

'We can't give up.' Vince paced the floor. 'She must survive, or her mother's death was for nothing.'

'Look at her, Vince. Not a day old and so innocent. She doesn't have a name or any idea that she is an orphan.' Alice blinked away the tears burning behind her eyes. 'Tomorrow she'll be taken to some cold orphanage and placed in a cot alongside other cots and await her fate.'

'She's a baby though. I expect couples select babies more than they do older children. It's Libby and Timmy I feel sorry for. What if they are all split up?' He rubbed his eyes wearily. 'I wish I knew a family who could take all three.'

'So do I.' As she spoke the baby opened her mouth and drank. 'Oh, look! She's drinking.'

Vince knelt beside Alice and watched intently. 'Good girl.'

'Who me or the baby?' Alice joked, full of relief.

'Both of you.' Vince's gaze met hers for a long moment before he stood and added more coal to the fire.

Alice concentrated on the baby, but she wanted Vince next to her again with that look of tenderness in his eyes. If Libby hadn't banged on the door, they would have been lovers by now...

# Chapter Ten

Alice woke to something touching her face. Opening her eyes, she smiled at Libby who leaned against her on the sofa. 'Good morning.'

'Timmy needs the pot.'

'Oh.' Sitting up, Alice looked at Vince who slept in the winged backed chair with the baby in the crook of his arm. The sight made Alice's heart twist with a deep primal emotion.

'Is there a potty?' Libby whispered.

'Yes. Upstairs. In the bathroom.'

'I know that, but Timmy can't reach to pee in it.'

Alice blinked. 'I see. Yes, of course. He needs a stool or something. Let's find a box for him to stand on.' She rose and went with Libby into the hallway to see Timmy coming in from the kitchen pulling up his short trousers.

'Where have you been?' Libby scowled at him like a mother hen.

'I pee pee outside.' He grinned, scratching his head.

'I said to stay upstairs.' Libby glared at him.

'Now, there's no harm done,' Alice soothed. 'Shall we have a cup of tea? Maybe we can make some breakfast?' Alice didn't own any skills in the kitchen, but she could make toast over a flame if needed.

'Where is mam?' Libby asked, sitting at the kitchen table.

Alice paused as she found the bread in a cupboard and turned to the girl. 'Well, you see...'

Vince came into the kitchen, his hair ruffled, stubble on his jaw and his handsome face showing the effects of a sleepless night. He handed the baby to Alice. The look in his eyes told her he'd heard the question. 'Now, Libby, Timmy. I have some news.'

He sat at the table with them, giving them a gentle smile. 'Sadly, your mother was very ill. She didn't have the strength to survive the birth of your baby sister.'

'She died?' Libby asked incredulously. 'Mam's gone?' Tears welled and her chin wobbled. 'She's not ever going to be with us again?'

'I'm afraid so.' Vince took her hand in his. 'I know you must be very sad and frightened.'

'But who will look after us?'

'You mustn't worry about that right now.' He glanced up at Alice, concern in his expression.

'But I want my mam.' Tears dripped over Libby's dark eyelashes. 'I want to go home.' She folded her arms on the table and, bowing her head, wept heartbrokenly.

Tears clogged Alice's throat at the tragic scene. Timmy didn't know what was going on and sat on the chair swinging his legs.

Vince took a deep breath, then picked up Libby and cradled her on his lap. 'You cry, sweetheart. It'll make you feel better.'

The baby began to whimper and Alice, tears blurring her vision, walked up and down the kitchen, trying to soothe the baby. She could hardly believe this terrible event had happened and she was now involved in it. When she'd left her home last evening, she never expected to witness a birth and a death and to feel so sorry for three children she'd not even known existed until last night.

After a few minutes, Vince wiped Libby's eyes with his handkerchief. 'There now. Shall we have some breakfast? I imagine you are both hungry?' He gave a wan smile to Timmy.

'Bread!' Timmy piped up.

'I'll make toast.' Vince placed Libby back on her own chair. 'And tea. I have some jam, too.' He looked at Alice. 'I'll make up a bottle.'

'Yes.' She nodded for the baby's crying grew.

'For someone so tiny, she has some lungs on her.' Vince quickly lit the stove and put the kettle on the gas.

'When do you think Doctor Hemming will come for them?' Alice asked him as he sliced the loaf of bread.

'Come for us?' Libby, a sharp little girl, sat up straighter. 'Who is coming for us?'

'Doctor Hemming, sweetie.' Alice tried to lighten her voice to sound enthusiastic.

'But why?'

'Because you'll need to go and live elsewhere now. And soon a lovely couple will come and take you to their home and you'll become a family.'

Libby stood, horror on her pretty face. 'I won't go!'

'Darling, you have to,' Vince said. 'You'll be adopted and have a new life.'

'No! I want to stay here! I want my mam!' Libby ran out of the kitchen, down the hallway and out of the front door before Vince had chance to stop her.

'Libby!' they both called after her.

'Go, Vince,' Alice urged him as he ran out of the house.

'Bread?' Timmy asked, reaching for a slice with a dirty hand.

'Yes.' Alice passed him a slice, realising how filthy he was. The baby continued to cry, and Alice felt overwhelmed. She had to lay the baby on the table and try to read the instructions on the can to prepare the powdered milk. Timmy asked for more bread and the kettle whistle shrieked and the baby screamed.

Frazzled, she took the kettle off the boil and read the instructions. Hands shaking, she prepared the bottle, while Timmy called for more bread and the baby grew red in the face from crying. She didn't know if she'd made the milk properly, and it was so hot it burned her hand when she tested it. She ran the bottle under the tap and let it sit in the sink, while she quickly sliced more bread for Timmy, smearing each slice with strawberry jam and passing it to him.

Finally, she picked up the baby and rocked her while she kept testing the temperature of the bottle. Despite the coldness of the room, she felt sweat trickle under her clothes at the pressure.

'Madam? The door was open.' Doctor Hemming came in, wearing a grey suit and black coat. He looked about the debris of the building work.

'Libby has run away.' She paced the floor, rocking the baby. 'She's taken the news badly.'

'Understandable.' The doctor peered at the baby. 'She seems a fighter. I didn't think she'd last the night.' He frowned at the jam-smeared face of Timmy. 'He'll need to be cleaned up before I take them to the orphanage. Then I'll come back for Libby, if you find her. If not, well...' He shrugged as though a young girl missing on the streets was a common occurrence.

'No, you can't take them without Libby. We'll find her,' Alice declared. 'They must go together.'

'It won't matter much. They will likely be adopted separately, anyway.' His stiff tone just incensed Alice.

'I would prefer it, Doctor Hemming, if they were taken together as a family.' She could also match his tone.

'Madam...' he huffed condescendingly. 'You do not understand.'

'My name is Lady Mayton-Walsh, Doctor Hemming,' she snapped. 'And what I understand is that these three children are now orphans. Their fate is to be institutionalised. I would like for the situation to be as unpleasant as possible.'

'There is no such thing in these circumstances,' he replied uncaring. 'They are now wards of the parish. If they are extremely lucky, some kind couple will take them in, but the chances are indeed slim. The baby might be taken, but the other two? Unlikely and certainly not together.'

'We must try, Doctor.'

'Forgive me if I sound harsh, but this is a world *you* are unaware of, but it is *my* world and I acknowledge the way things work in this part of London. Couples from good families do not come here to adopt the children from the East End. These children will likely spend their whole life in an orphanage until they are old enough to go out to work.' He picked up his bag. 'I must go. I have much to do. I shall call back this afternoon and take the children then.'

'No, there is no need for you to concern yourself, sir. Mr Barton and I will deliver the children to the orphanage ourselves.'

He gave her a stern look. 'But there are forms to attend to, certain regulations that must be adhered to, especially since adopting became legal four years ago in nineteen twenty-six. Things must be done correctly. I'll not have my good reputation besmirched by any underhand dealings.'

'Underhand dealings? What do you mean?' Alice hadn't a clue what he was talking about.

'If you take the children, then I wash my hands of the whole process.'

'Very well.' Alice tested the milk again and found it lukewarm. She offered it to the baby and was thankful when she stopped crying and began to suck. 'Mr Barton and I want only the best for the children.'

He paused by the door with a deep sigh. 'Then taking them to an orphanage isn't the right way to go about it, even if it is the legal way. The best option for these children is private adoption.'

'What do you mean?'

His left eye twitched. 'There are many advertisements in the newspapers offering up babies. You could do the same and that way you can vet the possible adopters.'

'Advertisements?' The fact shocked her.

'You've never seen them?' That shocked *him*.

'No. I have no need to pay attention to such a thing.'

'Believe me, it is true. Many a childless couple are desperate for a child, and there are many unwanted babies in the world.' Again, he spoke in a matter-of-fact way. 'Newspapers are happy to run advertisements.'

'You have done this yourself?'

'Not personally, but I know of those who have. It usually serves as a benefit to all parties.' He watched the baby drinking the milk. 'Do you want me to come back and take the children?'

'No.' Alice held the baby tighter. Some instinct told her that she couldn't trust Doctor Hemming to handle the situation with consideration and kindness. 'Good day, Doctor.'

'I'll go and see that the undertakers take Mrs Morris.' He nodded and walked out of the house.

Alice stared down at the baby, her mind whirling with the situation she was in. She and Vince must either take the children to the orphanage or place an advertisement in a newspaper like they were selling a bicycle, or a motor car...

She thought of the advertising she had in *Sheer* for gloves and scarves. Could she place an advertisement for three children as though they were goods to be sold?

The door opened and she turned to see Vince walk in holding Libby's hand. Dirty tears on Libby's cheeks showed her despair and Alice's heart went out to her.

'I found her by the canal.' Vince wiped a shaky hand over his face, his eyes wide.

'What's wrong?'

'She nearly fell in, and I honestly felt unable to breathe I was so scared.' He looked shaken and pale.

'But she's safe. That's all that matters.' She gave him the baby. 'It's been a traumatic night and morning. Sit down and I'll make us some tea.'

Libby sat quietly at the far end of the table, head down, not talking even to Timmy who was eating his third slice of bread and jam.

Alice quickly boiled the kettle again and spooned tea leaves into the teapot. She was a novice in the kitchen, but she knew how to make a pot of tea. She kept glancing at Vince, who looked tormented. 'Is there something else?' she asked, pouring a cup of tea for him.

'I promised Libby she wouldn't go to the orphanage.' Guilt was written across his handsome face.

'Oh, Vince,' Alice murmured, alarmed.

'I know, but she was crying, making a scene. Dock men working nearby were asking questions about why I was chasing a little girl...' He raked his fingers through his hair. 'It was becoming rather tense. Libby was frantic and screaming. She vomited and then nearly fell into the canal. I didn't know what to do...' He sounded helpless.

Alice placed a hand on his shoulder. 'You were in an impossible situation. This *whole* situation is rather a complete mess.' She went on to tell him about what Doctor Hemming said as she made slices of bread and jam for Libby.

'Advertisements?' Vince stared at her, then he got up and went into the scullery. He returned with a pile of newspapers in one hand, the baby asleep in the other arm. 'Look through these.'

Seated at the table they searched the newspapers and within minutes found advertisements.

'Listen to this,' Vince said. 'Offered for adoption. Four-months-old baby girl. All rights waived.' He looked across at Alice. 'There's an address to write to.'

Alice stared at him. 'How frightful. Are you saying we should place an advertisement in the newspaper for the three of them?'

'I don't know what I'm saying.' He gazed down at the baby he held. 'It seems obscene to put them in the newspaper like unwanted puppies.'

'Then what do we do? Go to the orphanage in Poplar?'

'I don't know. I really do not have a clue.'

'We have to make a decision. Perhaps if we spoke to the manager of the orphanage, are they even called managers? Wardens?' She shook her head, her thoughts flying about her mind like a leaf in a gale. 'Whoever. If we speak to them and tell them we absolutely want the children to remain together maybe they will listen to us? I can pay them some money...'

'It's worth a try.' Vince nodded.

The builders arrived, preventing any further discussion. Vince ushered Libby and Timmy out of the kitchen into the front room where they would be out of the way.

Alice quietly mentioned to Vince that Libby and Timmy should have a bath, and she could go and buy them new clothes. 'They need to look their best. It'll give them a better chance.'

'That's true but I can't look after all three of them.' Vince nodded to Happy's apprentice who wheeled in a wheelbarrow. 'This is a building site,' he said to Alice.

'How can I go shopping with them?' She smiled at Libby who was watching them keenly. 'I'm meant to be at the office. The Brannings are coming today to talk about the sale.' She stared down at her clothes, which needed washing. 'I need to change.'

'Can you not take them back with you to your house?' Vince rubbed a hand over his face. 'I'll get the men sorted here and then come to you.'

'I suppose there is no other alternative. Esme can see to them. Oh, and when you leave here stop at Harrods and buy them some clothes.'

His eyes widened. 'What do I know about buying children's clothes?'

She gave him a superior glare. 'About the same amount as I do! Ask an attendant.' She gathered the baby in her arms and collected her and the baby's bag. 'Come, Libby. Take your brother's hand and follow me.'

'Where are we going?' Libby's voice sounded belligerent. 'I want to go home.'

'You're coming with me. To my home. For a lovely bath.'

Libby dug her heels in. 'Mr Barton? Can't I stay with you? You have a bath.'

Vince knelt down in front of her. 'Go with Alice, there's a good girl. Have a nice bath and I'll be there as soon as I can. I'll bring you a present.'

'You promise?'

'I promise. I'll be with you as soon as I can.'

Reluctantly, Libby pulled Timmy behind her as Alice walked outside. The cold day and low grey clouds did little to lift the tense atmosphere.

Alice gave the baby to Libby to hold while she drove. The car was icy cold, the windscreen fogged instantly. Busy morning traffic made the drive through the city slow and treacherous.

By the time Alice pulled up in front of her townhouse in Notting Hill, the baby was crying, Timmy felt sick, and Libby was mutinously tight-lipped.

Trying not to lose her temper, Alice ushered them inside and upstairs to the parlour, bypassing Esme's incredulous stare.

'Run a bath, please, Esme.' Alice held the baby. 'Is Mrs Jones in?'

'Yes, madam. Just a few minutes ago.'

'These children, Libby, Timmy and the baby are staying here for a few hours. They need a bath, some decent food. They've had a ghastly time of it.' Alice lowered her voice. 'Their mother died last night, a neighbour of Mr Barton. They are orphans now. Later, we shall take them to an orphanage.'

'Poor lambs.' Esme smiled sadly at them.

Alice wiped her tired eyes. 'I need to be at the office for a meeting. I must leave them in your care, I do apologise.'

'That's fine, madam. I'm sure we'll get along just fine.' Esme smiled at Timmy. 'He looks a bit peaky.'

'He didn't enjoy the car journey.'

'We've never been in one before that's why,' Libby said defensively. 'I wanted to stay with Mr Barton.'

'Well, you are here now.' Alice sucked a controlled breath, knowing the little girl was grieving and had lost not only her mother but her home too. She was bound to be frightened. Vince was the only person she knew and trusted. Softening, Alice patted her shoulder. 'Mr Barton will be here as soon as he can. In the meantime, Esme will care for you.'

Alice turned to Esme. 'Take Libby and Timmy with you to the bathroom. I need Mrs Jones to feed this one while I wash and change.'

Mrs Jones, a grandmother, was delighted to hold the baby. Alice told her briefly the story of what had happened, and the older woman took it in her stride. She knew instantly what to do and before long the baby was wearing a clean napkin and sucking on another bottle of milk. 'She'll be fine with me, madam. You go along.'

Alice hesitated, touching the baby's soft cheek, not wanting to leave her. 'I apologise for dumping the children on you and Esme, Mrs Jones, but I must get to the office. I'll only be a few hours and Mr Barton will be here as soon as he can, too.' She glanced at the clock and hoped the Brannings just didn't turn up at the office this morning expecting to see her there early.

'Right you are, madam. Esme and me will see to them. I'm good with children.'

'Thank you, Mrs Jones.' Alice exhaled with relief.

Popping her head around the bathroom door, Alice smiled as Timmy and Libby were splashing in the bathtub, which Esme had filled with bubbles from Alice's expensive hair wash.

Esme scrubbed Timmy's back with a flannel and Alice's fragrant Pears soap. 'They're thick with dirt, madam. I'll have to refill the bath again to get rid of the mucky water.'

'They will smell nice, if nothing else,' she said to Esme.

'Look at me!' Timmy piled bubbles on his head and laughed an infectious laugh that made them all chuckle, even Libby.

'I'll give them a good wash and then they can wear old blouses of yours until you can sort something else out.'

'Mr Barton is bringing them some clothes. Mrs Jones will help you until I return.' She caught Libby's eye. 'Be good. Mr Barton will be here soon.'

Alice fled to her bedroom and pulled out a cream woollen dress and fresh underwear. She washed and changed quickly, brushed her hair and pulled on a black beret and black boots.

Within an hour, by driving faster than she should, she was sweeping into the office, her black sable cloak swinging out behind her. She'd love a cigarette, her nerves were on edge, but she'd been trying to give up the habit since last summer because Simon had said it was like kissing an ashtray.

Sitting behind her desk, she sorted through the post.

Winifred entered with invoices to sign and her diary. 'Madam, Mr Branning and his wife called ten minutes ago and asked if the appointment in an hour is still happening. I agreed since you have nothing else in your diary for today.'

'Yes, thank you.' Alice forced herself to relax. She had time to prepare before the Brannings arrived. She stood and went to the drawers in the cabinet on the far wall. 'Have tea and coffee ready for them, and pastries. Send someone out for them. Also have a bottle of champagne chilling in the cupboard.'

'Champagne?' Winifred was rarely surprised.

'Yes. If this deal happens, we'll want to celebrate.'

'There's a bottle of Moet in a locked drawer of my desk. Will that do, madam?'

'Perfectly.' Alice signed her signature on the invoices.

Winifred read from her notebook. 'You've an appointment at eleven tomorrow with the printers. A meeting with Mr Miles Flint from Flint's Emporium of Silks and Satins. He's wanting us to showcase his latest shipment of fine materials.'

'I'd forgotten about him. Dash it.' Alice scribbled a note in her diary.

Winifred continued. 'In the afternoon you have your hairdresser's appointment at three and high tea at four thirty with Mrs Frankston at the Savoy. The House of Frankston is celebrating their second anniversary and I believe she wants *Sheer* to showcase their latest designs in evening gowns. That's what her assistant told me on the telephone.'

Alice nodded and opened an envelope, which was an invitation to a ball in March held by design company, House of Worth. She went every year. Saw the same people and ate the same food and drank the same champagne.

Winifred turned the page in her diary. 'Thursday you have five appointments, no forgive me, that should be six, as well as dinner at eight with Mr and Mrs Starling from Starling Sporting Equipment. I believe they wish to continue their association with us this year. In the morning, your first appointment is with—'

'Stop.' Alice's head was starting to throb. 'I need a cup of tea.'

'Certainly, madam.' Winifred left her and closed the door.

Standing, Alice went to the window and looked out on the Thames. The grey river mirrored the grey clouds. She longed for spring and summer when the light altered and became brighter, the days warmer and longer. Winter was so depressing. A seagull flew past, soaring on the breeze. Below on the street, people hurried by, wrapped in scarves and coats as the cold stiff breeze blew bare-limbed trees.

Today she might have sold her business. The one thing she had cared for and loved for years. She gripped her hands together, expecting her emotions to be high, and they were but at the back of her mind were the thoughts that this afternoon, she and Vince would be taking three young children to an orphanage and that was making her feel ill.

A knock preceded Winifred, carrying a tea tray. 'The Brannings have arrived early.' Her stern expression revealed what she thought about that. Punctuality was one of Winifred's personal commandments. In her opinion a person arrived exactly at the time they were meant to, not early or late, exactly on time. 'They are taking off their coats.'

Alice returned to her desk. 'Show them in.'

She shook hands with Mr Branning and his beaming wife who couldn't hide her excitement.

'Oh, I cannot tell you how thrilling this is!' Mrs Branning stared around the office. 'We noticed the other people busy working in the other offices. What a fabulous idea to have the dividing walls to be made mostly of glass. So modern!'

Alice smiled and ushered them to a chair each. 'Glass partitions affords more light into the rooms for the artists. Their drawings depend so much on finding the correct colours. In the summer I encourage them to take themselves outside and sit by the river in the sunshine. Natural light is an artist's best friend.' Alice poured the tea.

Mr Branning placed a folder on the desk. 'We were surprised to receive your invitation to call today.'

'I can understand that. At our past meeting I gave you every indication that I would not be putting *Sheer* on the market.'

'But you've changed your mind?' Mrs Branning leant forward eagerly only to sit back when her husband put a gentle hand on her arm.

Alice nodded. 'I have given the idea considerable thought over Christmas and talked extensively with my family about it. I have decided to sell *Sheer*.'

'May I ask why?' Mr Branning asked calmly.

Alice glanced down at the papers on her desk, her full diary... 'I no longer feel the urge, the drive to continue with publishing the magazine. I have reached the heights of success with it and taken it as far as I wish to take it. There is room in the market for *Sheer* to be global. New York, Paris, Rome and so on. But that would take a lot of work, more than I wish to do. I have spent the long hours creating this magazine from scratch. I've achieved all I set out to do, but to continue successfully, *Sheer* needs to change and adapt. It needs fresh eyes, fresh ideas, fresh people...'

'And you have other things you wish to do?' Mrs Branning asked quietly.

Smiling slightly, Alice lifted her teacup. 'I believe I do, Mrs Branning. In my twenties I relished the buzz of creating this magazine, but I'm in my thirties now and I feel it's time for a change. I've had my fill of meetings and being responsible for everything. I want to slow down and have some time to consider my future.'

'Well then,' Mr Branning said, opening his folder. 'Shall we get down to business?'

Taking a deep breath, Alice picked up her pen and readied herself to write a new chapter of her life.

# Chapter Eleven

Alice turned off the motor car's engine and sat with her hands on the steering wheel. Wind blew dead leaves along the gutters mixing them with bits of paper and rubbish not secured in bins.

Beside her on the seat were signed contracts that the Brannings had prepared and which they had gone over with Alice's solicitor, who thankfully arrived at the office within half an hour of her calling him. They spent the next couple of hours going over the contract and then Alice signed it.

*Sheer* was sold. Done.

The price had been generous.

The Brannings' delight wonderful to witness.

But not so the reactions of her staff when she and the Brannings faced them and announced the news. However, the Brannings' compelling charm soon won them around, that and the promise that all their positions were safe.

She glanced up and saw the curtains twitch in her front room. Slowly she climbed from the car, dreading the afternoon to come. Lead-laden feet took her to the front door and upstairs to the wide landing. The sound of laughter reached her first. Libby's then Vince's. She couldn't remember the last time she'd heard Vince laugh.

The parlour door opened, and Esme came out, flushed and eyes bright. 'Oh, madam. You're back. My apologies I didn't hear the front door.'

'Sounds like fun in there?' Alice hesitated in the doorway.

'Yes. Mr Barton was giving Timmy horseback rides around the room.'

The vision made Alice grin. 'Has the baby been well?'

'Very much so. She's taken her bottles each time. Mrs Jones has hardly put her down for a minute. She's been doing everything one handed.'

'I've been gone longer than I expected.' She heard the hallway clock chime three o'clock. They would have to rush to Poplar to the orphanage before it became too late.

She walked into the parlour only to stop and take in the scene. Vince sat with Timmy on his lap, Libby right beside him as he read them a story. Timmy wore clean pressed shorts of dark grey and a navy pullover, long socks and polished black shoes. Libby, her black hair brushed and tied with red ribbons, wore a white dress with pink flowers printed on it, white socks and black shoes. They had been transformed. No longer did they look like children from the Docklands. Instead, they'd have fitted into any drawing room of her acquaintances.

Vince looked up and smiled at Alice. 'You're home.'

She nodded. Her throat constricted at the homely scene. Her heart banged out of time. *This.* This was what she wanted. A family of her own. She wanted Vince's babies. That was the future she envisioned and craved.

He held up the book. 'I've nearly finished reading it to them.'

'Then we shall go?' To linger would be torture for them all.

The happiness fell from his handsome features. Sadness filled his brown eyes. 'Yes...'

She sat and waited patiently for him to finish the story, noting that his voice held a tremor to it now. Esme brought in the baby, which also wore a new clean nightgown and white knitted booties and bonnet. Alice's heart melted as she took her in her arms and gazed down at the tiny pink face. She looked so innocent, so vulnerable. She didn't even have a name.

All too soon, Vince finished the story and stood up. He held out a hand to Libby and Timmy. 'Remember what we talked about?'

Libby hung her head. 'I don't want to go.'

'We'll find you a nice family. I promise.' Vince helped them put on their coats.

Mrs Jones and Esme came to the front door to wave the children goodbye as Vince carried Timmy and followed Alice downstairs and out to her motor car. He drove while she sat cradling the baby and Libby and Timmy remained quiet in the back seat.

'I wish I could drive slower,' Vince murmured as they reached the narrow streets of Poplar.

She couldn't answer him. The baby gave a little murmur and she rocked her in her arms.

The iron gates to the orphanage stood open and the drive curved before a large sandstone building with two identical wings on either side.

'Perhaps we should have found an establishment in the country?' Alice murmured.

'This is where the children are from, their roots. Being here, close to the sound of the docks will be comforting,' Vince reasoned, turning off the engine.

Libby gripped Vince's hand and he carried Timmy in one arm, while Alice hugged the baby to her as they waited for someone to answer the large double doors.

A young woman, dressed in uniform of steel grey showed them through the wide dim corridors to the warden's office. They heard the chanting of voices learning the alphabet as they passed one room. A boy of about ten years old stood outside the door, his face to the wall, obviously as some form of punishment. The corridor was bitingly cold.

Alice's stomach churned as they were invited into the warden's bleak room.

A man rose from behind a desk and removed his glasses. This room was marginally warmer than the corridors, at least it had a small fire blazing. 'Good day.' He shook Vince's hand and inclined his head to Alice.

While Vince spoke, informing him of the children's past and their circumstances, Alice summoned all her courage to give a reassuring smile to Libby who peaked at her from behind Vince's leg, still gripping his hand.

All three of them seemed too small for this huge building. The starkness of the corridors had grated on Alice's nerves. Where was the colour, the toys, the laughter of children's voices? She'd never entered an orphanage before and hadn't been expecting something resembling a hospital. Her naivety annoyed her.

'Thank you for considering our orphanage, Mr Barton,' said the man, who introduced himself as Mr Toothby. 'We will be delighted to take in these three children, and your generous donation will ensure that they are well taken care of.'

'Not just taken care of, Mr Toothby,' Alice interjected, 'but they must be kept together.'

'We will certainly try our best, of course. However, sometimes possible clients are looking for a certain age and sex, you understand. Babies are very popular, naturally. Easily moulded, even as young as three are sort after.' He looked at Timmy, then at Libby and frowned. 'Older than that it becomes more difficult.'

'We want them to remain as a family,' Alice added, feeling the man didn't care and that the children were simply inmates.

'And we shall certainly do our best to make that happen, madam.' Mr Toothby opened a drawer and pulled out a thick ledger before pulling a bell rope beside the fireplace behind his desk.

'It is a requirement,' Vince stated, a muscle in his jaw throbbed. 'We would like to be consulted on all possible candidates.'

'That is hardly feasible, sir.' Mr Toothby scowled. 'We have a great many children and clients to deal with every day. We cannot spend our time waiting for other parties to have their say. You have brought the children here into our care. You must give us the freedom to select what is the best option for the children. Now, their names?' he asked, pen poised.

Vince eyed him haughtily. 'Libby Morris, aged five.'

'Birth date?'

Frowning Vince gazed down at Libby. 'When is your birthday, sweetheart?'

Libby, eyes wide, mumbled something softly that Vince had to bend down and ask her to repeat it. Then he straightened and faced Toothby. 'She says in the summer.'

Mr Toothby nodded. 'I can consult the parish records at the church. Likely they were all christened at St Anne's. It's the nearest church to where you say the children lived. The boy?'

'Timmy Morris, aged two. He's three at Easter.'

'Timmy or Timothy?'

'Timothy,' Libby piped up, glaring rebelliously at Mr Toothby.

Toothby wrote in his ledger. 'And the baby?'

Alice stared at Vince. 'She hasn't a name.'

'We can name her,' Toothby declared, not looking up as Vince told him her date of birth.

'No...' Alice gazed down at the sweet little face.

'Choose a name, Alice.' Vince smiled tenderly.

'Mariah.' She touched the baby's cheek with a fingertip. 'Yes, Mariah.' She didn't know where the name came from, but it was a pretty name that she'd liked for a while. A name she might have given her own daughter should she ever have one, and it was looking doubtful she ever would.

'Mariah Alice,' Vince informed Mr Toothby.

Alice blinked away sudden tears at Vince's thoughtfulness of adding her name to the baby's.

Mr Toothby finished writing and pressed a buzzer on his desk.

The door opened and an older woman entered, wearing all black. She nodded to Mr Toothby.

Another younger woman followed her into the room and with a shy smile took Timmy from Vince's arms and beckoned Libby to follow her.

Libby shrank behind Vince, who squatted down and cupped Libby's cheek. 'Listen to me, Libby. Go with this nice lady and I'll come back and visit you tomorrow.'

'No. I won't go. *You* said I didn't have to go.' Tears filled Libby's eyes, washing the blueness of them to grey.

'I'll come back.' Vince held her shoulders. 'I'll visit everyday until you find your new family.'

A sob broke from Libby. 'No. Please. Don't leave us here.'

The older woman in black took the baby from Alice. The wrench made Alice gasp. Arms empty, she wanted to snatch the baby back, but she knew she couldn't. Mariah wasn't hers. Yet, something primal wanted to state the opposite.

Timmy crying now because Libby was, wet himself, earning a stern glare from the woman who held him.

'He's only two...' Alice told her.

'I suggest a quick exit,' Mr Toothby ordered the women and children out.

Alice cringed as the other woman pulled Libby screaming from Vince's legs. Timmy's wails could be heard echoing along the corridor.

The door shut and Alice felt her knees buckle. It was all absolutely hideous.

Vince, pale, took her elbow, giving her strength. 'We shall return tomorrow, Mr Toothby.'

'There is no need to do that at all, Mr Barton. In fact, you doing so will only cause more upset to the children. They must adjust to being here, especially the older girl.'

'Libby. Her name is Libby,' Vince growled between clenched teeth.

'Yes, yes.' Mr Toothby replaced his glasses. 'I will write when we have successfully placed the children. Thank you again.'

Dismissed, Alice held her head high as they left the building, but grateful that Vince held her arm for her legs were shaking.

In the car they sat for several moments in silence.

'Have we done the right thing?' Vince whispered, pulling out a cigarette case and lighting a cigarette.

'What choice do we have? They need parents, a family.' She took the lit cigarette from his fingers and took a deep drag on it. The tobacco and nicotine hit her senses. Her hands shook as well as her legs.

'I feel the biggest cad for leaving them,' Vince said through the cigarette smoke.

'What else could we do?' She closed her eyes, feeling hot tears behind her eyelids.

'Alice.' He reached for her as a tear fell, one then another, faster until she was sobbing into his chest.

'Sorry,' she mumbled after a few minutes, straightening up, wiping her eyes and nose with his handkerchief. 'It's been a terrible day.' She sucked in a ragged breath. 'I sold *Sheer. I sold Sheer!*' She gasped at the enormity of what she'd done. 'And now this. Libby's screams... Timmy's wailing... Baby Mariah...'

'I'll never forget this day as long as I live.' Vince flinched. 'Ghastly. I feel so guilty.'

'Exactly. It's rather affected me more than I imagined it would.' She waved the white handkerchief towards the building. 'I feel so wretched, Vince, and I've only known the three of them for less than two days.'

'I broke a promise to Libby.' He rubbed two hands over his face in anguish. 'Bloody hell. I'm so used to Libby and Timmy sitting on my front step, or on the stairs inside chatting to me as I worked. They didn't deserve this.'

Alice stared blindly into her lap. 'God, can we just go somewhere and get terribly drunk?'

Vince started the engine. 'My thoughts exactly.'

\*\*\*

A door slamming woke Alice. She rubbed the sleep from her eyes, becoming aware she was lying on Vince's sofa with a blanket over her. Happy and the other builders were bringing in their tools. 'Morning, madam.'

She raised her hand in acknowledgment, the morning light hurting her eyes, her head already starting to pound. Around the floor lay numerous bottles of wine and spirits, evidence of the night she and Vince had. A night to drown out their sorrows, to reminisce, to laugh quietly at fond memories, to be sad at missing lost loved ones. They didn't speak of the children, but the scene of Libby screaming as she was taken away loomed large in the room, like a shadow hiding in the corners. They drank toasts to the past and to the future. And the whole time she just wanted him to take her to bed and make love to her. He didn't.

Her tongue felt furry, and she was thirsty. Pushing herself up off the sofa, she realised Vince wasn't in the room.

He wasn't in the kitchen either, but she found him outside in the yard sitting on an upturned crate in the cold, smoking a cigarette.

'Did you sleep at all?' she asked, blinking in the morning sun. The air was crisp, the skies blue and cloudless. Her head throbbed.

'No.' He crushed out the stub of the cigarette on the dirt with his boot and stood. 'Tea?'

She shook her head, then wished she hadn't. 'I'll go home. Bathe. Change my clothes.'

'Of course.'

He walked with her through the house and outside to her motor car. 'Do you see the Brannings today?'

She opened the car door and climbed in. 'Yes. They want to spend the day with me, learning how the business is run. I'm rather not in the mood for it, really.'

'No.'

'Best to keep busy though.'

'Yes.'

She desperately wanted to stay with him.

'Thank you for everything, you know, with the children.' He bent into the car and kissed her cheek, then shut the door. He raised his hand in farewell and returned inside.

The whole scene was detached, cold. So unlike Vince. She sighed deeply. Last night, when drunk, the old witty Vince had returned. He'd made her laugh until she cried. Now, he was the quiet, closed man who'd lost everything, including someone else's children.

When she reached home, Esme was on the telephone.

'It's Mrs Forster, madam.' Esme handed the black and gold receiver to Alice.

'Prue, dearest? Is everything all right?' she asked.

'Yes, fine,' Prue answered. 'I wanted to get you before you left for the office.'

'Is something wrong? Is everyone well?'

'Nothing is wrong. Other than me being the size of an elephant.' Prue's delicate laugh filled Alice's ear. 'Everyone is fine. Your mother has taken Henry horse riding before breakfast and your father and Brandon are in the morning room having their breakfast. I've got a busy day ahead and wanted to ring you before I forget.'

'Forget what?'

'The reason I'm calling is that Grandmama is turning eighty this year. We are holding a special birthday party for her on the twenty-ninth of March. It's a Saturday. Put it in your diary.'

'How wonderful.'

'Grandmama is insisting on a huge party because it might be her last. Her words not mine, you know what she's like. Everyone must be there, of course. So, invite everyone you know. She wants a huge turnout. Grandmama says she might not make another year, but she'll outlive us all I think.'

Alice chuckled. Adeline Fordham was a wonderful woman, funny and smart and still as sharp as a tack.

'I'll post your invitation with all the details, but I just thought to telephone you as well,' Prue continued. 'We're holding the party in London, as it's simply easier for everyone to travel to London. I'll be enormous, naturally. The baby is due only a week or two after the party, but Millie, Jeremy and the boys, plus Mama, are coming over from France to do all the organising of it and Cece and Ross will be coming from Scotland a week before, so I shan't be doing all the work.'

'You must let me know if there's anything I can do to help,' Alice said.

'Just turn up is the main thing. Grandmama thinks the world of you, as you know. I've not been able to contact Vince. Is he still living with you?'

'No. He's at Limehouse permanently now.'

'Does he not have a telephone at his new house yet?'

'No. He barely has walls.'

'How utterly provincial.' Prue laughed again. 'Will you tell him about it? Grandmama will want him there, too.'

'Absolutely.'

'You're a star. Best go. I'm starving for my breakfast. Oh, are you coming to Yorkshire soon or before we come to London in March?'

'I may come up next month for a few days.' Alice took a deep breath. 'I sold *Sheer*, Prue. Signed the contracts yesterday.'

'Oh! Gosh!'

Silence stretched between them until Prue spoke. 'You actually did it.'

'Yes.'

'I thought you might change your mind. It's been such a large part of your life, mine too actually.'

'Yes, it was, and you were there right from the start.'

'I've enjoyed every moment of it, truly.' Prue sighed. 'I can't believe it.'

'It needed to be done. The fun had gone out of it.' She was still in shock that she'd gone through with it.

'How do you feel?'

'Relieved. Sad. Unsure. Glad.' The mix of emotions still whirled through Alice.

'You're bound to feel like that. *Sheer* was everything to you for years. It took some courage to start the magazine, going up against *Vogue*, and it's also taken immense courage to sell something that was so utterly special to you. I'm so proud of you.'

'Thank you. Will you tell Brandon and Father for me? Tell them I'll telephone tomorrow.'

'Consider it done. And bravo, absolutely bravo!'

Alice smiled hearing the praise in Prue's voice. 'Thank you.'

When she replaced the receiver, she turned to see Esme and Mrs Jones waiting for her. Mrs Jones rarely came out of the kitchen. 'Is something the matter?'

'We just wanted to know how it went with the children,' Esme said.

Tiredness overwhelmed Alice. 'They were accepted, especially with Mr Barton's donation.'

'Will they be kept together?' Mrs Jones asked, worry in her small eyes.

Alice shrugged, her gut churning at the thought of the children in that cold building surrounded by strangers. 'It wasn't promised.'

'Poor little pets.' Mrs Jones sniffed and returned to the kitchen.

Alice couldn't think about Libby, Timmy and Mariah. She just couldn't.

Feeling even worse, her head aching like a thousand hammers were smashing against her brain, Alice wanted nothing more than to go to bed for the rest of the day. But she couldn't, wouldn't.

The Brannings *needed* her guidance.

The staff *needed* her to help them adjust to the new owners.

And she *needed* to keep busy to take her mind off Vince and the children.

# Chapter Twelve

Two days later, Alice ushered the Brannings out of her office with a smile and a wave. The couple had wanted to come each day to discuss all aspects of the business. They kept Alice on her toes as she went through all the processes of creating the magazine each month. Although Mr and Mrs Branning were a lovely couple, their keenness and energy overwhelmed Alice. Now *Sheer* was no longer hers, she felt surplus to the staff meetings, held by the Brannings, and with each passing hour, she took another step away from the business. The future of *Sheer* was no longer hers to worry over, or to plan.

Winifred shuffled some papers as Alice closed the door on the Brannings. 'I'm glad it's them who you sold to, madam. Their enthusiasm is boundless. We, the staff and I, feel relieved that the Brannings are so passionate. It's spurred us all on to work with a new sense of purpose.'

'How pleasing to hear, Winifred.' Alice felt a tinge of jealousy, but it soon passed.

The telephone rang and Winifred answered it. '*Sheer,* how may I help you? Oh, Miss Stuart.' Winifred glanced at Alice. 'Yes, she's right here.'

Taking the receiver from Winifred, Alice experienced a pang of guilt for not being in touch with Sally or Helen or any of her friends lately. 'Sally, dearest.'

'You are a difficult woman to get a hold of!' Sally said with a huff. 'I have telephoned your house every day for over a week.'

'Yes, Esme did mention it. Sorry. I'm terribly busy.'

'Well, not tonight you aren't. No matter what you are doing, cancel it and come out with me.'

'Sally, really... I—'

'Absolutely, unequivocally no excuses!' Sally butted in. 'I've not seen you for simply ages. When did we last go out dancing? You're becoming rather dull, Alice darling. We positively must go out tonight. Helen and all the gang are coming.'

Alice tried to think of an excuse. 'I've been terribly busy, sweetie.'

'Yes, yes, I know you are a clever businesswoman and I do nothing all day but have long lunches and go shopping, but seriously, darling, it is rather glum not seeing you. I have so much to tell you.'

'Oh?' She knew Sally would tell her many hours' worth of gossip the minute she saw her.

'I shan't talk on the telephone, as walls have ears. So, we'll meet at Claridge's for cocktails, just you and me and then go on somewhere for dinner with the others. Say, eight o'clock?'

'I'd love to, but—'

'Alice! You are becoming a bore, truly you are. I shall simply get married without you!'

That shocked Alice. 'Married?'

'Well, yes. You know? The whole church and gown thing. Say I do and all that.'

'Who are you marrying?' This was such surprising news.

'Gordy, of course.'

'Of course.' Alice gave a false laugh. 'Silly me. Of course, Gordy. Congratulations!' Was she so out of touch with her friends that she didn't realise Sally and Gordy were that committed to each other? The relationship between Sally and Gordy had been on and off for years. One minute they were passionate and loving and the next both seeing different people. Alice had long given up on keeping straight regarding what they were doing.

'Gordy proposed last week in Rome.'

Alice didn't know they were in Rome. Goodness. Did she even deserve friends?

'We got home yesterday, and I've been trying to get a hold of you since he proposed to squeal about it! I rang every day from the hotel.'

'Dearest, I'm so sorry. Though I'm undeniably thrilled to bits you're engaged.'

'I knew you would be, old bean. We've much to talk about. The wedding and everything.'

'Gosh, how exciting.'

'Will you meet me tonight?'

'Certainly.' Though she was tired, she would have to spend time with Sally. Maybe it would be just the thing she needed. A night out with Sally was always fun, even if she regretted the hangover the next morning. Perhaps several hours talking to Sally, someone from her own world, would put her thoughts in order about Vince, *Sheer* and the children. Heaven knows she needed a few hours of light entertainment and Sally usually provided that in spades.

'Toodle pip, darling.'

Hanging up the receiver, Alice sucked in a breath. Sally and Gordy to marry? Another of her friends to become a couple, to be a family.

'That's nice, Miss Stuart is to marry. Such a lovely lady,' Winifred said, overhearing as she filed away some papers.

'Yes, she is.' Alice agreed.

'Speaking of weddings. Maisie is getting married in the summer, did you know?'

Surprised for the second time in the space of ten minutes, Alice stared at her secretary. 'Maisie? Our Maisie. Prue's former assistant?'

'Yes. Her Herbert proposed a few days ago.'

'I didn't know.' Even more out of the loop, Alice couldn't summon a smile. 'We must get her something.'

'I've already thought of that. I know how preoccupied you've been with the sale and everything, that's why I waited to tell you until you had a spare moment. Shall I go to Selfridges and purchase something for the happy couple?'

'Indeed.' She nodded, feeling wooden. The awful feeling of being left behind descended on her again. She had to shake it off.

It's not as though she'd never been happy before. She had been, desperately so with Tom, even if it was for such a short time. She had married him and felt wanted and desired. But the war had ended their time together before it really began. Tom's death seemed so long ago now, over ten years ago. Since then, she'd spent the years having fun and creating *Sheer*. She had no regrets. None at all.

However, she couldn't get rid of the feeling that everything was rapidly changing now, and she was adrift in the wake of it.

The telephone rang again, making her jump. Winifred answered it, sitting at her desk, pencil in hand.

Alice waited by her office door as Winifred's expression changed. 'Yes, sir. She is right here.' Winifred handed the receiver to Alice. 'It's Mr Barton. He's in a state.'

What now? Heart thumping, Alice grabbed the telephone. 'Vince?'

'Alice, come quickly.' He sounded panicked.

'What's happened?'

'The children have run away from the orphanage.'

Her stomach flipped. 'Good God. I'm on my way.'

'Meet me at my house.'

'I'll be there as quick as I can.' She threw the receiver onto the desk and dashed into her office for her bag before plucking her hat and coat from the stand near the door. 'Winifred. There's an emergency. I'll not be back today.'

'Yes, madam. I'll telephone Miss Stuart and cancel tonight?'

Swearing very unladylike under her breath, Alice nodded. 'Explain it's an emergency. I'll call her tomorrow.'

Alice ran through the other offices, ignoring the staff's stares as she hurtled towards the stairs, too impatient to wait for the old creaky lift to take her down to the ground floor.

She sped through the traffic, blind to the whistle-blowing policeman at an intersection, and weaved through the motor cars, lumbering lorries, horse-drawn wagons and cyclists. Clouds covered the blue sky, blotting out the sun and threatened rain. She prayed it wouldn't happen until they found the children.

It seemed like forever before she was screeching to a halt at Island Row. She saw Vince running back past the houses, coming from the direction of the docks.

She climbed out of the car. 'Tell me everything.'

He bent over, panting. 'A policeman knocked on my door an hour ago, saying Toothby had reported them missing this morning. There's a search happening around the orphanage but there won't be enough policemen to cover so much ground.'

'Is it just Libby?'

'Libby took the baby and Timmy with her.'

'Sweet Jesus!' Alice gripped the car door. 'Libby isn't old enough to take care of a baby not even a week old!'

'We need to find them.' Vince ran a hand through his hair, which was already standing on end as though he'd done it numerous times today. He wore work clothes and hadn't shaved.

'I'll drive around.' She climbed back into the car.

'I'll go along the Cut again. Happy and the other men are out searching, along with some of the neighbours. Mr Woo has gone to speak to the Chinese community and ask them for help.'

'You go down to the docks. I'll go on the other side of Commercial Road.' She reversed the car out of the Row, nearly colliding with a lorry. She spun the wheel and roared off.

Scared for the children's safety, she drove through the narrow streets, getting lost, finding dead ends, and asking women walking, carrying shopping bags, if anyone had seen three small children. No one had. Why would they? The warren of streets and lanes around the docks were perfect hiding spots for people not wanting to be found. Numerous children played in the gutters, but none would talk to her or answer her questions.

Mariah. All Alice could think about was that tiny baby. What was Libby thinking of taking her baby sister out into the winter weather? And Timmy, his little legs would tire so quickly. Were they frozen and hungry on this grey damp day? Timmy crying, the baby turning blue with cold. Images flashed through Alice's mind as she turned one corner after another. She felt ill and anxious and terribly afraid.

On Pekin Street, part of the Chinese community, Alice pulled the car over and spoke to some young Chinese children. Their English was perfect, but they also spoke in their native language to the adults standing in front of a shop asking if they'd seen the children. Head shakes and solemn faces didn't need translating. They hadn't seen them.

Alice drove on, becoming more desperate. She parked the motor car and ventured into narrow mean alleys. Men whistled as she passed, some offered her a good time, while others eyed her up, their gazes lingering on her jewellery. In one street, a homeless man grabbed her leg as she passed. Alice screamed and ran from him back to the safety of her motor car.

She kept driving, entering deeper into the docklands. She stared at unkempt women standing in the streets chatting, filthy children at their feet playing on the cobbles. Alice asked them each time if they'd seen three children, giving their descriptions, but each time the women shook their heads or turned away without answering as though speaking to a person of a higher class was forbidden. One dishevelled woman threw a bucket of dirty water over Alice's motor car, scaring her, but the woman's friends just laughed and told her to clear off.

For hours, she drove, circling back to Vince's house to check to see if he had found them. Each time he shook his head. She stopped by the orphanage several times to see if the police had found them and returned them, but the answer was always no.

Desperate, she crossed East India Dock Road and headed south towards the docks again. She scanned both sides of the road, willing them to be there. Light was fading fast. She dreaded to think of the three of them out in the night air. Were they huddled in an alley somewhere, shivering with cold? Did they have rats for company or were strangers wondering who they belonged to? Mariah would be wet and need her napkin changing and a warm bottle. Tears welled as Alice thought of the baby suffering at such a young age. Libby might cope, maybe even Timmy, but a newborn baby would die so easily from exposure, and it grieved Alice deeply to think of it happening.

After hours of driving, her petrol getting low, she turned and headed back to Island Row, hoping Vince had succeeded in finding them.

The light was nearly gone as she slowed down to let an old woman cross the road. The motor car's engine spluttered, surged and the spluttered again before dying completely.

'Blast!' Alice, angry at herself for allowing the petrol to get so low, sat fuming. A horn tooted behind her. Once out of the car, she went to the lorry waiting behind.

'There is absolutely no point in you sitting there with your hand on the horn. I have no petrol.'

'No petrol?' The driver scratched his chin. 'You'll need to shift your motor, luv. It can't stay there all night.'

Hands on hips, she stared up at him. 'And what would you like me to do? Push it?'

He mumbled something about women drivers to the other man in the cab. 'We'll help you shift it to the side. That way people can get past.'

'Thank you.'

A few minutes later, with much heaving and puffing, the lorry driver and his passenger, a wiry young man, had pushed Alice's motor car to the side of the road, and she'd collected her bag from inside it.

'Thank you for your help.'

The driver tipped his cap. 'No worries. You can get petrol on Commercial Road. He shuts up shop at six.'

'Your assistance is appreciated.' She walked away as he drove off. Finding petrol for her car was not at the top of her priorities. She'd walk back to Vince's house first, wanting to know if he'd found the children.

The dark narrow streets of Limehouse weren't familiar to her. Worried she'd become lost, she walked quickly, looking for anything she'd seen before which might give her a clue to where she needed to walk.

Down a narrow winding lane, the tang of the river thick in the air, Alice strode as fast as she could in her heeled boots. Dockers, their work done for the day, gave her side-long glances. One man whistled and she gave him a haughty stare. A beggar sitting against a building held out his hands, pleading for coins.

A woman coming the other way shook her head at Alice when she slowed to search in her purse for a few pennies. 'Don't give him any. He only goes straight to the pub with it.'

Alice nodded her thanks. 'You haven't seen three children around here, a five-year-old girl carrying a newborn and a little boy?'

'Gawd no. Are they lost or just playing games?'

'They ran away from the orphanage.'

'Poor souls. I hope you find them before much longer. They'll not last a cold night out in the open. Good luck.' The woman continued walking.

Sighing in despair, Alice turned into another road. She didn't know where she was. The road was deserted. She kept going, apprehensive of being out on the dark streets. Thinking she'd taken the wrong turn yet again, she came to a corner pub. Men were going in or coming out of it. She hesitated, thinking to go in and ask for directions, when the sound of crying made her spin on her heel. Beside the pub was a small narrow walkway, completely in darkness. The crying came again.

A cat jumped out, running for its life across the road. Chasing it was Timmy, calling for it.

'Timmy!' Alice nearly fainted at the sight of him.

Timmy paused, head swivelled towards her, but he wanted the cat and took off after it. A small lorry was coming down the road. Instinctively, Alice lunged for Timmy as he dashed past, heedless of the lorry.

Screeching brakes filled the air. The front of the lorry hit Alice's hip as she leaped, pulling Timmy away with seconds to spare. Knocked to the ground, her head hit the road, but she didn't let go of Timmy.

Yells from men near the pub and Timmy's wails echoed in her ears. Two men rushed to kneel beside her.

'You all right, luv?' An older man bent over her, looking concerned. 'There now, little one. You're not hurt, I don't think. 'Ere, Gav, hold this little fellow for a minute.' The old man lifted Timmy away from Alice, so he could help her to sit up.

'I'm fine.' She shook badly. Her hip throbbed as well as her head.

'Get this lady a brandy!' the old man yelled.

'Timmy?' She searched the crowd of men, looking for the little boy. She felt sick.

'He's here. He's here.' A different man plucked him from another set of arms and passed him back to Alice.

'Are you hurt?' Alice asked Timmy, checking his body with shaking hands.

'My knee.' His chin wobbled.

She examined his knee to see a scrape that had pin-pricks of blood on it. 'I'm sure it hurts you, darling, but you'll be fine. Where's Libby and the baby?'

Timmy looked around as if not sure. Alice's heart dropped. Was he all alone? Then she saw Libby emerge from the shadows into the golden light cast by the pub, holding the baby whose blanket fell away from her little bare legs and draped on the ground.

'Libby!' Alice stood and limped towards her, pain shooting up her body. 'Thank God you're safe.'

Tears streaked down Libby's cheeks. Her hair looked as though it had not seen a brush in days.

Neither Libby nor Timmy wore a coat. Libby's face was pinched with cold. 'Is Timmy hurt?'

'No, he's fine. He fell on me mostly.' Awkwardly, for Timmy didn't want to be put down, Alice scooped Mariah out of Libby's hold and held her in her other arm. She peered at the baby in the weak light, hoping she wasn't ill. 'We've been so worried, Libby. You shouldn't have left the orphanage, especially not with Timmy and Mariah. They are too little to be out on the streets in winter.' Alice fought her anger at the girl.

'You left us!' Libby's bottom lip trembled. 'I hate it there.'

'Excuse me, madam?' A man wearing a brown suit came to stand next to Alice. He was about Alice's age, and pleasant looking with a cultured accent which highlighted that he wasn't a docker. 'Do you want a lift in my motor car? I can take you home.' He smiled kindly. 'I'm a doctor. Doctor Geoffrey Garrett. One of the men came to my house and asked me to come. I live up the road.' He waved behind him to indicate. 'Or you could come to my house, and I can examine you there?'

'Could you take us home, please?' She knew Vince would be worried out of his mind now it was night and the children out in the darkness.

'Yes, certainly.'

'That would be very kind of you, Doctor Garrett.' Alice nodded gratefully. Her hip throbbed terribly. She thanked the men for their kindness. From her bag she took out a ten-shilling note and gave it to the old man. 'Buy some drinks for yourself and the others as a thank you from me.'

'Right you are, madam.' He tipped his hat at her.

'Come this way, and here let me take the baby for you.' Doctor Garrett gently took Mariah from Alice. 'She's a bit cold.'

'Yes. It's a dreadfully long story.' Alice glared at Libby who, for a second, stood her ground. '*Libby*, come along.'

'You're hurt?' the doctor asked, watching her limp towards his car parked down the street.

'The lorry collided with my hip. It's awfully sore.'

'I'll examine you once we're inside, if you'd like?'

'I'm sure it's nothing more than a bump.'

Within minutes, they were pulling to a stop in Island Row, so close in fact to where Alice had been hit that Alice felt stupid for not finding her way by herself.

'The warren of streets can be confusing in the dark,' Doctor Garrett said when she mentioned it to him as they climbed from the car.

Vince was turning the corner into the Row when he spotted them. 'Alice!'

'I found them, Vince.' She held Mariah as Doctor Garrett picked up Timmy.

'Libby.' Vince knelt and held the girl to him. 'I was so worried.'

Her mutinous face held the trace of fresh tears. 'You left us! You didn't come back! They smacked me for asking for you!'

'I'm sorry. Very sorry. But you shouldn't have endangered your brother and sister.'

'I wasn't leaving them.' She glared at Vince.

'Shall we go inside?' Tiredness overcame Alice. She was cold, aching and thirsty.

'Where is your car?' Vince asked her as they went into the front room, which was deliciously warm.

'I ran out of petrol.'

'Then she was involved in an accident,' Doctor Garrett chimed in. 'She's hurt her hip. I'd like to examine her.'

Vince's eyes widened. 'God Almighty, Alice!'

'I'm fine.' She waved away his concern. 'I just need a cup of tea desperately. This is Doctor Garrett, by the way.' She made the introductions.

Ten minutes later, sitting by the fire, with tea and toast, Alice watched Doctor Garrett give the children a few checks and declare them healthy, though Mariah's crying meant she was hungry.

'The baby is becoming dehydrated,' Doctor Garrett told them with concern. 'I can take her to the hospital for milk.'

'Not without me.' Alice stood up and winced as pain shot through her hip.

'And you'll be examined, too. No arguments.' The doctor's kind smile, but serious gaze told Alice she had no choice.

'I'll give these two a nice warm bath and put them to bed.' Vince stood and shook Doctor Garrett's hand. 'Thank you for everything.'

'You're welcome, Mr Barton. The hospital might keep them overnight to monitor them. I can bring them back in the morning.' Doctor Garrett gently took Alice's elbow, his manner kind and attentive. 'Shall we go, Mrs Barton?'

'Oh, we aren't married, and these aren't our children,' she told him, then saw a flash of something in Vince's brown eyes before he turned back to Libby.

Doctor Garrett tilted his head inquisitively. 'Forgive me, I shouldn't have assumed.'

'As I said, it's a long story.'

'I'm sure you can fill me in on the way.' Doctor Garrett helped her to the door. 'It sounds a fascinating story.'

# Chapter Thirteen

Vince slept badly. On waking the following morning, he instantly went upstairs to the bed to check Libby and Timmy were still there. He'd put them to bed after their bath, and they'd fallen asleep almost instantly, especially Timmy. Libby had barely said a word to him since her outburst when she got out of the doctor's car.

Now, as he boiled the kettle on the gas stove and stirred the porridge, he kept an ear cocked for any movement upstairs. He'd checked on them numerous times during the night, but they'd hadn't woken, probably exhausted from their escapade.

He buttered toast, aware he needed to buy more bread, more of everything, really. But he had enough oats to make porridge and set them on the stove top to simmer.

His attention wandered to Alice, hoping she was not in too much pain from her hip and had been able to rest in hospital. He'd seen the way Doctor

Garrett had looked at Alice. He knew the signs when a man was interested in a woman, and the good doctor was certainly that.

He sighed deeply. What if Alice was attracted to the doctor, too? Could he cope with having the woman he loved turn her attentions to another? Could he stop it? Did he have a right to do so?

They had kissed only last week. A glorious moment in his life when he'd finally been able to kiss and hold the woman he'd loved for years. But since that kiss, they'd been thrown together in a myriad of problems. The other night they had drank too much, and as much as he wanted to take Alice to bed and make love to her for hours, it hadn't been the right time. He wanted their first time to be special, unhurried and definitely not tainted with too much alcohol.

Alice meant the world to him. She was the one he wanted to spend the rest of his life with but how could he when he wasn't the same man he used to be? What did he have to offer her? He could no longer match the wealth of her other suitors like Simon or any man of their class. He'd fallen low not only in income but prospects. He didn't have a grand house to offer her, a comfortable lifestyle she was used to, and he couldn't offer her marriage and expect her to live a simple life.

From upstairs came the sound of the lavatory being flushed. Moments later, Libby came into the kitchen, again that wariness in her expression.

'Good morning,' Vince said.

She silently slipped onto a chair at the table, not looking at him.

'Are you hungry? Some porridge? With honey?' He doled out a small portion into a bowl and spooned a honey swirl over the top of it. He placed the bowl in front of Libby. 'A glass of milk?'

She ate quietly, not responding to him.

He left her to eat and went upstairs to check on Timmy, who was stirring. 'Good morning, little man.'

'Pee-pee.'

'Oh, right. Yes, Of course.' He helped the little boy, finding it all such a new experience. As he was pulling up Timmy's shorts, he had an awful thought that Libby might have run away again. He shouldn't have left her alone.

Grabbing Timmy, he raced as fast he could downstairs without dropping the boy, and into the kitchen. Heart pounding, he tried to relax on seeing her eating her porridge. She hadn't run away. At least not yet. He walked to the front door and locked it and did the same to the back door and pocketed the keys. She'd not be escaping any time soon.

'I thought we might go to the shops after breakfast? We need some food.' Vince kept his tone calm, a smile on his face as he helped Timmy with his porridge. 'Libby? Shall we do that?'

Her answer was a small shrug.

'Alice and Mariah will return later from the hospital. Shall we buy a cake?'

'Cake!' Timmy crowed and clapped.

'If you send me back, I'll run away again,' Libby suddenly spoke.

His stomach clenched. Guilt filled him. 'Now, Libby. That's not a sensible thing to say. You're too young to be on your own. You can't take care of yourself, or Timmy or Mariah.'

Despite the scared gleam in her blue eyes, she raised her chin. 'I'll leave them there.'

'You want to be out on the streets by yourself?' He couldn't help but to admire her stubbornness and her spirit.

'I hate it there!' She ran from the table and upstairs.

Vince went to go after her, but Timmy spilled his cup of milk and he had to clean it up.

What the hell was he going to do? These children needed a home, a family, but to take them back to the orphanage seemed too cruel. He couldn't go through another horrendous scene of leaving them, or feel the dread of hearing Libby had bolted again. Yet what was the alternative?

The idea to keep them wormed into his brain, but the reality was he lived in a run-down house that was more a ruin than a home. He couldn't have three small children living here, and to rent somewhere else would take his attention and money away from this house. Plus, he'd have to hire a nanny because he couldn't raise three small children on his own without help. Although he had a little money put aside after the estate sale, it wasn't enough to pay a live-in nanny's wage. He needed that money for his future, to invest in something substantial to give him an income for the rest of his life. However, how could he turn his back on these helpless children? It was a hopeless situation.

'More?' Timmy raised his cup for more milk, his blue eyes beseeching.

'We don't have any more, little man.' Vince felt terrible disappointing the boy which proved he had no idea about being a father.

Nothing was going how he expected it to. Secluding himself away from all he knew, rejecting his old life, and focusing on rebuilding this house was meant to be his solution to losing everything. He'd been prepared to never marry Alice, to not spend the rest of his days wining and dining, enjoying himself to the limit. He accepted that it was all gone.

Instead, he became determined to throw himself into so much activity it never gave him a moment's time to think or feel. Rebuilding this house, and then maybe another, was to be his new life. He'd come to terms with it, and in a strange way was actually embracing the challenge.

Only, now, he had three small people to consider. Three small people and Alice, who refused to walk away from him as so many of his friends had done when the family became bankrupt.

Vince gazed down at Timmy who looked up and smiled at him, melting his heart and destroying all his common sense. He knew he had to step up. Just like in the war, lives were at stake, and he had a responsibility to face this battle full on and protect them. He'd survived the war and brought a good deal of his men through it, too.

Perhaps it was time to fight once more.

***

Alice held Mariah as Doctor Garrett drove them to Vince's house at midday. She'd spent the night unable to sleep due to the pain in her hip, which thankfully was only bruised and nothing worse. Also keeping her awake had been the plans swirling in her mind. Through the dark hours of the night, she'd thought of many scenarios of what her future might look like, and each one always included the children.

The Morris children needed a home, and she wanted a family. Gazing at Mariah, touching her soft pink cheek, Alice felt a glow of warmth she'd never experienced before. This baby had been born in front of her, she'd held her within minutes of entering the world. Fate, or whatever was out there controlling their lives, had brought Mariah into Alice's life. The torment she felt taking Libby, Timmy and Mariah to the orphanage would never be forgotten, and she believed she wasn't capable of doing it again. Handing those three little souls over to strangers felt wrong, and although Alice hadn't known the children long herself, she knew they needed her as much as she needed them. She could make them a family.

Sometime before dawn, she'd decided to adopt the children with or without Vince's approval. Once she'd made the decision, she felt elated and frightened at the same time. This was what she was missing. A family of her own. For so long she had shied away from the thought of settling down and having children. Believing instead she wanted her career as a businesswoman. *Sheer* had been her baby, her driving force, only *Sheer* wasn't enough. *Sheer* didn't make her feel whole. Not anymore.

In the beginning, creating the magazine had fitted in with her crazy fast lifestyle. She'd enjoyed travelling to different countries, attending wild parties and boozy dinners, the weekends away at country estates, the race car meetings, the elite horse racing carnivals where she spent days in marquees socialising and drinking and never seeing one horse race during the entire meet. She sat and watched friends play cricket at Lord's, she'd shopped at Harrods, dined at the Savoy, danced at the Ritz and the days, weeks and years had gone by in a dizzying swirl of partying.

Yet, at night, when she was alone, tired and lonely, she would think of Brandon and Prue, of their deep love, their delight in having Henry, and wonder if she really was as fulfilled as she thought she was.

Lying in the hospital bed, she came to realise that she wanted more than her partying lifestyle. She wanted a family of her own.

Now she just had to tell Vince of her decision and hope he approved.

'Here we are,' Doctor Garrett said pulling to a stop in Island Row. 'How do you feel?'

Alice gave him a grateful smile. 'Fine. Sore but fine.' Then she noticed her car parked further along. 'Oh, that's a relief to see it here, but how I wonder?'

He ran around the car and opened her door for her. 'I could have taken you home to Notting Hill rather than here.' He seemed confused when she told him she wanted to return to Limehouse when she had a home in Notting Hill.

'I need to speak with Vince and see Libby and Timmy.'

'Of course.' He reached into his coat pocket and pulled out a small card. 'My details are on my card. Don't hesitate to contact me for anything.'

'Thank you. You have been such a tremendous help.'

'Perhaps we can meet again? Dinner one night?'

Alice stared at him, wishing she was still that woman who would have said yes in a heartbeat. That woman who'd have gone dancing with handsome doctor and sipped champagne with him until the wee hours. But she wasn't that person anymore. She wanted more than that.

'I don't think that is a good idea, sorry, but thank you for the offer.' She gripped the bag of bottles and cans of powdered milk for Mariah, which he took from her to carry to the house.

Vince opened the front door, Timmy in his arms. 'We've been watching out for you.'

'Is everything all right?' she asked, walking gingerly across the narrow lane to him.

'Yes.' His reassuring smile gave warmth to his eyes.

'You found my car.'

'Yes. I paid a few lads to go and find it. A Rolls Royce isn't that difficult to find in this area. We, Libby, Timmy and I, filled it with petrol and then drove it here.' He bent to kiss her cheek.

'You're a marvel!' Alice grinned at Timmy. 'How are you, sweet one? Been a good boy?'

Timmy nodded, one arm around Vince's neck, the other arm cuddling a soft material bear to his chest.

'What have you got there?'

'A bear. Mine.' Timmy held out the bear and then quickly cuddled it close again.

'He's a lovely bear.' Alice followed Vince inside, the doctor trailing behind them.

'I went out to the shops this morning before we sorted out your car.' Vince sat Timmy on the sofa in the front room, where Libby sat on the floor drawing with chalk on a slate board. 'I needed food and bought them a little present each to make them happy.'

Doctor Garrett crouched next Libby. 'That's a very good drawing.'

Libby quickly rubbed the picture out with her hand and turned away from him.

Alice and Vince exchanged worried glances.

Doctor Garrett slowly straightened. 'May I have a word with you both?'

Vince nodded. 'Libby, we are just going into the kitchen to make some tea. Look after Timmy for a moment.'

On the way to the kitchen, Vince first went to the front door and locked it, before he joined Alice and the doctor in the freezing kitchen.

'It's so cold in here.' Alice snuggled Mariah closer to her.

'I know and I can't understand why. The heating isn't working in any room except the front room. Happy will be back tomorrow and we'll sort it out.'

'This room, no, I should say this whole house isn't suitable for children, especially a newborn baby.' Doctor Garrett looked around him at the various stages of building work happening. 'What are your plans for the children? Libby's behaviour is demonstrating that she's likely to run away again if they are returned to the orphanage.'

'I'm frightened she'll run away from here at any moment. That's why the doors are permanently locked.'

Doctor Garrett frowned. 'She's a troubled child, but it's not surprising considering her past.'

'She was left alone to look after Timmy a lot.' Vince folded his arms in thought. 'They spent more time here than with their mother in recent months and then for her to die...'

Doctor Garrett pulled his coat around him tighter. 'I could take the children with me. There is an older couple I know who take in children.'

'No!' Alice stepped forward making both men turn and stare at her outburst. 'The children will stay with me. I'll take them to my home where it's warm. Now. This minute. Esme will be wondering where I am. I need to change, and the children will be fine with me.' She was babbling, eager to convince Vince that she wanted the children and the best place for them was with her.

'Are you well enough?' Doctor Garrett asked with genuine concern.

'Absolutely.' She beamed.

'The children are well enough here, Alice,' Vince said. 'The front room is warm. I have bought plenty of food. I *can* take care of them.'

'I know that, but my house is safer than here.'

'These children have lived in slum housing all their lives, they are used to a bit of hardship,' he defended.

'But they don't have to any longer.' She turned from Vince to Doctor Garrett. 'Thank you for all your help.' She walked from the kitchen and into the front room. 'Libby, Timmy, get your things, You're coming to live with me.'

Libby jerked up. 'Not at the children's home?'

'No. Gather your things.'

'Alice, really, they are happy with me.' Vince came behind her. 'I want them to stay.'

'I shall leave you both.' Doctor Garrett stood in the hallway. 'You have my card, Lady Mayton-Walsh. Good day to you both.' With a nod he put on his trilby hat and walked out.

Alice collected the bag with one hand, Mariah asleep in the other.

Vince gazed down at the baby in her arms and then over to Timmy and finally to Libby, who stared at him with wide dark-blue eyes. 'I want to keep them myself.'

She stared at him, shocked that he wanted the children. 'So do I.'

'You want to keep them?' The surprise was evident in Vince's question. 'You?'

'Yes, me. Why not me?' she snapped.

'Because children aren't your thing. Everyone knows that.'

'Perhaps that was true only a year ago, but lately I have been feeling that I'm missing something in my life. I've thought a lot about this, all night and yesterday. It's been there in the back of my mind ever since we left them at the orphanage.'

Vince stood, hands on hips. 'Children are not kittens, Alice. You cannot give them away once you're tired of playing with them.'

'That's absolutely rude of you to say such a thing to me,' she snarled. 'What gives you the right to judge me and my intentions? I've never heard you say you wanted children either.'

'I wanted children, of course I did.'

'You've never said it to *me*,' she replied angrily.

'Because I couldn't.'

'Why?'

'Because I wanted children with *you*!' He shrugged and thrust his hands into his trouser pockets.

'Me?' Shocked, she stared at him, the children forgotten for a moment.

'I've always wanted you, but you never wanted me.' He shrugged. 'I understood that.'

She couldn't think straight for a minute. Mariah was becoming heavy in her arms, the bag also. 'Why haven't you ever mentioned this before?'

'I was never someone you took seriously. I was your brother's best friend, your jester, your dinner partner when there was no one else. The safe option when you couldn't be bothered with relationships or when Simon or some other fellow had bored you.'

'Good God,' she breathed. 'I never knew you felt like that.'

'Don't get me wrong. I enjoy our friendship. It means the world to me, but I want more, Alice. So much more.'

'As do I,' she murmured.

His brown eyes widened then dulled. 'More with me, or someone else?'

'With you,' she confessed.

'I don't believe you.'

'That's your choice.' She shifted Mariah more comfortably.

'You never gave me any inclination that you wanted more than just friendship.'

She tossed her head in annoyance of being wrong-footed by his declaration. 'Neither did you.'

'I have *loved* you for years, ever since I was a foolish youth visiting your family home in Yorkshire in my school holidays.' His voice was soft, as though afraid to say the words that might condemn him.

'You love me...' She spoke tenderly, afraid to believe the words. 'Not just as a friend?'

'No, not just as a friend.'

They smiled shyly at each other.

'Pee-pee!' Timmy shouted, scooting off the sofa.

'I'll take him.' Libby got to her feet and taking Timmy by the hand led him upstairs.

Vince took a deep breath and expelled it. 'Well, now it's all out in the open. What shall we do about it?'

'I have absolutely no idea.' Emotion tightened her chest and the turmoil she felt was reflected in his eyes.

'And now we have these three to think about...' Vince glanced at Mariah.

Alice felt the wetness of the baby. 'She needs changing. If you'll excuse me.' Glad to escape into the kitchen, Alice felt such conflicting emotions she didn't know how to act or think. Vince wanted her. That's all that went through her mind as she changed the baby on the kitchen table into a fresh napkin.

'Alice.' Vince came to stand beside her. 'We need to talk about all of this.'

'Yes.' She couldn't look at him and concentrated on the baby.

'This is where they belong. It's what they know.' He frowned at her. 'You are suggesting to uproot them even more than they already are by proposing to take them to Notting Hill?'

'Surely its better than staying here in an unfinished house?' She re-wrapped Mariah in the blanket.

Vince scooped her up into his arms as Alice tidied away the napkin and wiped down the table. 'I know it's not ideal...'

'The children need to be in a warm and safe environment. I can provide that.'

He nodded, unable to argue the fact. 'And us?'

She sucked in a breath. 'Come for dinner tonight. We'll talk properly.'

'With no alcohol.'

'Maybe just one...' she joked.

His smile was slow but loving. 'I'll be there for seven.'

'Come earlier. You can help put the children to bed.' She gave him a long lingering look, then stepped to the front door, calling for Libby and Timmy.

The drive home was a blur, her thoughts and emotions in a whirl. Vince's confession about his feelings kept repeating in her mind. He wanted her. They could be together, with the children. She would have her happy ever after.

Libby was subdued as she drove, but Timmy chatted the whole way. He seemed a happy little fellow despite his terrible beginning in life.

Esme whooped with delight on seeing the children, calling for Mrs Jones, who came running out of the kitchen, nearly crying in joy.

'I need a bath, Esme.' Alice sighed after telling them both of everything that had happened.

'Of course, madam. I'll see to it now for you.' Esme gave Mariah to Mrs Jones and ushered Libby and Timmy into the kitchen with Mrs Jones, who was telling the children that she'd make them a special meal, and what pudding did they want?

Alice limped upstairs into the parlour, driving the motor car had caused her hip to ache in protest at the constant movement. A pile of mail waited for her on the sideboard, and she flipped through several envelopes before opening the one from her lawyer in regards to the sale of *Sheer*. She had final papers to sign, and he wanted her to visit him as soon as it was convenient.

The telephone rang next to her, and she answered. 'Lady Mayton-Walsh speaking.'

'Alice!' Sally's shrill tone filled her ear. 'Where have you been? Dear God, I thought you'd died or gone to a different country, or deary Yorkshire which is just as intolerable.'

'There has been a lot going on, sorry. Forgive me for not meeting you the other night.'

'You didn't attend the theatre last night either, or Ronnie's shindig the day before. It was a frightful hoot, really it was. Where have you been? Esme couldn't tell me.'

'Yes, sorry. I know I've been a disgraceful friend.' She closed her eyes, just wanting to soak in the bath.

'What is going on with you? I simply must know, old bean. It's all rather glum without you to have fun with.'

'I doubt that, Sal. You find fun wherever you go or whoever you are with.'

'Maybe so, but it is positively much juicer if you are with us. Gordy says howdy do, by the way. He's been jolly good about listening to me whine over your disappearance. Where have you *been*?'

'It's all rather complicated, actually.' Alice sighed tiredly.

'Oh, splendid! Tell me everything.'

'I sold *Sheer*.'

Sally's gasp was loud. 'Gordy! Alice has sold *Sheer*! Can you believe it?' Sally shouted obviously not covering the mouthpiece, so Alice's ear rang.

'Sally, stop shouting, for heaven's sake.'

'Apologies,' Sally said, speaking normally again. 'Gracious, Alice. *Sheer*. You really did it. Well done, old bean!'

'Also...' Alice took a deep breath. 'I'm going to adopt three orphan children.'

Sally's peal of laughter shocked Alice, then offended her.

It took several moments for Sally to control herself. '*Adopting children*. That's the funniest thing I've heard you say in simply ages. Gordy!' Sally yelled again. 'Gordy! Alice just made a joke about adopting some children. Isn't that hilarious! Alice, of all people! You are a card, Alice, truly you are.'

That Sally thought she could joke about such a thing, irritated Alice beyond belief. 'It's the truth. I was witness to a birth in Limehouse while visiting Vince. The mother died, leaving three children behind.' The hard tone of her voice finally penetrated Sally's hilarity.

'But why must *you* take care of them? Isn't there family or an orphanage they can go to?'

'There are no family to take them, and Vince and I tried the orphanage, but the eldest girl, Libby took her brother and baby sister and ran away. While looking for them I was hit by a lorry and spent a night in hospital.'

'Hospital? Were you hurt?'

'My hip is badly bruised, and I banged my head.'

'Goodness.'

'The children are here with me now. So, I must go.'

'Wait. You cannot drop that on me and then simply hang up,' Sally demanded. 'Meet me for dinner tonight at the Ritz. I feel I might have to talk some sense into you, seriously I do.'

'I've made my mind up and won't change it no matter what you say.'

'I won't believe it,' Sally said, sounding annoyed. 'I won't let you ruin your life by taking in three homeless children from the slums of the East End. It's unheard of. Unimaginable! That is not what people do, at least not our sort of people. You will ruin your life.'

'Well, I don't see it as *ruining* my life, but rather *adding* to it.'

'You are beastly to do this to me, Alice. I know you can be stubborn but to hinder yourself with some street children is not the answer if you're feeling lonely or upset at selling *Sheer*. Find another project. Start another business, travel or something. I know, we'll go and spend a few months travelling around Europe. My uncle has recently bought a chateau near Lyon. We'll go there first and then cross over into Italy. Shopping in Milan, that's just the ticket.'

'No.'

'Alice, listen to me.'

'No.'

There was a long pause, before Sally made a small noise. 'I know of a fine nanny service in Kensington that my cousin has used. I'll get the name of it. An excellent nanny or two will be just what you need. They can take care of the children and you can get on with your life. Then there's boarding school right up until they are adults. It didn't do us any harm. Pay for them but you don't need to destroy your life for them.'

'They aren't objects to be pushed to one side.'

'Nor are they your responsibility! What on earth do you know about being a mother for God's sake?'

'I can learn.'

'They aren't even of our class. Adopt a child if you must but why choose the dregs of the slums?'

'Goodbye, Sally.'

'Alice—'

Alice put down the receiver before she said something she would later regret and covered her eyes with a hand.

'Madam?' Esme stood by the stairs. 'Your bath is ready.'

Alice nodded. 'And you'll make up the spare room for Libby and Timmy. Mariah can sleep with me.'

'Very good, madam.'

'I shall go shopping tomorrow and buy what we need.'

'It's exciting, madam.' Esme grinned. 'They're lovely little things.'

'They will change our lives, Esme.' She didn't know if she was saying it to herself or to Esme.

The maid shrugged. 'Only in a good way, madam. My mam said children were a blessing and my mam is never wrong.'

Alice smiled and went for her bath. The long soak relaxed her better than anything else. For a short time, she thought of nothing but the warm water soothing her bruises. She cleared her mind of Vince, the children and the conversation with Sally and let the water lap gently over her tired body. Her right hip was a mass of dark colours while both knees were scraped from where she landed on the road. The sleepless night before was catching up on her. She yawned repeatedly, wishing she could close her eyes and sleep.

The door opened and Esme came in carry a warm towel. 'That Timmy is a sweetie. He's jabbering on like he's our best friend, bless him. Libby's quiet though. She's not spoken hardly at all.'

'The trauma of her mother's death, being left at the orphanage and then running away has left its mark on her,' Alice answered, stepping out of the bath to dry herself. 'She doesn't trust anyone anymore and we have to treat her delicately until we earn her trust again.'

'Poor little dear.' Esme took away the clothes Alice had discarded. 'With Mr Barton coming I've laid out your red woollen sheath dress, which is non-restrictive around the hips, but still stylish enough for familiar visitors.'

'Very thoughtful, thank you.'

Once dressed, Alice went down to the kitchen and spent an hour with the children. Holding Mariah, she encouraged Libby to do some more drawing and taught Timmy to count to five, before business called her away. She had letters to write, telephone calls to make and accounts to deal with.

Thankfully, Esme offered to take Libby and Timmy for a quick walk around Ladbroke Square Gardens as the sun was lowering, while Mrs Jones kept an eye on Mariah who slept in padded box.

'It's not a very auspicious start, is it?' Alice had said looking down at the baby sleeping in the box.

'It'll do for now.' Mrs Jones grinned, rolling out pastry.

'I'll make some calls. We'll have furniture by this evening!' Determined, Alice telephoned Harrods and placed an order. Then she telephoned Winifred and asked her to ring an agency dealing with nannies.

'Nannies?'

'Yes. I have some children staying with me.'

'Very good, madam. Are you coming into the office tomorrow, madam, or shall I allow the Brannings to deal with what needs to be done?' Winifred asked.

'No, I won't be coming in. I was in an accident and spent the night in hospital.'

'Goodness gracious! Are you badly hurt, madam?'

'Just some bruising. Can you relay to the team that I won't be in the office for the rest of the week, please? Oh, and the Brannings... They might as well take over now while I'm not there. I know I was meant to meet with them and take them to the printers for introductions, but I won't be able to make it. Reassure them that they have free use of my office, which is actually there office now.'

'I will, madam. I shall help them in any way I can.'

'Can you pack up my personal belongings, please Winifred? I shall collect them in a few days.'

'Of course, madam.'

'You are a treasure, Winifred. I'll speak to you soon.' Hanging up, Alice sat at her desk and continued writing her letters, answering the numerous invitations to parties, balls, art gallery exhibitions, and so on. All events she normally would have attended, but which now held no interest. She needed to be home with the children. They were her priority. Settling them into their new life was her only focus, that and Vince.

Her stomach flipped at the thought of him arriving soon. The man who was her friend, someone she'd known since childhood, had suddenly become the most important person to her. It baffled her that he'd been in her life all this time, yet not once had she seen him as a possible suitor until a few months ago. It didn't make sense to her. It was as though she'd been blind and now the shades have been lifted allowing her to see everything fresh and new.

She'd been aware of Vince's handsomeness, his wild flirtations with women, his cheeky manner and disastrous relationships which never lasted longer than a month or two were a part of him, a part of what made him so loveable as a friend. He'd been her right-hand man throughout building *Sheer*. They laughed and spent countless hours together in all manner of ways from tense editorial meetings with the *Sheer* team to dancing to jazz at three in the morning in some basement club in Soho. But never once, in all that time, did she think of him as the man she wanted above all others. Not until she learnt he'd proposed to Diana, only then did she realise how much she'd taken him for granted. The thought of losing him to Diana had changed all her perceptions and made her wake up to what was right in front of her.

Tonight, they would talk about it. Be honest with each other. Discuss the future, their needs and wants...

Her pen poised mid-air as she wondered if they'd go to bed and make love?

A shiver of desire flooded her, and she smiled secretly in delight.

# Chapter Fourteen

By that evening, Alice and Esme had changed one
of the two spare rooms into a nursery for the
children with the help of the delivery men from
Harrods. Two single beds had replaced the ornate
double bed and a cot now stood in the corner.
A small bath on a stand, which had a removable
top to use as a changing table, was placed by the
window. The tall wardrobe was filled with dresses
for Libby, shirts and shorts for Timmy, new shoes
and new coats one in red for Libby and one in
grey for Timmy. The set of drawers contained
new nightwear, shawls and lacey white gowns for
Mariah.

Toys were littered over the floor as Libby and
Timmy played with the array of gifts Alice had
bought. Spinning tops, a miniature doll's house, a
wooden train set, books, chalk and slate, paints, a
rocking horse that Libby adored, and a tin truck
and a doll. Their cries of delight brought tears

to Esme, and Alice's throat choked with emotion seeing such joy on their dear faces.

'They'll be too excited for sleep, madam,' Esme joked.

'Does it matter?' She smiled. 'They've had nothing all their lives. Their mother struggled to keep a roof over their heads and food in their stomachs. A few toys are the least they can have.'

'You're giving them more than that, madam. You're giving them a life so different to the one they would have lived if their mother survived. Because of you, these children will never be hungry again. They will have an education, a future of their choosing...' Esme sniffed back tears. 'Libby won't have to work in a factory, or Timmy on the docks. Mariah won't have to marry young and have a child every year to a man who beats her or is drunk more times than not.'

'Oh, Esme,' Alice gasped, seeing the despair in the younger woman's face, but knowing she spoke the truth. These children would escape the poverty of the East End.

Esme wiped her eyes with the bottom of her apron. 'Whatever else you do in life, madam, nothing will top this.'

Alice gently squeezed her arm in thanks. The little clock on the small mantle above the narrow black fireplace chimed six times. She frowned, excepting Vince to be here by now.

'When do you interview the first nanny, madam?' Esme asked, helping Timmy to right a train carriage that had fallen off the rails.

'Friday afternoon. Winifred telephoned to say she had organised for two possible candidates. One at three o'clock and one at four.' Alice fiddled with her strand of pearls. The idea of having a nanny looking after the children was practical, of course, but she felt ridiculously jealous of another woman being in the house and dealing with the children.

However, she had to be sensible. It was the done thing to have a nanny. Every family of her class had a nanny or two. She couldn't spend every moment with the children, even without the long hours she'd normally spend at the office, she was still a busy woman. A small part of her wondered if that would be true? Afterall, without *Sheer* what would she do with her time? Lunches with Sally or Helen, dinner parties, shopping and all those activities that she used to squash into the day between editorial meetings and deadlines would now be more leisurely.

She needed to do something though. She remembered Vince mentioning his plan to buy old houses and renovate them. She had said she'd be happy to partner with him in that. If they were to be a couple it could become a family business. Would he allow her to be his partner in every way?

The doorbell rang and Esme went downstairs to answer it.

Alice smiled at Libby on the rocking horse. 'One day you might have a real horse to ride. Would you like that?'

Libby's eyes narrowed in thought. 'Do you ride?'

'I do, yes. My horse is in Yorkshire stabled at my parents' house.'

'Would you ride with me?'

'Of course, sweetie. I would like that immensely.'

Libby nodded and kept rocking. It was the most she'd said all day. The poor child was still anxious, her eyes watching everything and everyone.

'Me?' Timmy chimed up, not even knowing what they were talking about.

Alice knelt down beside him. 'Yes, you, too.' She ruffled his light brown hair and he grinned up at her in his innocent and trusting way, so different to Libby. She knew at that moment she could never let anything happen to these children. She had to keep them safe.

Esme entered, a hand on the doorknob. 'Madam, there's a gentleman waiting for you in the drawing room. Doctor Geoffrey Garrett.'

'Doctor Garrett?' Intrigued, she stood. 'Stay with the children.'

'Refreshments?' Esme asked. It was her job to bring in a tray of refreshments when guests called, but the children couldn't be left alone.

'If needed, I'll go to the kitchen myself and ask Mrs Jones.' Alice checked her reflection in the mirror on the landing. Her hair needed cutting, the bob she wore was touching the collar of her dress. She peered closer, happy to see no grey yet amongst her black hair. Though with the last couple of weeks she'd not be surprised if they started appearing!

In the parlour, the handsome doctor stood by the fireplace, which glowed with red coals. He turned as she entered and smiled. 'Lady Mayton-Walsh, I hope you don't mind my unexpected call?'

'Not at all.' She noticed that outside it was completely dark and after inviting the doctor to sit, she went and drew the curtains across the sash windows.

'I simply wanted to check on you. Make sure you were resting.'

'That is most considerate, thank you. As you can see, I am well. A little sore, obviously, and tired, but nothing a good night's sleep won't cure.'

'Indeed.' He sat with his hands on his thighs and gazed around the stylish room.

'Drink? Or are you on duty or whatever it is called?'

'No, I'm not on duty, and, yes, a drink would be lovely, thank you.'

'Cocktail or a whiskey, or tea?'

'Whiskey with water, please.'

From the small bar in the corner of the room, Alice poured him a shot of whiskey and water and passed it to him. 'How did you find me?'

'I have my sources.' He chuckled. 'Your name is not common.'

'That is true.' She didn't know how to feel about him finding out where she lived. He'd gone to some trouble to visit, and she wasn't sure why.

He took a sip of the golden liquid. 'Are the children well?'

Alice took a seat opposite him, not having a drink herself. A glass of wine would have been perfect, but she was waiting for Vince to arrive first. 'Yes, completely well. They are upstairs playing. Mariah is asleep but she has been drinking her bottles of milk and has plenty of wet napkins which the hospital said to look for.' Was he checking up that she was looking after them properly?

'Excellent. If you have any doubts about Mariah, simply take her back to the hospital.'

'I have my own doctor in Kensington. If I am concerned about the children at any time, I shall visit him,' Alice said.

'Of course.' He paused. 'I know when we were in the motor car that you didn't want to go for dinner with me, but I can't seem to get you out of my mind.' He shrugged, the material of his expensive suit moving smoothly. 'I'd like us to become better acquainted. Is that possible?'

Alice clasped her hands together, thinking quickly. At any other time, she'd have said yes and gone to dinner with him. He was not only handsome but a doctor, one who was obviously kind and compassionate for he worked in the poor areas of East London when he could easily work somewhere more exclusive or have a private practise, yet he cared for the poor. This kind of man would be a perfect companion, his good looks would turn any woman's head. However, not hers, not this time. Vince was the only man she thought of, the man she wanted a future with and a family.

'The answer is still the same?' Doctor Garrett asked pre-empting her answer, a wry smile lifting the corners of his mouth.

'I'm sorry, but if I'd met you six months ago it might have been a different answer, but I must be honest, I'm in love with Vince.'

'Then he's a lucky man.'

'We've been friends for years, most of my life, but suddenly it's grown to something more and I owe it to myself and him to see where it goes, to give it a chance.' She didn't know why she was explaining it all to him.

He rose and threw back the last of his drink before putting the glass on the small table next to the sofa. 'I wish you all the very best.'

She stood and walked with him to the door and retrieved his coat and hat for him from the cupboard. 'Goodbye, Doctor Garrett.'

'Keep my card... Just in case.' He kissed her cheek and left the house.

Alice closed the door and leant against it for a moment. She'd said no to Doctor Garrett, and to Simon Delamont. Two men who wanted her. Two men who could give her very different lives. Neither of them was Vince though. Neither of them gave her the twist in the stomach, or the thump of an erratic heartbeat as Vince did. Still, she'd rejected good men. Vince better be worth it. She chuckled at herself and then went upstairs to the children.

Another hour passed without Vince arriving. A little annoyed he'd not come early as promised, she bathed the children, laughing at Timmy blowing the bubbles Esme made, again with Alice's good hair shampoo soap bought from Selfridges.

It grew later and Timmy fell asleep on the sofa, while Libby yawned fighting sleep wanting to see Vince.

By eight o'clock, Alice was fuming. She put the children to bed and gave Mariah a bottle, before putting her down in the cot. Libby wanted Vince to put her to bed and Alice had to work hard to convince her that she'd see him in the morning. Once again, Libby's trust was broken, and she turned away from Alice and faced the wall, cuddling the doll Alice had bought for her.

Alice stayed in the nursery while the children slept, looking out the window at the dark street below. All was quiet, only the odd taxi drove by, a strolling neighbour returning home. A cat stalked the shadows, but other than that there was no movement. No Vince.

Tired herself, Alice gave up on him. He'd obviously changed his mind about coming to the house. Had he regretted opening up to her, telling her his feelings? Their friendship had slipped into something more, emotions bared. Had that frightened him off?

Could they really have a relationship? Was it possible after all these years of friendship? Had he decided he'd made a mistake?

She undressed, washed and donned a silk nightdress, her mind swirling with thoughts. At every slight noise she'd pause, expecting it to be Vince, hoping it was.

She checked the children once more, leaving their door open so she could hear Mariah if she cried during the night.

Alice tried to read a book for an hour but the lack of a decent sleep in days made her eyes heavy. She snuggled down in the bed, annoyed and disappointed that Vince hadn't arrived. She'd been so looking forward to talking to him, spending some time together to discuss the future. Now she doubted they had one. He'd changed his mind and it hurt.

A few times during the night she woke to Mariah's little cries. At three o'clock she gave her a bottle of milk in the kitchen, sitting by the warm aga. Drowsy, she managed to stay awake enough to see that Mariah drank a few ounces.

By five the next morning Mariah was crying lustily. Alice quickly took her downstairs to the kitchen and made her another bottle. While the bottle of milk cooled in a jug of cold water, Alice changed her napkin and crooned to her. Although hungry, Mariah stopped crying and settled a little.

Alice was feeding her the bottle when Mrs Jones let herself in from the back stairs that led down from the street.

'Oh, madam. Did you have a bad night with her?'
Mrs Jones took off her outdoor things and hung
them up.

'No, she was quite good, really. She had a feed
at three. But she was very hungry by five and
has taken this bottle very greedily.' Alice smiled
proudly, lovingly. Holding Mariah gave her such a
sense of happiness.

'Well, if you'd like, I can get her wind up if you
want to go upstairs and lie down?'

'I don't need to lie down, but I will go up and
dress. Libby and Timmy will be awake soon.'

'I'll start making breakfast.' Mrs Jones refilled
the kettle before taking bacon and eggs from the
larder.

The door opened again, and Esme came in all
smiles at seeing Alice and Mariah in the kitchen.
'This is strange coming in and seeing this sight,
madam.' She laughed.

'Indeed. In years past I'd be returning home
from a party at this time of the morning, not up
feeding a baby.' Alice grinned. 'My wild reputation
is lost now I'm afraid.'

'And all the better for it, madam,' Mrs Jones
murmured wisely. 'Take the baby, Esme, so
madam can see to herself.'

Esme did as she was told and arms feeling empty,
Alice gave a lingering look at Mariah before going
upstairs.

Libby and Timmy still slept, and Alice took the
opportunity to wash and dress in a rose-coloured
wool dress with long sleeves and a flat collar. While
brushing her hair she heard the children wake
and chatter to each other. It sounded odd having
children in the house, but also comforting, as
though it was a natural occurrence.

Ready to face the day, Alice walked into the nursery. 'Good morning, sweet ones.'

Timmy raced to the bathroom, grinning as he sped by Alice. 'Good boy,' she told him, before turning to Libby. 'Are you hungry for some breakfast?'

'Is Mr Barton here?'

Alice sighed and shook her head. 'Not yet.'

'I want to see him.'

'So do I,' Alice admitted. He'd not only let her down but Libby, too. The girl had been through enough and Vince needed to earn her trust again. At the moment he wasn't going about it the right way.

'Can we go to him?'

She hesitated in answering. She didn't want Libby to see Vince if he had changed his mind about them. In fact, *she* didn't want to see him *at all* if he'd changed his mind. However, the future had to be decided.

Alice perched herself on the chair by the fireplace and beckoned Libby to her. The girl hesitated and then took a few steps, stopping beside Alice's knee as though frightened to come any closer.

Taking Libby's hand, Alice stroked it. 'Sweetie, you know I want the best for you and your brother and sister, don't you?'

Libby stared unblinkingly.

'And you know I want you all to stay here with me, to live with me in this house. For us to be a family, yes?'

Libby frowned but didn't take her hand out of Alice's grasp.

'Do you want to be here, too? Would you like me to take care of you?'

'And Mr Barton?'

'Forget about Mr Barton just for a moment,' Alice said gently. 'Would you be happy living here with me? I could become your guardian, the person who is responsible for you. Would you like that?'

'We wouldn't have to go back to that place?'

'The orphanage? No. You'd live with me until you're old enough to decide for yourself what you want to do.'

'You wouldn't leave us?' Libby's eyes stared into Alice's. 'Not ever?'

'I wouldn't leave you. Not ever. I promise. You, Timmy and Mariah would be adopted by me, I'd become your parent... your new mother.' Alice let out a pent-up breath. She was making an enormous decision, but one that felt completely right.

Libby took a step closer. 'We'd stay with you always?'

Alice's heart broke at the constant reassurance the child needed. 'Always, my darling.'

'We'd belong to you?'

'Yes. You'd become my children.'

'Truly? You won't leave us at some horrible place?'

'Not ever again.'

'Good.'

Relieved, Alice relaxed slightly. 'Let us get you dressed and then breakfast will be ready.'

Libby followed her to the wardrobe and selected a pretty pink and white dress. 'Is this mine?'

'All yours. Shall we put it on?'

'And me!' Timmy raced into the room, his pyjamas not pulled up properly.

'Yes, sweet boy. We'll get you dressed too.' Alice's heart melted as he hugged her leg, his face beaming with joy. He was such a loveable child.

It was gone nine o'clock before Alice felt able to leave the house. She'd spent the time eating breakfast with the children and holding Mariah. Esme was told not to do her normal duties and instead look after the children today. Alice had errands to run and must call in at the solicitors. She'd like to book an appointment to have her hair cut as well but overriding all her tasks was the desperate need to speak to Vince. To confront him about not coming to the house last night or even this morning. Surely, he knew that Libby was fragile. Why hadn't he come to reassure the child? Alice wanted to know why he was avoiding her, too.

A slow anger was building as she sped away from the house and towards the city centre. Before doing anything, she'd go to Limehouse and confront Vince. She wanted answers.

By the time she'd driven through the heavy traffic around the docks, she was frustrated and irritated. The morning rush of workers and transport slowed her down while her anger mounted.

On Island Row, she parked the motor car. Two men were talking outside of the last house in the row and watched her as she left the car. Alice knocked on Vince's door and waited. She'd expected the door to open quickly. Usually Happy or one of his workers were about, but there was no movement in the front window, no sound of hammering, so sign of them even being here.

She knocked loudly. 'Vince!'

No answer. Her anger grew. Where was he? Was he out getting supplies for the building work? Or had he made his way to her house, and they'd missed each other?

'Blast!' she cursed. Impulsively, she turned the door handle and was surprised when it gave, and the door opened. 'Vince?'

She stepped inside. Why hadn't he locked the door? 'Vince? Are you out the back?'

The front room was empty, cold. The fire hadn't been on. She shivered inside her thick fur coat. 'Vince?' she called up the stairs before going along to the kitchen.

On the table she saw a half-made sandwich, a bottle of milk and a cup of cold tea. Vince was many things, but untidy he wasn't. Something felt odd to her that he'd leave the house without tidying the kitchen table. Rats were a problem around here. Nothing was left out to encourage them into the house. She glanced out of the back door but there was no sign of him in the garden.

Something wasn't right. She could feel it. Returning to the bottom of the stairs, she wondered if she should go up. A tingle of fear shivered down her spine at the sudden thought that maybe Vince was up there, either sick, or not alone...

Never being one to back down from a challenge, or considered a coward, she steeled herself to climb the stairs. At the same time came a noise. Alice paused, one foot on the step. 'Vince?'

A noise came again, muffled. Alice glanced at the closed door of what would be the dining room. A room unfinished. The door was always closed to keep the heat in the front room.

Instinct made her step to the door and turn the handle. She flung open the door and gasped. Where the floor used to be was a gaping hole. The whole floor had collapsed into the cellar below. Shocked, Alice peered down at the blackness of it. This must be the reason why Vince wasn't here. He'd gone to get more building supplies perhaps?

She was about to shut the door when a moan reached her. She stilled. Had she heard correctly? Was it a rat? A cat? There was a sudden movement of something beneath a timber beam. Dust drifted up to her. The moan came again.

Then it hit her. Vince. Vince was down there!

She screamed his name.

Dropping her bag, she edged closer to the gaping, jagged hole. She had to get down there.

Inching herself down, placing her feet on a timber beam that slanted downwards, she grabbed hold of a piece of wood sticking out of the floor. Slowly, heart in her mouth, she lowered herself down, slipping on the beam every few inches.

'Vince. I'm coming.'

Halfway down, she stopped and bent low, peering, trying to see in the murkiness of the cellar. 'Vince?'

A moan was her answer.

'Darling, I'm nearly there. Hold on.' She couldn't see him, but she continued down the beam, grabbing hold of anything that might give her balance. Darkness closed in, the small window above no longer any use.

Suddenly, the beam broke beneath her. Her cry echoed around the cellar. She fell a few feet and landed on her knees on the brick floor. Her bruised hip throbbed in protest.

Gasping at the pain, she knelt and caught her breath. Deep shadows lurked in every corner. Broken beams and shards of wood criss-crossed the whole cellar. And there was the smell of gas...

Her eyes adjusted to the gloom and there, lying on his back under a large piece of the floor from above, Vince moaned.

Alice carefully picked her way over and under the debris to him, kneeling by his head. 'I'm here, my love.'

His eyes flickered and closed. Blood seeped from his hairline. His upper body was hidden in rubble. She needed help to get him out. It was an impossible task to do it by herself. 'Vince, I'm going to get help. I'll be back as soon as I can.'

Fearful of leaving him, she placed a kiss on his forehead, but his eyes didn't open. She looked up at the gaping floor above, knowing she'd have to climb the broken beams angling down, as the cellar stairs that went up to the kitchen door were blocked by rubble.

Like a monkey shimming up a tree, she grabbed a beam with both hands and climbed up on her toes. Her boots slipped a few times and the beam wobbled dangerously. Dust coated her, making her cough but she inched her way up until her fingers gratefully gripped the jagged floor above her head. Heaving herself over the edge, she lay for a moment, panting.

She didn't look back as she raced to the front door and outside. She stopped, realising she'd left her bag inside and hurriedly went back in to retrieve it before dashing for the car. Only then did she spot the two men still talking further down the row.

'Help! Please!' She ran towards them.

Both men threw down their cigarettes and jogged to her.

'What's wrong, luv?'

'My friend, he's trapped inside. The floor has collapsed, and he's buried in the cellar. I can smell gas.'

'Jesus!' One man, no more than twenty, scruffy and missing more teeth than he had, stared at his mate. 'We need the fire brigade or the ambulance!'

'You go, Larry, you're faster than me and get both of them!' his friend replied, pushing the other man on. 'I'll go and help the poor blighter if I can.'

'There's gas, Fred,' Larry warned.

'I'll be fine. Go, man!'

'He needs a doctor.' Alice ran back to the house with them. 'Doctor Garrett lives not far. Do you know him?'

'Aye, he runs a soup kitchen on the corner of Pennyfields and West India Dock Road. I know where he lives.' Fred, a small man with dark-green eyes, stopped at the front door. 'Larry run home and get me brother to run for the doctor.'

Larry waved and sprinted away.

Alice showed Fred into the collapsed dining room. 'Vince. Vince, I'm back. There's someone to help us.'

Fred took in the situation and shrugged off his threadbare coat and hat. 'I'll go down, miss. Hold this beam for me.'

Alice knelt and held the beam while Fred shimmied down it backwards into the darkness below. The beam trembled in her hands, and she wondered how much more it would take before breaking in half.

'Hell, it's mess down here.'

Alice watched Fred pick his way over the wreckage. 'He's over to the right. Shall I get a lamp?'

'No!' Fred yelled. 'Do not light anything. The gas is strong down here. Make sure no one has a cigarette anywhere near this place. Tell the fire brigade when they get here to have the gas turned off.'

Shaking with fear, Alice peered into the gloom. 'Can you see him?'

'Aye, I've found him. What's his name?'

'Vince. Vincent Barton,' she called down.

The noise of bricks and wood being moved carried up to her, that and billows of dust. She wanted to ask if Vince was still alive but couldn't get the words out.

'Miss? Can you throw down a blanket and a pillow? I can't free him by myself, but I can make him more comfortable.'

'Yes!' She scrambled away and into the front room where she found two cushions on the sofa. Then she raced upstairs and pulled the blankets from the bed. It was only as she was running back down the stairs did, she think that the upper floor might be unstable, too.

'I've got them.' She waited until Fred was in view and then threw them down to him.

After what seemed an eternity, Larry came into the house panting. 'They're coming.' He bent over, trying to catch his breath. His thin body shaking at all the effort.

'Thank you.' Alice wanted to do something for him, the man looked homeless, or simply extremely poor. He seemed ready to drop at any moment. 'Sit down. Rest.'

He slumped to the floor, face pale. 'I've not run like that in years...'

'I'll get you some water.' She quickly went into the kitchen and poured him some water.

'Thanks.' His blue lips smiled as she handed it to him. He gulped it down and then pushed himself to his feet. 'I'll wait outside and direct them here.'

Alice knelt by the edge and stared down at the rubble below and although not a praying woman, she prayed to whoever or whatever the fates were to keep Vince safe and alive.

She kept her vigil for another twenty minutes until she heard a commotion outside and then Doctor Garrett was kneeling beside her. 'Vince is hurt. Oh, God, I can't bear it. You must help him, please.' The sight of the doctor, of help arriving, made her chest tight and tears burn behind her eyes. 'Please save him. I beg you.'

'Calm down. I'll do the best I can. I would have been here sooner but was stitching up a deeply cut knee on the docks.' He shrugged off his coat and placed it beside her with his hat. 'I'm coming down,' he called.

'A man is down there with Vince.' She held the beam for him, not feeling strong enough and was glad when Larry knelt beside her and took a firmer grip. Together they held the shaking wood until Doctor Garrett was safely down and then lost in the dark.

'You need a rest, miss,' Larry whispered.

'I'll rest when I know Vince is safe.'

Larry turned his head at a noise outside. 'Someone is here.' He left and she gazed down at the blackness, trying to see any movement.

'Can you move aside, madam?' A burly fireman came beside her and took stock of the situation. 'I can smell gas.'

'Yes.' She slowly rose to her feet.

'Right, outside now.' He took her elbow.

'No, I can't leave Vince!'

'You can and you will do, madam!' He led her outside, ignoring her protests, his strong fingers clamped on her elbow.

Immediately instructions were shouted to the other firemen. Alice stood across the street with Larry. They were told to not come any closer.

'If the gas catches it'll blow this whole street,' Larry murmured, taking another step back, his eyes worried.

The firemen took ladders down from their truck and started knocking on doors, telling residents to evacuate the buildings. Larry soon was helping them, leaving Alice alone to stand and watch, feeling so helpless. Mothers with crying babies and young children, old men and women began gathering at the end of the street. A policeman walking by took charge of them, his whistle blowing any time a cheeky child slipped the cordon and skipped towards the house.

A sleek W & G Du Cros ambulance arrived, its paintwork shining. Two officers jumped down and opened the back doors, a stretcher litter was taken inside the house.

Alice itched to go in after them but caught the senior fireman's eyes and he silently shook his head. She was desperate for news. A cold wind blew down the row and she huddled into her coat, guilty to have such a warm garment when the rest of the street's inhabitants were shivering in thin coats or none at all. She'd gladly have given her coat to one of them, but she wore nothing very warm underneath, just her dress and a silk slip. She couldn't risk catching a chill when Vince needed her.

For another hour she waited, her feet frozen, her nose cold to touch. More fire brigades arrived and two more policemen. Families were allowed inside their homes, the gas securely turned off, though a few remained out in the elements their curiosity overriding their concern of the cold.

Then suddenly there was movement. The two ambulance men came out carrying Vince on a stretcher litter, Doctor Garrett not far behind.

Alice ran to them, not caring of anything but seeing Vince.

'He's unconscious, Alice,' Doctor Garrett told her. He was covered in dust, his attention on Vince. 'He's going straight to Poplar Hospital.'

Her heart twisted. 'He'll survive though, won't he?'

The glance he gave her didn't seem hopeful. 'He's in a bad way. Prepare yourself.'

She thought her legs would give way beneath her, but he caught her to him as they lifted Vince into the back of the ambulance.

'I'll drive you to the hospital.' Garrett led her over to her car.

In silence they drove the short distance to the hospital. He turned down Brunswick Road and then right in Athol Street and parked the car.

Without speaking, Garrett took her arm and they walked into the west wing of the hospital. He told her to wait, and he'd come and fetch her as soon as he'd seen Vince and had some news. 'I maybe gone some time. Don't fret. I'll be back as soon as I can.'

She sat in a high-ceilinged corridor on a cold wooden bench, watching nurses and doctors walking by, the odd patient on crutches. She stared down at her dress, filthy and covered in dust and dirt from kneeling, her hands were grimy, and two nails were broken that she hadn't even realised.

The day drew on. Through the windows, she watched the wind whip the clouds across the sky. Once again, she longed for summer. For the blue skies, for the warmth, the flowers and the smiles that a sunny day put on people's faces. She wanted to take the children to the parks, watch them run in the sunshine. She thought of Libby, of telling her that Vince was sick in hospital. The poor girl will be scared. How was she or Timmy to understand how ill he was? Their young lives had been filled with tragedy, they didn't need this added to it.

She closed her eyes for a while, sick of looking out the window, a headache throbbing and her hip aching.

'Lady Mayton-Walsh.'

Alice sprang forward having dozed.

Doctor Garrett came towards her, a soft expression on his face. 'Sorry it's been so long.'

'How is he?' Alice jerked to her feet, noticing it was dim in the corridor now. A light had been switched on at one end and out the window dusk was falling.

'Alive. Just.' He took her arm. 'Come with me. You can see him only for a minute, then I'll take you home to rest.'

She didn't argue with him, her only thought was to see Vince. He linked her arm through his and walked with her through the corridors of the hospital to the room where Vince lay surrounded by several nurses who were attending to him.

Alice gasped. He looked dead. The paleness of his face, his complete stillness unnerved her. She hesitated in the doorway. Vince lay, his head heavily bandaged and with a cage covered by a blanket over his body. She fought back tears, not wanting to be weak. Vince needed her strong and capable. Slowly she went to him, her eyes on him, only him, not all the paraphernalia around him.

'He's sustained a lot of damage,' Garrett murmured. 'His chest was trapped, squashing his lungs. He has broken ribs, internal bruising and he received a serious knock on the head. They've drilled a small hole in his skull to allow the pressure to ease in his brain.'

'No!' She swayed in shock. Was that even such a thing? Surely, he would die from that alone? Her heart twisted in agony at the notion of losing him.

Garrett took her arm and sat her on a chair. 'He's in a critical state. The next few hours and days will be vital.'

'He must live.'

'He'll not be moved to the men's ward until he's stable.' Garrett checked the notes a nurse was writing down.

Alice focused on Vince. He looked pale, eyes closed. She took his hand gently, not wanting to hurt him. 'Vince,' she whispered. 'It's Alice. I'm here. You're safe now. All you have to do is jolly well get better.' She stroked his check, slight stubble was shadowing it. 'You must pull through. I need you. The children do, too. We all want you home.' She swallowed back tears. 'I love you so much. Fight, my darling. Fight for us.'

'We really must leave him to rest.' Doctor Garrett stepped beside her. 'He won't wake for hours. Come back in the morning.'

She nodded and brought Vince's hand up to kiss it. 'I'll be back first thing, my darling.' She hated walking away, every part of her wanted to stay by his side, but the nurse's stern looks made her finally turn away.

'I'll drive you home.' Doctor Garrett walked beside her down the corridor.

'No...' Suddenly she needed to be by herself. 'Thank you, but I'll be perfectly fine.'

'You can't drive, not after the day you've had.'

'I can. I'll take it slowly. Besides, it's out of your way.'

'I don't mind.' His smile was comforting.

'Thank you, but really, I insist. I need to be on my own.' She shook his hand. 'You have been absolutely amazing. Truly, you deserve a medal.'

'Hardly.' He looked embarrassed. 'If you're sure you'll be all right?'

She smiled and quickly walked away before she cried. She waited until she was in her car before breaking down and sobbing. Vince nearly died, still could. The shattering thought brought her undone. She cried until her head pounded.

Then, wiping her face with a handkerchief, she finally started the engine and drove carefully home to the children.

# Chapter Fifteen

Alice paced the floor of the parlour, glancing out of the window at any sound. She'd telephoned Brandon and Prue last evening and they'd managed to get the night train from York to London. They'd be arriving that morning.

Upstairs, Esme played with the children. Libby had taken the news of Vince's accident badly, putting herself to bed and not speaking again. Timmy, too young to understand, had carried on as normal, his cheery manner and giggles gladdened Alice's sore heart. Last night she read them a bedtime story of Peter Rabbit, which had caught Libby's interest. The girl was fascinated by books and Alice needed to enrol her in a school. That task was put on the top of her bulging list of things to do.

Throughout the night, she'd tossed and turned, exhausted but her mind too fearful about Vince to allow her to sleep. So, she had risen early and gone to the children's bedroom. Mariah as though sensing her unease woke and Alice had taken her down to the kitchen and fed her a bottle, content to just sit and hold her, even when the baby had fallen asleep again.

The sound of a car brought her to the window. She sighed in relief as Brandon and Prue climbed out of the taxi. She rushed downstairs to open the door, hugging Brandon before he had a chance to step inside.

'There now.' He returned the embrace. 'Calm down. Everything will be all right.'

She leaned back, tears dripping over her lashes. 'You cannot promise that at all.' She stepped from him to hug Prue. 'Thank you for coming so quickly.'

'As if we wouldn't. Poor darling Vince.' Prue touched her face, her eyes soft with concern. 'You look awful. And crying! Goodness, I don't think I've ever seen you cry. Come on, let's sort this out.' Taking her hand, Prue led her back up to the parlour, while Brandon carried the suitcases inside.

'I'm eager to see these three orphans you've taken in,' Prue said, taking off her outerwear. 'But they can wait a little longer.' She sat on the sofa, her stomach large with child. 'Now, Vince. What is the latest?'

Brandon divested his coat and hat, his expression closed. 'Have you telephoned the hospital this morning?'

'Doctor Garrett called me an hour ago. He knew I'd be frantic and that I had a telephone.'

'And?' Brandon prompted.

'Vince survived the night, but he's not woken yet.' Her chin wobbled. Her emotions were a mess, and she fought the constant need to cry, which was so unlike her. She never cried. Even when her first husband died, she had only allowed herself a day to wallow, to mourn and then she'd picked herself up and carried on, throwing herself into war activities. However, this accident with Vince had turned her into a blubbering sop.

'We'll go to the hospital and see what we can do,' Brandon decided, picking up his coat. 'I should have kept the taxi. Have you got your motor? Poplar, isn't it? God knows how he's being treated there. Why he had to live in the East End I don't know. We should talk to someone about having him moved to a better hospital. I have a friend, a surgeon, who works at St Thomas's Hospital. We'll have him transferred there straight away.'

'Slow down!' She rubbed her forehead. Brandon was taking control and although she needed him here, he was moving too fast, making decisions without consulting her. 'Brandon, he's too ill to be moved,' Alice panicked. 'He was lucky to make it through the night. I won't have him disturbed.'

'Let us speak with the doctors first. Shall we go?' Brandon snapped, worried for his best friend.

'Brandon, stop.' Prue pushed up from the sofa, an annoyed frown on her face. 'I know you're worried. You've been beside yourself all the way down here on the train but calm down. Alice needs us just as much as Vince, more so, as he is being cared for by medical staff. Now, let Alice take me up to meet the children, and then when they are comfortable with me, Alice can go with you.'

'There's no time for any of that,' Brandon said impatiently, then immediately apologised.

Prue kissed his cheek. 'I know you're concerned. Just give us five minutes.'

Alice, grateful that Prue was staying with the children, opened the door to their bedroom. The large room was littered with toys, but Libby and Timmy seemed happy enough. Esme was changing Mariah's napkin and smiled happily when she saw Prue.

'I have come to help you, Esme,' Prue said, bending down beside Timmy. 'Hello, I'm Mrs Forster. I do like your train set very much. My little boy, Henry, has one just like it. Shall we play?'

Timmy grinned and quickly showed Prue how to link the engine to the carriages.

Prue glanced up at Libby. 'What a splendid rocking horse, Libby.'

Libby frowned at her. 'You know my name?'

'Why, yes. Alice has told me all about you. We are best friends and I hope I can be your friend, too.'

Libby shrank back. 'You aren't taking me away?'

Alice went to her and held her around the waist. 'Sweetie, I told you. You are staying here with me. No one will ever take you away. I promise.'

Libby gazed up at Alice. 'When is Mr Barton coming home?'

'As I told you last night, he's very sick. He needs to stay in hospital for a little while.'

'He won't die like my mam?'

'We simply don't know, dearest. But whatever happens, you're safe here. This is your home now.'

'So,' Prue said brightly, 'I think we should have a tea party!' She clapped her hands, grinning at Libby. 'You can be the host of it, Libby. Can we arrange that, Esme?'

'Absolutely, madam.' Esme placed Mariah in her cot and left the room.

Prue grasped Alice's hand. 'Go. Brandon will be downstairs pacing like a caged lion. The children will be fine with me and Esme.'

'Oh, I have appointments to engage a new nanny this afternoon.' Alice had forgotten about them. Her commitments were stacked high. She'd not been to the office, nor seen the Brannings.

'You trust me to interview them?'

Alice nodded. Prue knew her very well and was a mother herself. Henry's nanny was a lovely country woman who adored Henry. That's the same kind of person Alice wanted for the children.

'Leave it to me then. Concentrate on Vince.' Prue kissed Alice's cheek and then declared that Libby should tell her all about the doll's house and Timmy simply must give her a turn at the spinning top.

Reassured that the children would be fine, Alice hurriedly left the room.

At the hospital, a nurse showed Alice and Brandon to Vince's room. He lay exactly as he was when Alice left him the evening before, eyes closed, not moving.

'Well, old chap,' Brandon murmured, patting Vince's arm. 'What a to-do this is. I must confess I don't like to be scared like this. Are you paying me back for that time I fell on the mountain in Italy, and you had to carry me down in a storm?' he joked before sobering. 'Payback is noted, good friend.'

Vince didn't open his eyes or move.

They sat opposite each other on either side of Vince's bed. Alice held Vince's hand, silently begging him to open his eyes. 'He's so still. I can't bear it, truly I can't.'

'You love him,' Brandon stated suddenly.

Alice glanced at her brother. 'I do.'

'How astonishing. I never expected you to fall in love with Vince. You've known him since you were a young girl and never considered him as a love interest.'

She gazed at Vince's handsome face. 'No, I didn't, not at all. Then when he announced he was engaged to Diana... well... something changed in me.'

'You expected him to always be by your side, yours alone to have. The thought of him being taken away woke you up to new feelings.' Brandon smiled as though pleased.

'That is it exactly.'

Brandon crossed one knee over the other. 'Emotions can be extraordinary things. Vince has loved you all his life, I think. Wouldn't admit it to a soul though, but I knew.'

'We haven't properly talked it through. We were going to discuss the future the night of his accident.'

'Discuss it?' Brandon frowned. 'How formal.'

'Yes, I suppose it sounds that way. My feelings for Vince are new and rather surprising after all these years. For Vince, his feelings have been hidden for so long, it's not something either of us are used to voicing.' She smiled softly at Vince, willing him to wake up. 'I didn't even realise I loved him until a few months ago. It crept up on me without warning. I needed time to process the meaning, the consequences.'

'Love has no rules, dear sister,' Brandon said fondly. 'I'm happy for you both, if that's truly what you both want.'

'It is. We want each other, and the children. To be a family.'

'Mother and Father are still in shock about the children,' he told her. 'I am, too, I suppose. Are you absolutely certain this is what you want?'

'They are orphans. Vince loves them and so do I. It surprised me how quickly I grew feelings for them. I watched Marish being born. I helped her to take her first breath. It was truly a magical event and I felt honoured to be a part of it. Then her mother died and all I wanted to do was hold the baby and not let her go. Vince and I both tried turning our backs on the children. We placed them in an orphanage, but Libby ran away, taking Timmy and Mariah with her. Searching for them frightened me terrifically. I thought I'd never see them again and then I knew I needed to take care of them.' She let out a long breath. The strength of her feelings still overwhelmed her. The recent events had taken a heavy toll on her emotions.

'Prue says it'll be great for you, to have children to love and care for, and to have that love given in return. You've been alone too long. Now you have sold *Sheer* you can devote your life to the children and perhaps slow down a little. Your frantic life needs to be let go.'

'Absolutely. I didn't realise how unhappy I was until the children came into my life. They bring me unexpected joy. They bring us both joy, for Vince adores them, too.'

'Will you marry him despite his loss of fortune?'

A warm glow flooded through her chest. 'I hope so, yes.'

'And become plain Mrs Barton?'

'There's nothing I want more. We will adopt the children and we will all be Bartons.'

Brandon stood and gave her a wink. 'Then this chap needs to wake up and make an honest woman of my sister. I shall go and find a doctor and see what's to be done.'

Left alone with Vince, Alice leaned over and kissed him lightly on the lips. 'Please wake up, darling. We all need you desperately, especially me.'

But Vince remained still and unresponsive.

For two days, Alice spent most of her time by his bedside, Brandon also. Vince remained unresponsive, unmoving. The worry mounted with each hour as Alice sat watching him, begging him to stir, to wake up and smile at her.

Day and night merged, Alice only knew the difference because Brandon insisted she went home to bed each night. Though, of course she didn't sleep but lay staring at the ceiling waiting for the hours to pass, or she'd creep into the children's bedroom and watch them sleeping, or give Mariah her bottle. Then, when daylight broke, she would return to Vince's side and hold his hand.

On the third day after the accident, Alice sat beside Vince's bed. Brandon had gone to speak to a nurse about making two cups of tea for them.

'Lady Mayton-Walsh?' Doctor Garrett entered the room. He'd been a constant sight in the last few days. 'How are you today?'

'I'm well, thank you.' She felt the opposite, if truth be told, but she didn't mention the state of exhaustion and numbness she felt.

'I have some news. I've just been informed by a friend, who is a local councillor for the parish where Mr Barton lives, that the health authority have confirmed that Mr Barton's house has been condemned and must be demolished.'

'What?' She stared in shock.

'I'm very sorry. Broken gas pipes and unstable foundations are the cause. Apparently overnight further subsidence has occurred. The adjoining wall to Mr Barton's house and his neighbour has collapsed.'

'Goodness, no! Was anyone hurt?'

'No, thankfully. The family heard the rumble and quickly vacated the building, so I was told. The authorities did an inspection this morning and declared the houses cannot be repaired to a suitable standard by Mr Barton within twenty-one days as is the rule. They are unliveable and while Mr Barton is ill, he cannot instruct his wishes or argue the case. Water is now flooding the cellars. The whole terrace will be knocked down and the people rehoused.'

'Gracious. Vince will be utterly devastated.'

'The hospital was informed because when Mr Barton is well, he cannot return to his residence, and we needed to be aware that any ongoing treatment cannot be done at his home.'

'He will come to live with me.' There was no question about it in her mind.

He nodded. 'Yes, that is what I presumed and that he wouldn't need to go to a convalescent hospital.'

'No. I shall hire a nurse if needed.'

'Very good.'

'I have to retrieve his belongings from his home.'

'Then I suggest you do it quickly before the house is boarded up and made secure until the builders can demolish it.'

Brandon stood in the doorway. 'What's happened?'

Alice grabbed her bag. 'Come, I'll tell you along the way. Thank you, Doctor Garrett.'

They drove to Island Row but found the entrance to the row barricaded. Brandon parked on Commercial Road, and they walked back to the terrace.

Alice saw Happy out the front of the house, his workers nailing boards over the windows. 'Happy!'

'Ah, madam.' Happy shook hands with Brandon when she made the introductions. 'Terrible business this is. I couldn't believe it when we heard the news. All that work and money wasted. How is Mr Barton?'

'No change. Still unconscious.' Alice stared at the house. 'Where were you on that morning when I found Mr Barton?'

'I'd gone to get more supplies. I'd told Mr Barton I'd be late arriving for work. I wish to God I hadn't gone now. I could have found him a few hours earlier.'

'Why did that room collapse?' Brandon asked.

'Weak foundations down in the cellar beneath. Though we didn't know about that until we'd finished some of the other rooms and then started to strip back the dining room. It wasn't an important room, Mr Barton said. So, we did the other rooms first. When we did turn our attention to the dining room, we noticed the cellar underneath had cracks in the walls, water leaked in at times when it rained. I told Mr Barton to not enter the cellar until we'd shored it up with timber posts and got an engineer down there. While we waited for an engineer to inspect the cellar, Mr Barton said to carry on with the rest of the other side of the house. He was eager to get as much work done as possible, to make it liveable. The engineer was due to inspect it this week. He came, of course, but it was too late. He still gave his findings to the authorities. They told me this morning to board the place up. The whole terrace is unstable and will be pulled down.' Happy shook his head sadly. 'These folks are all out of a home now.'

'A shocking situation,' Alice murmured, thinking of the poor families that rented from Vince now homeless.

'Will Mr Barton recover?' Happy asked quietly.

'He's in a rather terrible state.' Alice sighed deeply. 'He's had an operation on his skull and his chest was crushed, his lungs... It's very serious...' Her voice trembled.

'God bless him.' Happy shook his head. 'He's a good man. Decent.'

Alice felt her throat tighten. She took a deep breath, needing to focus. 'We need to gather Mr Barton's things.'

'Aye, of course.' Happy straightened briskly. 'We've put some stuff into crates already. I was going to store them in my timber yard until he was well enough to collect them.'

'Thank you. Can you still do that, please? We'll organise collection as soon as Mr Barton is out of hospital,' Alice said, injecting positivity into her tone. 'But we do need his clothes and personal things.'

'Aye, aye.' Happy opened the door into the dim house, the place Vince had been so proud to work on, to make his home. Now, with the windows boarded, a dismal gloom filled the rooms as though the house knew its fate.

'Let me go up, madam.' Happy put a hand out to bar the way inside. 'I'll collect all his clothes and bring them down. We have to be quick. We aren't meant to be inside.'

'Miss?'

Alice spun around and smiled at Larry and Fred. 'I am so pleased to see you both. I wanted to say thank you for all your help.'

Larry shrugged. 'Anyone would have done what we did.'

Fred agreed. 'How is he?'

'Not great, I'm afraid.'

'No. A night spent buried in a cellar is bound to make you unwell.' Fred stared down at the road.

'I'm here to collect some of his belongings. The whole terrace is condemned.'

'Aye, we heard this morning.' Larry's dirty face looked stricken. 'Me sister has no where to go and has six kids. I live with her, but I'm not worried about meself. I can sleep anywhere. Slip into a warehouse and kip the nights there, but she and the little 'uns...'

'Me aunt is coming to live with me and the missus,' Fred added. 'Couldn't see her on the streets, could we? Though how we'll manage I don't know. I've not had work for three weeks.'

'Try not having any for three *months*.' Larry scratched his head under his cap. 'I'm not even fussy anymore in what I do.'

'I told you not to argue with the stevedore, but you didn't listen,' Fred mumbled.

'Stevedore?' Alice asked curiously. She'd never heard the word before.

'A stevedore is a cargo loader on the wharf. The one we had, where we used to work, was a right tyrant,' Fred supplied. 'He's hated us ever since we went on strike in twenty-six.'

Larry muttered, *bastard*, under his breath, but Alice heard him. She knew the East End suffered in the General Strike, and conditions for dockers were not favourable for job security.

Unemployment was rife in the area and living conditions were below average, slums in fact. She only had to look around this very row to see how poorly people lived.

'It's a ghastly business.' Alice felt terrible for them. She reached into the car and grabbed her purse out of her bag. She had four ten shilling notes and she gave them two each. 'This might help you both, for a little while at least.'

'Nay, miss, we can't take your money,' Fred protested.

'Yes, you can, for your families. You helped my friend, probably saved his life by going for assistance as quickly as you did. It's the least I can do. I wish I could do more.'

'Ta very much.' Larry tipped his hat to her, tucking the notes into his trouser pocket.

'I wish you both well.' Alice returned to the house just as Happy carried down two suitcases from upstairs.

Brandon took them from him. 'Thank you. If you can manage to get the rest out without injury to yourself, of course, we'd appreciate it.'

'Will do, sir.' Happy shook hands with them both. 'I'll take what I can to my timber yard.'

Alice gave Happy her card. 'In case you need to contact me about anything.'

'Right you are, madam.'

Driving back to the hospital, sadness filled Alice. 'Vince is going to be so upset when he learns the terrace is to be pulled down.'

'He should never have gone to live there in the first place,' Brandon tutted. 'He's a gentleman not a docker.'

'It was something that he owned when he'd lost everything else. Now it's worth nothing.' Alice gazed out of the window as the hospital came into view.

'He can sell the land. Start again. His pride won't allow him to live off you for any length of time. Be prepared for that.' Brandon parked the car and helped her out.

'Then we need to get him involved in something then. Like the building company. Now I've sold *Sheer* I can invest in the building company and that will give Vince a goal to look forward to.' She sounded more confident than she felt. Vince was fiercely proud. He'd take nothing from her, she knew.

'All that can wait.' Brandon took her elbow as they walked to the hospital. 'Let us get him well first.'

*** 

Noise filtered into Vince's subconscious. He fought against it. The noise continued, disturbing him. He didn't move or open his eyes, but lay still, trying to determine what the noise was, what it meant. The pitch became low, deeper, but then was joined by another sound, higher. The two tones joined and became indistinguishable, then faded. Silence. He relaxed and then there was nothing.

Something disturbed him again, annoying him. A touch. He wanted to respond but couldn't. There was nothing he could do. Panic attacked him. Rushing up through his consciousness, pulsating through his brain, causing a sharp stab of agony. He cried out. What was happening? He couldn't see or move. He felt restraints, more pain, then quiet, serenity, no more discomfort...

He woke with a start. He stared at a white ceiling. A blurred face appeared over him. A woman he didn't know. His chest tightened in panic.

'There now, Mr Barton. Rest easy. You're in hospital. I'm Nurse Elton. Stay calm. You've woken up from a very long sleep.'

Hospital.

Vince slowly moved his head, feeling the resistance of bandages. The nurse came into focus more clearly.

She smiled at him. 'How do you feel?'

'I...' He licked his lips, and she quickly wiped a damp cloth around his mouth.

'Are you in pain?'

He frowned, wondering if he was. Something certainly wasn't right with him, but he couldn't identify what it was. 'I don't know.'

She smiled again. 'I'll fetch the doctor. You must stay still now. Don't try to move until we come back.'

Left alone he lay staring at the ceiling. Slowly he lifted his hand, half afraid to do so. The movement cause a twinge in his chest. For some reason he couldn't breathe properly just shallow breaths, which alarmed him. He knew he needed to breathe to stay alive. God what was wrong with him? He started to panic. His fingers touched his bandaged head.

'Ah, the patient is awake!' An older man in a white coat entered the room with the nurse and came close to the bed. 'Do you know your name, sir?'

Vince blinked, wondering if it was some kind of test. 'Vin... cent... Bar...ton.'

'Excellent. Perfect!' The doctor turned to the nurse and issued rapid instructions and she left in a hurry.

His throat dry, Vince tried to speak again but the doctor held up his hand, stopping him.

'Now, my good man. I'm going to examine you and then if I'm satisfied by my findings, we'll make you more comfortable, yes? And there's a very pretty lady out there desperate to see you. She's been waiting days for you to wake.'

Alice. Vince instantly wanted to see her, then registered the word *days*. 'Alice... waiting days?'

'Ah, you know who I mean then. Bravo. Yes, three days in total since your accident.' The old man grinned. 'Right, let us begin.'

A long time later, Vince felt exhausted from all the prodding, tests and questions, but at last the doctor gave permission for Alice to come in. Vince was surprised and pleased to see Brandon with her.

She ran to him and kissed him on the lips, not caring who saw. 'You gave me such a fright. Don't ever do that to me again.'

'I'll try not,' he replied softly, his head and ribs aching, but she had kissed him, and he wanted to relish it just for a moment.

'What's the verdict, Doctor? Is he *sensible*?' Brandon asked, giving Vince a cheeky wink.

The doctor finished writing his notes. 'Pneumothorax. A collapsed lung, but that will improve with rest. We've taken the chest tube out. He has broken ribs on the left side as well as bruising and soreness elsewhere on his body. More importantly, his head wound is responding to treatment and that Mr Barton has woken and spoken gives us great hope for a full recovery in time.' He peered over the rim of his glasses. 'Ten minutes. That's all you have. You can come back tomorrow for a short time, but Mr Barton needs complete rest. He *shall* have it.' The doctor's stern glare prevented any argument. He walked out with the nurse hurrying behind him.

Alice gripped Vince's hand. 'There now. That's wonderful news, isn't it?'

Tiredness overcame him, the best he could do was a small smile.

'We'll have you home before you know it,' Brandon declared.

Alice whipped around to scowl at him. 'Brandon!'

Vince sensed something was wrong. 'Alice?'

'It's nothing, nothing at all.'

'You're lying.' He watched her. She always was a terrible liar.

Brandon sat on the chair beside him. 'Listen, old fellow. There's some bad news about your house.'

'He doesn't need to know now, Brandon,' Alice snapped.

'Tell me,' Vince murmured. Over the last hour, his memory of the accident had come back, and he knew he'd been in some kind of a mishap at the terrace house. He'd fallen, or something had fallen on him.

'The house has unstable foundations. The wall between your house and its neighbour crumbled. No one was hurt though, but the damage is severe. Water is flooding into the cellars now and everything is rather volatile,' Alice explained gently. 'The gas pipes are broken as well. The authorities have condemned the whole terrace. Everyone has to move out.'

'They are tearing it all down?' He couldn't believe it.

'Yes. The whole terrace will be flattened. You'll just have the land,' Brandon told him.

'I'm homeless.' After all the hard work he'd done to make the dwelling liveable, comfortable. That was his home. He'd spent money on it. What was he going to do now? His head pounded. And his remaining tenants... they'd be homeless.

Alice rubbed her thumb over the back of his hand. 'Do not worry. You'll come and live with me. The children will be so *absolutely* delighted to see you.'

Vince winced. He'd not thought of the children once since waking up. What was wrong with him to not think of them? He wanted to be their father, to have a family, yet he'd not given them a thought. Perhaps it was a sign he shouldn't adopt them. He had no home to give them now, but Alice did. Alice had it all. A nice house, money... What did he have to offer anyone? Nothing. Alice and the children deserved more than that.

'Vince?' Alice prompted.

'I won't be a burden on you.' He gazed down at her hand holding his, not able to meet her eyes. He slipped his hand away from hers. 'I'm not the man you deserve, Alice.'

'I think that is for me to decide.' Her voice sounded hard. 'Don't you dare turn away from me, Vincent Barton. I simply won't allow it.'

'Alice.' Brandon came to her side. 'Perhaps Vince needs some sleep.'

'Yes, I do.' He turned his head away and closing his eyes, he shut out her distraught face. He suffered a pain in his chest that had nothing to do with his collapsed lung.

# Chapter Sixteen

'He doesn't want to come here, Alice,' Brandon told her.

She stared at her brother in surprise. 'That is ridiculous. Where else will he go? Not to a hotel. He needs nursing. I can hire a nurse to take care of him.'

'He's coming home to Yorkshire with us.' Brandon's eyes held an apology. 'We'll employ a nurse for him.'

'It's only been three weeks since he was injured. Surely the doctor will not allow him to leave so soon?'

'He's recovering well and wants to leave. They want to book him into a convalescent hospital somewhere, but Vince won't have it. Insists he's had enough of doctors and nurses and hospitals. He only agreed to a nurse once I suggested that he come home with us.'

Alice glanced away, hurt. For the last three weeks, Vince had totally withdrawn from her. Last week he had told her that he didn't want her to visit him and made it quite clear that she should adopt the children without him. She'd been so angry she'd stormed from the hospital and not been back.

Instead, she'd spent her time on other things, enrolling Libby into a nearby school, buying her books, and treating the children to whatever she thought would make them happy. She wanted to make them feel settled, loved and secure. She spent long periods of time with them, holding Mariah, listening to Timmy's tales as he played with his toys, and joyously, she had begun earning Libby's trust slowly. A few days ago, she had visited her solicitor and formally applied to adopt the three children.

She'd hosted a farewell dinner at the Savoy for all the *Sheer* staff and the Brannings. Saying goodbye to them all, closing a chapter on her life had left her terribly emotional and she'd cried openly in front of her staff for the first time, making them all teary and wishing her the very best.

Her current emotional state was trying her patience. She'd always been a hard businesswoman, she had to be to make her magazine a success. However, lately, since meeting the children and then confessing to Vince her true feelings, then his accident, she felt as though tears were always hovering behind her eyes. Saying goodbye to Prue a week ago at the train station, she'd been in a flood even though she'd see Prue soon for her grandmama's birthday party at the end of March. She'd never been so emotional. A simple touch from Timmy's hand when he wanted to show her something, or a windy smile from Mariah made the tears well.

She must get a grip of her feelings. She was becoming a stranger to herself with all this crying.

'Alice?' Brandon tilted his head, a question in his eyes.

She'd not heard him, lost in her thoughts. 'Sorry?'

'I said, you need to give Vince some time. He's lost a lot in the last twelve months. The accident was the last straw.'

'But I'm here to help him. I told him how I felt about him. He said he felt the same.'

'Then perhaps you need to tell him again?'

She glanced at the clock. Twenty past two.

'Go and visit him.'

'He doesn't want me to.'

'And when have you ever listened when you've been told no?' Brandon smiled. 'I need to write some letters, anyway, so go alone.'

Alice left the room and found Esme coming up the stairs from the kitchen. 'I'm going out.'

'Very good, madam.'

'Tell Nanny I'll spend time with the children when I return.'

'Yes, madam. Though I don't think she'll be back for another hour or so. She promised Timmy he could feed the ducks at Hyde Park and Mariah has been fed so she's got a few hours before she needs to return. I told her I'd keep an eye on the baby while she was out.'

Alice's heart skipped a little at the notion of the nanny taking the children out for such long walks, but Miss Hilda Knatchbull was a delightful and trustworthy nanny. Prue had done a fabulous job in hiring her and making sure the new nanny was exactly the right fit for the children, while Alice had been spending days at the hospital. Nanny slept in the other spare room for now, but Alice was going to make the attic a bedroom for her, so she had her own privacy. She'd also wanted the other spare room vacant for Vince, but this news that he wasn't coming here, and instead going to Yorkshire with Brandon annoyed her tremendously.

She drove to the hospital, her anger at him growing with every mile. How dare he dismiss her and the feelings she had as though they were of no importance?

When she reached his ward where he'd been moved to, a long room he shared with five other men, she paused to gather herself. She straightened her navy-coloured skirt and long-sleeved cream silk bouse. Spring weather was starting to make an appearance in London as February drew to a close.

She spotted him reading the newspaper, sitting up in bed. He looked so much better than when she saw him last. There was colour on his clean-shaven cheeks and his hair, shaved short for the head operation was growing a little. She'd never seen him with such short hair, but it suited him.

Aware she was staring, she quickly walked up to the bed. 'Good afternoon, Vince.'

He lowered the newspaper onto his lap. 'Alice.' He looked shocked to see her.

'Brandon tells me you are returning to Yorkshire with him?' She cut straight to what was important. She couldn't stand small talk.

'That's true.'

'Why would you not come to me?' She hated belittling herself to ask the question.

'There is more room at the manor. You have a full house.'

'The children want to see you. Libby, especially, is missing you.'

'I'm sure you are handling them perfectly well without me.' He seemed uncomfortable.

'That is not the point, Vince. Libby wants to see *you*. *We* want you home with us.'

'Your house is not my home. My home has gone, along with everything else I had.'

'Not everything. I'm still here.'

'You are not mine.'

'I could be. I don't see why I'm not. I thought it was what we both wanted.'

Vince shook his head slowly. 'I have nothing to give you. I will not marry you as a man with nothing. I am *nothing*.' The statement was uttered coldly, harshly.

'A house isn't important to me, Vince Barton, but you are. Am I to beg?'

'It will do no good, Alice. I have made up my mind. There can be no us.'

'What about what I want?'

His expression tightened. 'You want to be lumbered with a homeless man? A man with very little income, a small amount of money in the bank and little else? A man with no future? Is that what you want, Alice, because I don't believe it, not for a moment.'

'I want you, Vince, just you. The rest we can sort out. The rest is simply details. We can grow a business together, and a family. It's all there ready for you to claim. Why won't you?'

'And live off your money?' He laughed mockingly. 'Not a chance, my lady.'

That he called her his old nickname brought her undone. Tears filled her eyes. 'You are rejecting me, Vince?'

'Am letting you go, finally. There's a difference. It is something I should have done many years ago.'

She swallowed the lump in her throat. 'I thought you were a better man than that. Obviously, I was wrong, very wrong. In truth, you are a coward.' She lifted her chin, summoning her courage. 'Never mind. Silly of me, really, to believe in you.' She turned on her heel but stopped at the bottom of the bed. 'The children and I don't need you. I don't need anyone. *I never have.*'

Back straight she walked away from him. This time she didn't cry. The tears stopped immediately, and a cold band of steel encircled her heart.

***

'You are still coming to the party, aren't you?' Prue asked her on the telephone.

Alice, hot and dusty from the long drive back from Margate, where she'd taken the children for a couple of days as they experienced a bout of unseasonably warm March weather, felt reluctant to commit. 'I don't know, Prue.'

'But Grandmama will love to see you. Bring the children and Nanny.'

'I'm undecided about going, but probably will not.'

'You must! I insist you come. We've hired a rather large marquee in the beautiful grounds of Dara Park in north London. One of Grandmama's friends owns it and everything is going to be delightful. You must come.'

'Is Vince going?' Alice murmured, irritated that she had to ask and annoyed her answer depended on what Prue said next.

'No. He's staying here. He says he's not up to a party. Vince is going to keep an eye on things here for us, as your parents are attending the party and want to stay in London for a couple of weeks to meet up with old friends. Then we shall all return together to Yorkshire in time for the baby to be born.'

Relieved that Vince wouldn't be coming back to London, made Alice relent. 'Maybe I will attend the party then. I haven't seen Millie and Cece for absolutely ages.'

'Excellent. I'll see you next week when we come down before the party.'

Alice replaced the receiver onto the telephone stand. From upstairs she heard the quarrelsome whines of two very tired children, though they had loved every minute of being by the seaside. For the first time in their lives, they had seen a body of water larger than the Thames. They had run on the beach, sifting the sand between their fingers and squealed with joy.

Alice had booked a large room in a hotel and spoiled the children with ice creams, fish and chips, donkey rides, which Libby adored, bags of sweets and no Nanny's rules. They stayed up late and rose late. Alice needed the break and she needed to spend time with Libby and Timmy. Nanny had stayed at home with Mariah, which gave Alice a stab of guilt, but she knew with Vince gone from their lives, that Libby needed cheering up. Alice wanted Libby to rely only on her, to be reassured that Alice wouldn't leave her. She was her adoptive mother and Libby needed to learn that Alice was trustworthy and reliable. They needed to create a bond that wouldn't break, no matter what.

But now they were home again. Libby was to return to her new school on Monday, which thankfully she liked, and Alice had to make some decisions as to what she was going to do with the rest of her life. She had recouped her losses from the stock crash last year with the sale of *Sheer*. So, money was not a problem at the moment. But aside from the children, she had to do something to keep herself occupied. Nothing too taxing, not like running a successful magazine that dominated her time and had her constantly travelling, but she must do *something*.

She loved fashion, which was why she started the magazine, and she had a talent for style and colour. Her thoughts ran to owning a high-end clothing shop, something small, yet tasteful. She could use her many connections to gain access to the latest designs by fashion creators who were acquaintances. She could easily fill a shop with clothes from companies who worked with her at *Sheer*.

Add to that, her address book was full of wealthy women who spent a small fortune on clothes every season. She knew they would come to her shop and select quality garments, unique pieces sold only in her shop.

Mariah's crying interrupted her thoughts. Spending time away from the baby had reinforced her commitment to raising her, and spending time alone with Libby and Timmy also showed her an avenue of love and joy she'd been missing in her life.

She knew they'd be fine, the four of them. She'd hoped Vince would be involved, but it wasn't meant to be, and as much as it hurt, she was determined to not let it affect her life, or the children's.

Going upstairs, she helped Nanny bath Libby and Timmy, then she read them a story to calm them down. Esme brought up a tray of soup and bread with an apple custard pudding for afterwards. Mariah was given her bottle, changed and Alice rocked her in her arms gently, humming a soft tune while the children finished their meal.

Nanny wiped Timmy's mouth. 'Would it be all right with you, madam, if I went home as soon as the children are settled? It's my Father's birthday and I'd like to give him his present. He'll be waiting on the street corner for me.'

'Heavens, Nanny, you should have said,' Alice admonished. 'Go now. I insist. I can see to the children.'

'I don't mind staying.'

'Nonsense. Go and be with your father for the evening. Be as late as you need, you've been tied to the house for three days with Mariah. You deserve a break.'

'Thank you, madam.' Nanny hastened up to the attic to change.

Alice, finding Mariah asleep, placed her in her cot with a small kiss and then cleaned up Libby and Timmy. They didn't protest when she said it was bedtime. Though Libby asked for another story, which she read to them. Timmy was asleep before she finished.

Giving him a kiss, she tucked in the blankets around him before turning to adjust the blankets around Libby. 'Sleep well, sweetie.'

Libby took her hand, keeping her by the bed.

'Is anything wrong?' Alice asked, unused to Libby reaching out for her. The child was still rather reserved in giving any affection, unlike Timmy whose favourite game was to smother Alice's face with kisses.

'I'm glad we came here,' Libby whispered as though admitting it cost her a great deal.

'I am too, darling, very glad. You and your brother and sister have made me so utterly happy.' Alice dared to brush away a tendril of long black hair over Libby's shoulder. 'I want the three of you to be happy, too.'

Libby nodded and nestled into her pillows more comfortably. 'Will you be our mam now?'

'I'd like to be, yes. Do you think you could call me Mama?'

'Mama...' The small girl tried it out on her tongue. 'Mama. I like that.'

Alice let out a pent-up breath, relieved. 'Me, too. Good night, sweetheart.'

Going downstairs, Alice had her meal in the dining room, soup to start with then salmon, but no pudding. Once Esme had cleared away, Alice told her and Mrs Jones to go home when they were ready. She would spend a quiet evening catching up on her correspondences and then an early night.

With the house quiet, Alice sat in the parlour at her small writing desk and opened her pile of mail. She answered several invitations to dinner parties and cocktail nights. She accepted some of the dinner invites, but declined the cocktail parties, chuckling a little at herself for saying no to wild drunken events that not so long ago were things she attended a few times a week.

How her life had changed.

Just as Vince's had.

She paused, wondering if, perhaps, Vince thought about her as much as she did of him.

The telephone rang and she dashed to answer it before the shrill tone woke up the children.

'Lady Mayton-Walsh speaking,' she answered breathlessly.

'Putting the connection through now,' the operator's voice tingled in her ear before a click

'Alice, it's me, Sally.'

'Oh.'

'Don't hang up.'

'Why would I do that?'

'We've not spoken since our beastly little disagreement, and I want to talk to you, to apologise. I said some nasty comments and I am truly very sorry. I had no right to say what I did. I'd had too much to drink but that is not an excuse. Gordy was furious with me. I haven't been myself since. I've felt ghastly.'

'Thank you for apologising.'

'You do forgive me, don't you?'

'I do.'

'Thank God!' Sally's voice was full of relief.

Alice could hear music in the background. 'Are you at a party?'

'Yes, a small one. I'm in Edinburgh with Gordy. We're at one of his cousin's house, a lovely chap, but I couldn't enjoy myself because we were playing charades and my partner choose to act out a book. He chose Virginia Woolf's *To The Lighthouse*... It made me think of you and I started crying. Gordy insisted I telephoned you immediately. Do remember when you picked that same book at the country house party in the Cotswolds we went to two years ago, remember?'

'I remember...' Alice did miss her friend, even though Sally could be a trial at times, she was her closest friend and they had been through so much together.

'And it took me absolutely forever to guess the word lighthouse and you were so funny trying to act out a lighthouse. We fell about positively laughing like loons.'

'We did.' Alice grinned to herself, recalling the wild weekend they'd spent after being invited to stay at a large old house by a friend of a friend. They'd partied hard, slept little and laughed until they couldn't breathe. Alice had argued with one chap about women drivers. She'd challenged him to a race around the estate grounds. She'd beaten him by twenty yards and nearly rolled a friend's nippy little Morris motor car in the process.

'Anyway, tonight, hearing about that book made me miss you dreadfully. I cannot live my life without you in it. Simple.'

Alice could hear the tears in her voice. 'I don't want to lose our friendship, either, but we are changing, or at least I am.'

'Yes...'

'To be my friend, Sal, you must accept the decisions I make, or try to understand them, and if not agree then at least support me. Friendship is about the good and the bad, the highs and the lows and respecting each other's choices.'

'It rather is...'

'I have adopted three children, Sal. Children that I have grown to love, that I wish to nurture and see grow into adults. They are my family and the only children I'll ever have.'

'Golly. You do *really* want them then?'

'Of course. I couldn't adopt children on a whim, like they were puppies.'

'You are very brave.'

'Perhaps, but the reward is having three little people totally depend on you, and in time I hope they will love me as much as I love them.'

'They will. How could they not? We all love you.'

'I'd like you to come and see them, get to know them. You can be their aunty.'

'Gracious. You know I am not great with children. What about that time Henry was a baby and he was sick all over me when I was holding him? I nearly dropped him as I gagged.'

Alice laughed, recalling the day it happened. It had been the first time Alice had taken Sally to see her tiny nephew. She'd gone home to Yorkshire to see the family and Sally had gone with her, as she adored Alice's parents.

'I promise I won't drop your children though,' Sally said.

*Your children.* The words swelled Alice's chest with love. 'Come soon.'

'Next week when we are home again.'

'Go and enjoy your party.'

'Can we have lunch, too?' Hope filled Sally's voice.

'We can, yes, and maybe some shopping?' Alice knew that was Sally's favourite thing to do in all the world.

Sally squealed. 'I haven't lost you to the nursery!'

'No.' Alice laughed. 'I can still do normal things like shopping. I just don't want to spend drunken weekends away anymore.'

'And we are still the very best of friends?'

'Always.'

'Good because I need a bridesmaid. You and Helen.'

'I'd adore that.' Alice smiled.

'Smashing!'

After finishing the call, Alice returned to her desk and wrote two letters, one to her aunt who lived in Singapore and another to a friend in Australia.

Knocking on the downstairs front door brought her head up. She wasn't expecting anyone, and not this late. Intrigued, she hurried downstairs to the entrance hall, and checking herself in the ornate mirror beside the coat cupboard, she unlocked the door and gaped at the man standing at the top of the steps.

'Alice.' Simon Delamont grinned sheepishly at her.

'Simon. This is a surprise.'

'A pleasant one I hope?'

'Come in.' She opened the door wider and stepped back for him to enter.

He stooped and kissed her cheek. 'I brought this.' He held up a bottle of champagne.

'Are you celebrating something?'

'A close call,' he drawled in his American accent.

She led the way upstairs to the parlour and found two glasses from behind the drinks bar. 'Care to elaborate?'

'My wedding has been cancelled.'

She laughed gently 'I didn't know you were engaged.'

He shrugged and popped the cork.

Alice winced, hoping the sound didn't wake Mariah.

As he poured the golden bubbly drink into the wide shallow glasses, he kept looking at her. 'She was no one you would know. An American from Texas. She's never been to England.'

'And why has your wedding been cancelled?'

'Because, despite our families wishes, Ursula and I weren't compatible. We should have been, but we weren't.' He handed her a glass.

'And so, you are back in London.' Alice sat on the sofa, and he sat in the chair opposite her.

'I am. For business and pleasure. My father wishes for me to strengthen our business dealings in London. The stock market crash hit us terribly, but we are rallying to some degree. Father wants to consolidate our finances here and then have me go on and do the same in Paris.'

'A busy man.' She smiled, sipping the delicious champagne that she knew would be one of the most expensive ever produced. Simon never did anything by half.

'I *am* a busy man, but not too busy to see old friends... and lovers...'

In a blink she knew what he wanted. He'd come back to her, to continue where they left off last year. To be her lover once more.

'Would you care to join me for dinner tomorrow night?' he asked, his handsome face breaking into a cheeky grin.

A part of her wanted to say yes, very much so. It had been forever since she'd been spoilt by a man. An age since she was taken out for dinner, plied with great food and wine. However, she knew Simon would want more than dinner. He'd want to spend the night in her bed. Did she want that to? Vince sprang into her mind. He was the only man she wanted to be in her bed, but he had rejected her. Should she look to another? A cry came from upstairs and instantly she had her answer.

Simon tilted his head towards the door. 'Was that a baby's cry?'

'Come with me.' She took him upstairs to the children's bedroom and opened the door.

In surprise, Simon stared around as Alice went to the cot and soothed Mariah who was stirring.

'Who do they belong to?' Simon whispered, his worried eyes on the baby. 'Is she yours?'

Alice gave him a wry smile. 'Concerned you might have left me pregnant?'

His eyebrows rose in shock. 'Did I?'

'No.' She shook her head and then checked on Libby and Timmy before coming to stand beside him in the doorway. 'So, my news is that I have decided to become their mother.'

'Christ!' His eyes widened.

She went back downstairs and waited for him to say something else.

'Why?' he asked, gulping his champagne.

'Because I want a family.'

'I can give you a family. Marry me. I'll give you as many children as you want.'

'Do you want children?'

'One day, yes.'

'But not three instant children that didn't come from you?'

His gaze dropped. 'That is not a question a man can answer immediately.'

'True.' She thought of Vince who had wanted to care for the children straight away. He never wanted them to go to the orphanage. Only later had he changed his mind about his role in their lives.

'You will not give them up?' Simon asked.

She shook her head. 'Never.'

'We can still have some fun though?'

She went to him and kissed his lips, tasting champagne. It would be the last kiss she ever gave him. 'Unfortunately, I cannot.'

'But why?'

'Because I don't want to get hurt, Simon. Because I have others to consider. I am putting their welfare first. They need a mother who is committed to them, not someone who is out all the time having fun until the sun rises. I am not that person anymore.'

'Surely a little fun can't be bad?' He winked.

She stepped back, seeing him for the man that he was, kind, generous, attractive, but also someone who couldn't and wouldn't remain faithful. He had a wandering eye and in years past she hadn't been too concerned, but now, she had to consider *her children*. And that changed everything.

'Good night, Simon.'

He nodded. 'Call me if you change your mind.'

She knew she wouldn't.

# Chapter Seventeen

Vince walked the sweeping grounds of the Forsters' estate which was built on a hillside overlooking the north Yorkshire coast. In the distance, the seaside village of Whitby hugged the jagged cliffs. The warm March weather hinted at a long dry summer to come. The morning sun on his back reminded him of the countries which bordered the Mediterranean, when he and Brandon had spent some time mountain climbing. Such happy years after the horrors of the war.

Slowly regaining his health, he'd started hiking in the countryside surrounding the estate. Sometimes, Brandon came with him, or Henry, but mostly he went alone. The long walks tired him out, allowing him to sleep at night instead of tossing in bed thinking of Alice.

At first, he thought walking would give him more time to think of Alice, but the opposite was true. While hiking, his mind was clear of all thought. He simply walked. Perhaps it was a condition gained when in the army. The long walks between battles, trekking between little French villages in all weathers. He didn't think or feel back then. It was a tactic to keep himself going when his body and mind had grown weary of death and slaughter.

But when he wasn't rambling the fields or striding along cliff tops, he felt caged at the manor. The Forsters were the nicest of people. He loved them as family. Yet, he felt idle, useless, a burden on them. A house guest with no date of departure. Not that they minded, of course they didn't, but he did.

He needed to think of the future, only the future seemed to stretch as a long and dull span of time. Was that why he was beginning to feel edgy, trapped? Did he need to travel again? Or simply move somewhere warm, idyllic? Away from all he knew? Perhaps he needed to find adventure again?

'There you are.' Brandon rounded the path.

'Are you ready to leave?' Vince fell into step beside him, back towards the terraced gardens at the rear of the manor.

'Yes. All packed. The train leaves at ten. So, we need to get going. Are you sure you don't want to come?'

'No.'

'Adeline mentioned you when she telephoned Prue this morning. You know how much the old dear adores you,' Brandon joked.

'I'll send her a large bouquet of flowers.'

'You'll be fine by yourself here?'

'Absolutely.'

'Can you please not walk too far and always tell one of the staff where you are going?' Brandon had a worried look on his face. 'I'd hate to think something might happen to you and you aren't found for days.'

'You're only going to London for just over a week, then you and Prue will be back.' Vince slapped him gently on the shoulder. 'I'm quite certain I will be fine in the short amount of time you are gone.'

Brandon paused on the step. 'Any message for Alice?'

Vince lifted his chin in defence of his tortured heart. 'No.'

'I wish you two would speak.'

'There is nothing to say,' he murmured. 'I am not the man for Alice. I never have been, it was just wishful thinking on my part all these years.'

'Prue heard that Simon Delamont has returned to London.'

His stomach churned. 'If Alice wants him, then good luck to her, and him.'

Brandon shook his head. 'You're a bloody fool, my friend. A *stubborn bloody fool* who is going to lose the woman he loves because of stupid pride.'

'How is it stupid pride to let her go? I am being honourable.'

'You're being an idiot.'

'Thanks.'

'You wear your honour like a badge, first Diana and now Alice.'

'What does that mean?' Vince grew defensive.

Brandon folded his arms. 'It means the man I used to know so well has changed and become this weak, insipid fool I do not recognise any longer. I'd like to have the old Vince back, please. The one full of laughter and courage. The man who had my back in every battle, up every mountain. The wild funny man who made me laugh until I thought I'd break a rib. Where has he gone?'

Vince felt worse than ever. He'd let down his best friend. 'I wish I was that man again, Brandon. But he's gone, along with my family's estate and wealth. I have nothing to offer her. I do not have a fortune like Delamont, that's for certain.'

'You have loved Alice for as long as I can remember. Love is all she wants from you.'

'While I live off her money? Live in her house?'

'For God's sake, man! This same argument yet again? You're looking for excuses, God knows why. You have some money left, you told me. You've sold the land that the terraces were built on. So, start a business and earn an income! Sell Alice's townhouse and buy one together.'

'How can I ask her to live a simple life while I sort out my future?'

Brandon cursed. 'You make it sound as though you're asking her to live in a miner's hut! Alice doesn't need all the glitz and glam of London, anymore. She needs somewhere solid, a loving home for her and the children. The children *you* once *wanted* yourself, might I add!'

'Go and catch your train.' Vince turned and walked away. The mention of the children gave him such grief. He felt the biggest cad to have abandoned them. He would never be able to look at Libby again. He couldn't bear to see the distrust and disappointment in her sweet little face.

'Vincent Barton survived the war for what?' Brandon called after him. 'To live a half life when good men died who'd give anything to have lived and be you!'

The words echoed across the gardens. Vince shuddered, shoulders bowed and pretended he didn't hear.

***

Festive garlands swathed from tree to tree, across the entrance to the marque and hung from windows of the impressive house of Dara Park. Hundreds of people mingled on the manicured green lawn. Women were dressed in all shades of pretty spring colours, wearing voluminous hats and gossamer scarves. Tables and chairs were scattered inside the marquee and outside, allowing guests to stand and chat or sit in the shade of umbrellas and take refreshments.

The sun shone and Alice felt a little sorry for the numerous staff carrying heavy trays of food from the house to the marquee, for the footmen in stiff uniforms serving drinks, the black clad maids collecting empty glasses and teacups and saucers. She was glad she wore a linen dress of apple green with white lace at the neck and sleeves. Her large, brimmed hat had one side turned up and was decorated with apple blossom.

'Goodness,' Nanny said, walking beside Alice, carrying Mariah. 'There are a lot of people.'

'Everyone adores Adeline Fordham.' Alice held Libby and Timmy's hands as they stepped along a pale gravelled path surrounding the house. She was proud of the children. Libby wore a yellow dress with yellow ribbons in her dark hair, while Timmy wore a sailor suit, his hair brushed neatly.

'Look!' Libby gasped at the small ponies being led about an enclosure with giggling children on their backs.

Alice grinned. 'Would you care for a ride?'

'Are they like the donkeys we went on at the seaside?'

'Similar, yes.'

Libby's gaze stayed on the ponies as they walked over the lawn.

'Alice!' Prue waved from a table at the entrance to the marquee.

Alice bent to Libby and Timmy. 'You remember Mrs Forster, don't you?'

They both nodded.

'Her little boy is here, too. He's called Henry. He's about your age, Libby.'

'Will he play with me?'

'I'm sure he will.' She smiled down at her as they reached Prue's table.

'I'm so happy you have come,' Prue gushed.

'I said I would.' Alice kissed her hot cheek.

'Grandmama is inside, we have placed her up on a small dais so she can see everyone. It's hilarious. She's as regal as a queen.'

'I'll go in and speak to her.'

'Have a drink first. Isn't it hot?' Prue dabbed her face with a handkerchief. 'I am melting like ice cream! Speaking of which...' She grasped Libby's hand. 'There's an ice cream man giving out ice creams to all the children. Do you see him over there?' She pointed to a man and his cart swarmed by eager children of all ages.

Libby nodded.

'Would you and Timmy like some?'

'Me!' Timmy jumped up and down.

'Then let us go and get some before it's all gone. My little boy, Henry is likely over there, too.' Prue heaved herself up from the chair and taking Libby and Timmy's hands she gave Alice a kind smile.

'Nanny can take Mariah into the house. There's a room for babies to sleep.'

'I'll take her in there now.' Nanny nodded and left with the baby.

'Alice, go and enjoy yourself. Grandmama is waiting to see you. These two are fine with me.'

Alice hesitated. 'Are you sure? I don't want you to tire yourself out.'

'I'm fine. Go.' Prue waved her away.

Left alone, Alice wandered over to the tent's opening, grabbing a glass of champagne from a waiter as she went.

'Alice!'

She spun, looking around the crowd to see who called her name, then she spotted Millie and Cece waving to her, and broke into a wide smile. Prue's sisters where good friends of hers, and she missed seeing them regularly. Millie lived in France and Cece in Scotland.

'It's been forever!' Millie declared, hugging Alice.

'Too long,' she agreed. Millie looked the same as always, black curls and warm eyes. She was dressed in a summer dress of sky blue and looked as stylish as ever.

'How are Jeremy and the boys? Jonathan and Charles must be so grown up now.'

Millie smiled. 'They are growing so tall. Jonathan's nearly ten and my height!' She laughed in amazement. 'But they are perfectly well and around here somewhere. The boys wanted to go boating on the lake down behind those trees, so Jeremy has taken them.'

'You look well.' Cece embraced her. 'When are you coming to Scotland to spend some time in the wilds?'

'When will you have me?' Alice joked, liking the white dress with spring blooms on it that Cece wore. Cece had arranged her red hair into a roll under her wide straw hat. She looked healthy and happy, and Alice glimpsed a small roundness to her stomach and laughingly raised her eyebrows.

Cece tilted her head and patted her stomach. 'You guessed?'

'Congratulations!' Alice kissed her cheek. 'Another little highlander! This baby will be number five? I've not seen your last baby boy yet! Sometimes Scotland is too far away.'

'I agree,' Millie chimed in.

Cece chuckled. 'Indeed, this is number five and I hope the last. Elizabeth, Alexander, Jamie, Hamish, who you've not seen, and now this one due in the autumn is more than enough for me. Grandmama says the Scottish air is to blame for us breeding like rabbits.'

Alice laughed, but felt a pang of jealousy. Cece and Ross were so happy. They lived on a sheep farm in a beautiful part of Scotland and rarely left it to come south. Ross was one of those calm and trusting men you could depend on with your life. 'Where are they all? And Ross?'

'Ross has taken Hamish inside, he was in need of a change. We brought a young girl with us who helps me with the children and lives at the farm. She's never been away from her village and is scared to death of London. The other three are probably with Mama and Jacques in the marquee.'

'How is Violet and Jacques?' Alice asked after the girls' mama and her French husband. 'Has Jacques recovered from his illness?'

Millie nodded with a worrying sigh. 'Mama didn't want him to come as his doctors said he must take things easy, but Jacques wouldn't dream of being left behind. He said to me on the boat as we came over that if he were to suffer another heart attack while alone, he'd not survive it. If he was going to die, then he'd rather do it with Mama and his family around him.'

'Saying that though,' Cece added, 'he looks as fit as a fiddle today. Good colour in his cheeks and laughing and joking with Grandmama. Mama is worried constantly, but, really, you just have to get on with it, don't you?'

'Very true. Life is too short.' Alice sipped her champagne, the delicious taste on her tongue. 'Is this one of your bottles from the chateau?'

'Yes.' Millie took a glass from a passing waiter. 'Chateau Dumont has supplied the party. As if we couldn't? Grandmama insisted it had to be our champagne.'

'Now tell us about these three children you've adopted.' Cece linked her arm through Alice's. 'Prue says they are little darlings.'

'They are. Prue has taken Libby and Timmy to the ice cream man and Nanny has gone inside with Mariah.'

'What a wonderful thing to do, adopt three small orphans.' Millie gave her a look of awe. 'That is such dedication.'

'I fell in love with them.' Alice shrugged. 'I couldn't help it. They were what I was missing in my life.' A small voice in her head added that Vince was also missing but she ignored it.

'Very honourable,' Cece murmured. 'Taking on another person's child is so rewarding. Ross did it with Elizabeth and he loves her the same as the boys, more so, I think, being the only girl. She has him wrapped around her little finger.' She laughed.

'And you sold *Sheer*?' Millie enquired. 'I couldn't believe it when Prue told me.'

Alice nodded, gazing over to the line of children waiting for ice cream. 'It was time. I could have kept going with it, but the interest was lost. I no longer felt the drive, the excitement like I used to. I didn't want to keep travelling to see the same people and talk about fashion and materials and which designer was better than that designer. I had become bored.'

'You needed something else... a new challenge,' Millie said, giving Alice's hand a squeeze.

'The six years of creating and making the magazine a success meant everything to me,' Alice paused, 'but... well... it wasn't enough, in the end.'

'And now you have three beautiful children to care for and love and worry over for the rest of your life!' Cece grinned. 'The future will be wonderful, I know it.'

'I'm so looking forward to it.' Alice's heart warmed at the thought. 'I can make a difference in their lives. Give them a chance to grow up with an education, a good home...'

Millie nodded. 'They are lucky to have you. You will fill their lives with love.'

'You don't think I've made a mistake?' Alice knew other people thought that. Sally did, so why wouldn't others?

'Tosh!' Cece exclaimed. 'Giving a warm and loving home to three orphans? How is that ever a mistake? As long as *you* want this.'

Alice took a deep breath. 'A single woman, in her thirties, creating her own family... Some people will think it odd.'

'Then they are fools,' declared Millie. 'The people who matter think you've done a marvellous thing. Do not concern yourself with negativity. As long as you and the children are happy, who cares what other people's opinions are?'

Alice heaved a sigh and relaxed. 'I'm so pleased we are together today. I needed to be with friends and who better than the Marsh sisters?'

'Who indeed?' Cece affirmed with a smile. 'Now we should go and see if Grandmama needs anything.'

'I must say happy birthday to her.' Alice saw Prue walking back with Libby and Timmy and waited.

'They are simply delightful, Alice,' Millie said when Alice had made the introductions.

'That looks delicious.' Alice bent down next to Timmy to wipe his chin with her handkerchief. The warm day was melting the ice cream quicker than he could eat it.

'Let us go inside,' Prue begged. 'It's far too hot outside.'

'You need to sit down before you have this baby on the grass,' Cece chided.

'I wish,' Prue groaned. 'Unlike your births, Cece, I didn't have a quick birth with Henry. I don't expect an easy time of it with this one either.' A flicker of fear shadowed her eyes.

'You'll be fine,' Millie soothed. 'Second ones can be less arduous.'

Alice followed the sisters into the entrance, wishing she could join in on the discussion, but childbirth seemed to be something she'd never experience.

Inside the marquee, which was set up with a dozen white-clothed tables, each displayed with a huge bouquet of spring flowers perfuming the air. Crystal and porcelain shone from the glow of multi-armed candelabras and white silk bunting criss-crossed the ceiling.

'How beautiful,' Alice breathed. She glanced down at Libby who gaped in awe. 'Isn't it pretty, Libby?'

The girl nodded. 'I like the flowers.'

'You can take some home later.' Cece gave her a wink.

Libby gave one of her rare smiles.

On the wooden dais sitting in a well-padded chair, Adeline Fordham, the sisters' grandmama, sat laughing with some of her guests. Her eyes spotted Alice and she held out both hands to her.

Alice gave her glass to Millie and hurried to embrace the old woman, who was a faded beauty. 'Happy birthday!'

'Oh, it is a happy one for sure. And now you are here. Let me look at you.' Adeline leaned back to peer at Alice as her other guests melted away. 'Stunning as always but too thin!'

'And you look marvellous,' Alice replied, taking in Adeline's glorious dove-grey satin dress embroidered with silver swirls and embellished with touches of white lace and pearls at the throat and sleeves.

'You approve? I do enjoy it when someone with high fashion knowledge approves of what I wear.' Adeline smoothed down the skirt. Her aged face was lightly powdered with only a hint of rouge. Her grey hair was swept up under a short, brimmed straw hat, its crown swathed in grey chiffon and studded with pearls to match her dress.

'Style and sophistication have always been two of your strongest qualities,' Alice told her, smiling.

'Not my wit and beauty?' Adeline challenged with a glint in her eyes.

'Must you have it all?' Alice laughed.

'Of course!' Adeline joked. She noticed Libby and Timmy standing behind Alice. 'And these dear children must be your new family?'

Alice took their hands and brought them forward. 'Yes. Libby and Timmy. The baby is in the house.'

Adeline's expression softened. 'It's a fine thing you are doing, Alice. Never doubt it. Promise me you won't.'

Close to tears, Alice nodded. 'I won't.'

'And where is Vince?' Adeline changed the subject in a blink of an eye. 'You two are usually thick as thieves. I hear he is still recuperating in Yorkshire?'

'Yes.' Alice stiffened slightly at the mention of Vince.

'He was very lucky to survive.' Adeline frowned. 'He was indeed fortunate that you found him. You saved his life. How scared you must have been.'

'It is not a day I wish to repeat again that is for certain.'

'Limehouse. What a place for him to live.' Adeline glanced at the children. 'But at least something good came from it. You have also saved their lives from one of poverty and disillusionment.'

'Disillusionment can also be felt in our class, too,' Alice murmured.

Adeline frowned, then looked at Millie. 'Dear, fetch me another glass of wine, will you? And Prue go and sit down and take the weight off your feet. Cece, take the children out to the ponies.'

No one argued and Alice was left alone with Adeline.

'So...' Adeline tapped her finger against her lips. 'Why do your shoulders bow? What unhappiness befalls you when you should be dancing with joy now you are a mother?'

'I am happy.'

'You don't fool me. I'm too old. I know when there is a deep unhappiness in someone. I've seen it too many times before. Is it Vince?'

Alice stared in surprise.

'Naturally, it is Vince. Men are usually the root of all our problems.' She chuckled. 'Tell me.'

'There is nothing to tell. That is the truth of it. For a moment I thought we might mean something more to each other, but after his accident he rejected me and the children. I don't understand it. He wanted to adopt them as much as I did, and I thought he wanted me as much as I wanted him.' She surprised herself by revealing so much but Adeline has a way about her that made you talk, knowing she would listen and counsel wisely.

'Men are stupid. It is a known fact,' Adeline declared with a wave of her hand. 'I love men. Truly, I do. However, without us women in their lives they'd be a very dull breed, indeed. Every man needs a woman, whether as a mother, wife or mistress. When a man has neither of those things, as Vince clearly doesn't, then he becomes too introspective,' she stated with a small pout. 'Vince has lost everything. He went from an adored son to a war hero to what? A son carrying a large fortune in debt, the highly eligible heir who, through no fault of his own, lost it all and ended up living in the slums of London. Is it any wonder he turned his back on everything, including you?'

'But I didn't care about any of that.'

'Dearest.' Adeline gave her a grandmotherly look. 'You might not care, but he certainly does.'

'Well, none of it matters now.' She didn't want to discuss his rejection at a birthday party, a celebration.

'Do you love him? Properly love him, I mean. Not any of that soft infatuation, but genuinely love him, the good, the bad and the ugly part of him?'

'I do.' It was the one thing she was decidedly certain of. 'When he had his accident, I thought... it was as though I couldn't breathe with the thought of losing him.'

Adeline nodded wisely. 'You are not a young silly girl. You're a woman of the world... and you know your own mind. But you are everything that represents what Vince lost...'

Alice blinked rapidly as the words sank in. 'I have to change who I am?'

'God no!' Adeline snapped. 'Never do that for anyone. However, you need to show Vince that he's better off with you than without you.'

'How do I do that?' She felt helpless and out of her depth.

'Brandon told me that Vince has loved you since you were teenagers.' Adeline smiled a secret smile. 'Give him *you*.'

Alice sucked in a breath. 'Seduce him?'

'Make his head spin.' Adeline gave a saucy wink. 'Vince is an honourable man, but no man can resist a beautiful woman when she is offering him herself. Trust me.'

Alice didn't know what to say. Could she do it? Could she seduce Vince to show him what he was missing?

'The other alternative is to forget him completely, my dear. It's one or the other.' Adeline clapped her hands. 'Now, let us drink some champagne and eat cake and celebrate life!'

Hours later, as the sun was setting, casting a golden glow over the park and most of the guests were leaving, Alice sat outside with Millie, Prue, Cece and their husbands. Either seated on deckchairs or sprawled on blankets, the adults chatted while their children ran about the lawns playing games.

'It's been a wonderful day,' Cece said, yawning.

'I don't want it to end,' Prue murmured, her head resting on Brandon's shoulder.

'Where is Grandmama and Mama?' Millie asked, accepting a cup of tea from Jeremy who had taken on footman duties and made cups of tea for everyone from the refreshment table while the real footmen began tidying away the debris of the party.

'Gone inside for a rest, apparently. Your mama is fussing over Jacques, poor man,' Ross said, keeping an eye on his two oldest sons as they tackled other children in a game. 'Alexander and Jamie are becoming too wild,' he spoke to Cece.

'Leave them, darling. They are boys. You say it all the time when they are running amok.' Cece stared across the lawn. 'Look at Elizabeth and Libby helping the man with the ponies.' Cece pointed over to the area where the ponies were being tied up, ready to be led home.

'They've become friends,' Alice said. 'Libby loves animals. I'm thinking of buying her a puppy. Something that is hers.'

'She will adore it.' Prue nodded in agreement, closing her eyes. 'I think I could sleep out here tonight. I don't want to move.'

'I doubt Mama would be pleased to see you do that.' Millie laughed.

'Grandmama would approve though,' Prue replied. 'She has done it in the past, when younger.'

'Adeline Fordham has done a lot of things in her past, if her stories are to be believed,' Jeremy joked.

'No one is sleeping outside, least of all you.' Brandon shook his head at his wife but took her hand and kissed it.

'Goodness, is that Vince?' Cece sat up straighter.

Alice whipped around, her heart beating rapidly. She stared at the man walking towards them, his hat pulled low. Yet, she knew that walk, knew that man and her stomach swooped.

Brandon went to him. They spoke for a few seconds then they walked back together. At the edge of the group, Vince paused, greeted everyone then stared straight at Alice.

Her mouth went dry. He looked thinner, yet healthier with colour on his face, his hair longer again. His brown eyes bored into hers.

Vince thrust his hands into his pockets of the grey suit he wore. 'Can I speak with you for a moment, please Alice?'

She rose on wobbly legs. Her gaze went to the house and standing on the terraced steps was Adeline, who gave a nod of encouragement.

Aware of everyone staring at them, Alice walked quickly away in the direction opposite to where the children played. Vince followed her. She went to the far side of the park into a stand of copper beech trees. Her thoughts flew around in circles.

Vince stopped by a trunk, the twilight darkening the area. A bird called high in the branches above their heads.

'This is a surprise. I believe you didn't want to see me.' She couldn't look at him and instead concentrated on a red squirrel which had frozen in fear in the long grass.

'I needed to speak with you. To apologise for my behaviour towards you.'

'I see.' He'd hurt her and she didn't know if she could forgive him right at this moment.

'I behaved badly. My actions were unforgivable. You have every right to never speak to me again and I would understand.'

She watched the squirrel dart away in the grass and in the next breath he was scrambling up a nearby trunk and out of sight.

'I'm sorry, Alice.'

'For which bit?' Her dull tone sounded strange to her ears as she looked at him. 'For giving me a glimpse of your feelings, feelings that you claim you've had for years, or the promise to care for the children only to abandon them, or for the future that could have been ours to share and enjoy and which is now in ashes?'

He winced.

'It is a lot to forgive,' she murmured, emotion clogging her throat.

He bowed his head and shuffled the toe of his shoe in the grass. 'I deserve your anger.'

'Yes, you do but you also deserve a life of happiness, Vince. Brandon told me that you do nothing but walk for miles in all weathers every day. You sound rather lost in purpose.'

'It gives me something to do, but, yes, you're right, I am.'

'What kind of life is that?'

He looked straight at her. 'I have no life. I would like one though.'

Her breathing grew short. 'You have plans then?'

'Perhaps. They depend on many things.'

'Such as?'

'Whether you can forgive me for one. I cannot live my life with you hating me, being disappointed in me.'

'I do not hate you, Vince. It isn't in me to hate you.'

He exhaled a long breath. 'That's a start then.'

'Lord, when you had your accident, I thought that was it. You nearly died and I couldn't cope with the idea of you never being in my life again. Doesn't that tell you how I feel? But you pushed me away...'

Silence stretched between them. A bird sang above their heads. Behind them something rustled in the grass.

'I'd best go,' Vince said, hands still in his pockets. 'I'll say happy birthday to Adeline first.'

She glared at him. 'And what of the children and me?'

'I can't stay, Alice. It would break me to see the children and then leave them again. And you...' He shrugged. 'I've already broken my heart over you.'

'Then let me heal it.' Without another thought, she strode over to him and kissed him. It was a bruising kiss, one full of anger and resentment. She wanted to punish him.

'Alice, God, Alice...' he murmured, his hands coming up to grasp her upper arms. He kissed her back with equal desperation.

She tore her mouth from his. 'You left me!'

'I was a fool! I'm sorry.'

They stared at each other, misery etched in their gazes.

'Will you leave me again?' Alice asked, before cupping his face in her hands and kissing him slowly, lovingly. It was a kiss of wonder, hope and longing. She showed him how much he meant to her and gave him a hint of the passion they could share.

'Never,' he groaned into her mouth.

She pressed her body against his, her hands gripping his shoulders wanting him more than air.

Vince held her hips hard against his, his mouth hungry for hers before kissing her neck, pushing aside the flimsy lace neckline.

Alice moaned. She felt alive, so startling alive. She pushed her fingers through his hair. 'I love you.'

'My darling.' He raised his head, desire in his eyes. 'I've loved you forever.'

She gave him a flirtatious smile. 'We can do this for the rest of our days. Tell me you don't want the same? I'll not believe you if you do.'

'I do, of course I do.' He sucked in a deep breath, sobering himself. 'We should talk sensibly though.'

She took a small step backwards. As much as she didn't want to stop kissing, he was right. They had to talk. Taking a moment to calm herself, she tidied her dress. 'Do you still want to buy and renovate old houses and then sell them on?'

'Yes. I feel that is where my passions lie. I want to build a property portfolio over time.'

'I want to open a clothing shop.'

His brown eyes widened. 'Interesting. You would be a success, you always are.'

'Not with you though it seems...'

He sighed heavily. 'I want you in my life, Alice, you and the children, but it will be a rough road as I rebuild my finances.'

'But you won't be walking that road alone, Vince. I'll be by your side every step of the way, but you must *let* me. Shutting me out will harm us. Your pride cannot be your shield, not against me. We can only be happy if you realise that I am your partner in life and in business.'

He reached out and held her hand. 'I've thought long and hard about that. I cannot take your money.'

'The money is from *Sheer*. You helped me build that. Tom's money is all gone. I lost it in the stock market crash. You won't be living off another's man's fortune.'

He bowed his head. 'That was my concern.'

'Then you should have spoken to me about it.'

'I felt I had nothing to offer you.'

'Did you ever realise it wasn't your family money or your pedigree I coveted? It was you. Once I knew I loved you more than just a friend, it was only ever the man I desired.' She took a deep breath. 'Would you still want me if I was penniless?'

His head shot up and he frowned. 'Of course!'

She gave him a sassy glare. 'It works both ways, Mr Barton.'

He chuckled. 'So, it seems.'

'Once we are married, it'll be *our* money.'

'Married?' His smile was full of wonder.

'You do not want me as your wife? Or the children?'

Vince stroked her cheek. 'I want all of it. I have always wanted you.'

'There is nothing to stop us, Vince. Believe it, please.' She didn't know what else to say to make him understand her sincerity.

'It sounds too good to be true. It's not easy to believe a dream can come true after years of wanting it.' He rubbed a hand over his face, as though weary of fighting his demons. 'I do not come to you completely destitute. What little I have is yours. I will work hard for us.'

She kissed him. 'We'll join forces together. Besides, we need to sell my house and buy somewhere else. A home of our own. The children need a garden to play in and we need a fresh start.'

He gave her a wry smile. 'You have it all planned out?'

She hesitated in answering. 'Don't I always?'

He laughed and kissed her again.

Alice gave him all the love she had in every kiss, every touch until breathing hard, they eventually broke apart.

'We should return to the party,' he murmured, resting his forehead against Alice's.

'We should. But you will come home with me tonight?' She didn't want to sound hopeful.

'Gladly.' He kissed her again. 'I'll stop being a fool.'

She grinned at him. 'That's a big call.'

Laughing, hand in hand they walked back to the rest of the group who cheered and clapped on seeing them smiling and together.

'Thank God for that,' Brandon declared, shaking Vince's hand. 'I thought you'd never come to your senses.'

'It was a close call,' Vince joked.

Nanny walked towards them carrying Mariah in her arms with Timmy tagging along behind, looking tired.

Alice took Mariah from Nanny and showed her off to Millie and Cece while Vince picked up Timmy and let him rest against his shoulder

There was a sudden squeal and they all turned as Libby broke into a run over the lawn, heading straight for Vince.

Vince passed Timmy to Prue and dashed towards the child.

Alice's heart leapt as the child did, straight into Vince's arms.

'You're not dead!' Libby sobbed, her thin arms around his neck. 'I thought you'd died like my mam.'

'No, darling.' He held her close. 'I've come back to you, and I won't ever leave you again.'

She raised her tear-streaked face to his. 'Do you *really* promise this time?'

'I do. I'm going to be your new papa.'

Libby glanced shyly at Alice. 'Like my new mama?'

Vince opened one arm to encompass Alice and Mariah into the embrace. 'We'll be a family, all of us.'

Timmy in fear of missing out, scrambled off Prue's lap and ran to hug their legs.

Heart full, Alice closed her eyes in utter happiness. She never thought she wanted a family of her own until it was thrust upon her, and she ached with love and gratitude for it.

# Acknowledgements

Dear readers,

Thank you for choosing to read Alice. This book is the conclusion to the Marsh Saga Series, and I hoped you enjoyed reading about all four women.

This was the first time I have written a book set in 1929/30 and a learned a lot through my research. The Stock Market Crash of 1929 was a deciding point in history as it led to the Great Depression in the USA and United Kingdom, which had a knock-on effect throughout the world. However, many of the wealthy people of London rode through that unstable time untouched, and London did recover quicker than the USA. London expanded in the 1930s. Building projects, especially the beginning of housing estates, knocking down slums and creating new housing became a financial boost during that time. While the north of England suffered with high unemployment, low production, such as in the coal mines due to the terrible price of coal at the time, the south of the country rallied well economically.

I wanted to touch on the fact that the sons who returned from WWI as heroes did not always come home to the same comfortable life they left. Many great country houses throughout the UK where lost due to high taxes and death duties needing to be paid and the heirs unable to afford the upkeep. The world had changed after WWI and the glory days of big country estates were dying. Ways had to be found to either keep the family's country seat or sell. I have a book of country houses which were lost between the wars and after WWII due to the huge financial cost to keep the estates viable. It's so sad to see such beautiful homes reduced to rubble, stand abandoned or sold to become a series of government institutions.

During my research I also came across a startling fact that adoption only became legal in England in 1926, and amazingly, advertisements were put in newspapers for unwanted babies. I didn't believe it until I saw it for myself. It is amazing what fascinating little nuggets of information researching can find.

If this is the first book you have read of the Marsh Saga Series, the order is Book 1 is titled, Millie, then there is an accompanying novella to Millie, titled, Christmas at the Chateau. Book 2 is titled, Prue and Book 3 is titled, Cece.

I would like to take a moment to thank all my lovely readers who choose to read my books. I cannot tell you how much it means to me to be able to write my books and know they give enjoyment to others. In this crazy world, we all need to find time to disengage from the outside world and escape somewhere new. That I can provide some escape and pleasure for others brings my such joy I can't even describe.

Receiving messages from readers makes my day each and every time. I feel utterly privileged to be an author. The support I receive from readers, friends and, of course, my family is something I will never take for granted.

Thank you.

AnneMarie Brear

2022

# About the Author

AnneMarie was born in a small town in N.S.W. Australia, to English parents from Yorkshire, and is the youngest of five children. From an early age she loved reading, working her way through the Enid Blyton stories, before moving onto Catherine Cookson's novels as a teenager.

Living in England during the 1980s and more recently, AnneMarie developed a love of history from visiting grand old English houses and this grew into a fascination with what may have happened behind their walls over their long existence. Her enjoyment of visiting old country estates and castles when travelling and, her interest in genealogy and researching her family tree, has been put to good use, providing backgrounds and names for her historical novels which are mainly set in Yorkshire or Australia between Victorian times and WWII.

A long and winding road to publication led to her first novel being published in 2006. She has now published over twenty-nine historical family